The Camera Fiend by E.W. Hornung

Ernest William Hornung was born in Middlesbrough, England on 7th June 1866, the third son and youngest of eight children.

Although spending most of his life in England and France he spent two years in Australia from 1884 and that experience was to colour and influence much of his written works.

His most famous character A. J. Raffles, 'the gentleman thief', was published first in Cassell's Magazine during 1898 and was to make him famous across the world as the new century dawned.

Hornung also wrote several stage plays and was a gifted poet.

Spending time with the troops in WWI he published Notes of a Camp-Follower on the Western Front during 1919, a detailed account of his time there. This was especially close to his heart as his son, and only child, was killed at the Second Battle of Ypres on 6th July 1915.

Ernest William Hornung died in Saint-Jean-de-Luz, in the south of France on 22nd March 1921.

Index of Contents

A CONSCIENTIOUS ASS
A BOY ABOUT TOWN
HIS PEOPLE
A GRIM SAMARITAN
THE GLASS EYE
AN AWAKENING
BLOOD-GUILTY
POINTS OF VIEW
MR. EUGENE THRUSH
SECOND THOUGHTS
ON PAROLE
HUNTING WITH THE HOUNDS
BOY AND GIRL
BEFORE THE STORM
A LIKELY STORY
MALINGERING
ON THE TRACK OF THE TRUTH
A THIRD CASE
THE FOURTH CASE
WHAT THE THAMES GAVE UP
AFTER THE FAIR
THE SECRET OF THE CAMERA
E.W. HORNUNG – A SHORT BIOGRAPHY
E.W. HORNUNG – A CONCISE BIBLIOGRAPHY

A CONSCIENTIOUS ASS

Pocket Upton had come down late and panting, in spite of his daily exemption from first school, and the postcard on his plate had taken away his remaining modicum of breath. He could have wept over it in open hall, and would probably have done so in the subsequent seclusion of his own study, had not an obvious way out of his difficulty been bothering him by that time almost as much as the difficulty itself. For it was not a very honest way, and the unfortunate Pocket had been called "a conscientious ass" by some of the nicest fellows in his house. Perhaps he deserved the epithet for going even as straight as he did to his house-master, who was discovered correcting proses with a blue pencil and a briar pipe.

"Please, sir, Mr. Coverley can't have me, sir. He's got a case of chicken-pox, sir."

The boy produced the actual intimation in a few strokes of an honoured but laconic pen. The man poised his pencil and puffed his pipe.

"Then you must come back to-night, and I'm just as glad. It's all nonsense your staying the night whenever you go up to see that doctor of yours."

"He makes a great point of it, sir. He likes to try some fresh stuff on me, and then see what sort of night I have."

"You could go up again to-morrow."

"Of course I could, sir," replied Pocket Upton, with a delicate emphasis on his penultimate. At the moment he was perhaps neither so acutely conscientious nor such an ass as his critics considered him.

"What else do you propose?" inquired Mr. Spearman.

"Well, sir, I have plenty of other friends in town, sir. Either the Knaggses or Miss Harbottle would put me up in a minute, sir."

"Who are the Knaggses?"

"The boys were with me at Mr. Coverley's, sir; they go to Westminster now. One of them stayed with us last holidays. They live in St. John's Wood Park."

"And the lady you mentioned?"

"Miss Harbottle, sir, an old friend of my mother's; it was through her I went to Mr. Coverley's, and I've often stayed there. She's in the Wellington Road, sir, quite close to Lord's."

Mr. Spearman smiled at the gratuitous explanation of an eagerness that other lads might have taken more trouble to conceal. But there was no guile in any Upton; in that one respect the third and last of them resembled the great twin brethren of whom he had been prematurely voted a "pocket edition" on his arrival in the school. He had few of their other merits, though he took a morbid interest in the games they played by light of nature, as well as in things both beyond and beneath his brothers and the average boy. You cannot sit up half your nights with asthma and be an average boy. This was obvious even to Mr. Spearman, who was an average man. He had never disguised his own disappointment in the youngest Upton, but had often made him the butt of outspoken and disastrous comparisons. Yet in his softer moments he had some sympathy with the failure of an otherwise worthy family; this fine June morning he seemed even to understand the joy of a jaunt to London for a boy who was getting very little out of his school life. He made a note of the two names and addresses.

"You're quite sure they'll put you up, are you?"

"Absolutely certain, sir."

"But you'll come straight back if they can't?"

"Rather, sir!"

"Then run away, and don't miss your train."

Pocket interpreted the first part of the injunction so literally as to arrive very breathless in his study. That diminutive cell was garnished with more ambitious pictures than the generality of its order; but the best of them was framed in the ivy round the lattice window, and its foreground was the nasturtiums in the flower-box. Pocket glanced down into the quad, where the fellows were preparing construes for second school in sunlit groups on garden seats. At that moment the bell began. And by the time Pocket had changed his black tie for a green one with red spots, in which he had come back after the Easter holidays, the bell had stopped and the quad was empty; before it filled again he would be up in town and on his way to Welbeck Street in a hansom.

The very journey was a joy. It was such sport to be flying through a world of buttercups and daisies in a train again, so refreshing to feel as good as anybody else in the third smoker; for even the grown men in the corner seats did not dream of calling the youth an "old ass," much less a young one, to his face. His friends and contemporaries at school were in the habit of employing the ameliorating adjective, but there were still a few fellows in Pocket's house who made an insulting point of the other. All, however, seemed agreed as to the noun; and it was pleasant to cast off friend and foe for a change, to sit comfortably unknown and unsuspected of one's foibles in the train. It made Pocket feel a bit of a man; but then he really was almost seventeen, and in the Middle Fifth, and allowed to smoke asthma cigarettes in bed. He took one out of a cardboard box in his bag, and thought it might do him good to smoke it now. But an adult tobacco-smoker looked so curiously at the little thin cross between cigar and cigarette, that it was transferred to a pocket unlit, and the coward hid himself behind his paper, in which there were several items of immediate interest to him. Would the match hold out at Lord's? If not, which was the best of the Wednesday matinees? Pocket had received a pound from home for his expenses, so that these questions took an adventitious precedence over even such attractive topics as an execution and a murder that bade fair to lead to one. But the horrors had their turn, and having supped on the newspaper supply, he continued the feast in Henry Dunbar, the novel he had brought with him in his bag. There was something like a murder! It was so exciting as to detach Pocket Upton from the flying buttercups and daisies, from the reek of the smoking carriage, the real crimes in the paper, and all thoughts of London until he found himself there too soon.

The asthma specialist was one of those enterprising practitioners whose professional standing is never quite on a par with their material success. The injurious discrepancy may have spoilt his temper, or it may be that his temper was at the root of the prejudice against him. He was never very amiable with Pocket Upton, a casual patient in every sense; but this morning Dr. Bompas had some call to complain.

"You mean to tell me," he expostulated, "that you've gone back to the cigarettes in spite of what I said last time? If you weren't a stupid schoolboy I should throw up your case!"

Pocket did not wish to have his case thrown up; it would mean no more days and nights in town. So he accepted his rebuke without visible resentment.

"It's the only way I can stop an attack," he mumbled.

"Nonsense!" snapped the specialist. "You can make yourself coffee in the night, as you've done before."

"I can't at school. They draw the line at that."

"Then a public school is no place for you. I've said so from the first. Your people should have listened to me, and sent you on a long sea voyage under the man I recommended, in the ship I told them about. She sails the day after to-morrow, and you should have sailed in her."

The patient made no remark; but he felt as sore as his physician on the subject of that long sea voyage. It would have meant a premature end to his undistinguished schooldays, and goodbye to all thought of following in his brothers' steps on the field of schoolboy glory. But he might have had adventures beyond the pale of that circumscribed arena, he might have been shipwrecked on a desert island, and lived to tell a tale beyond the dreams of envious athletes, if his people had but taken kindly to the scheme. But they had been so very far from taking to it at all, with the single exception of his only sister, that the boy had not the heart to discuss it now.

"If only there were some medicine one could take to stop an attack!" he sighed. "But there doesn't seem to be any."

"There are plenty of preventives," returned the doctor. "That's what we want. Smoking and inhaling all sorts of rubbish is merely a palliative that does more harm than good in the long run."

"But it does you good when the preventives fail. If I could get a good night without smoking I should be thankful."

"If I promise you a good night will you give me your cigarettes to keep until to-morrow?"

"If you like."

The doctor wrote a prescription while the boy produced the cardboard box from his bag.

"Thank you," said Bompas, as they made an exchange. "I don't want you even to be tempted to smoke to-night, because I know what the temptation must be when you can't get your breath. You will get this prescription made up in two bottles; take the first before you go to bed to-night, and the second if you wake with an attack before five in the morning. You say you are staying the night with friends; better give me the name and let me see if they're on the telephone before you go. I want you to go to bed early, tell them not to call you in the morning, and come back to me the moment you've had your breakfast."

They parted amicably after all, and Pocket went off only wondering whether he ought to have said positively that he was staying with friends when he might be going back to school. But Dr. Bompas had been so short with him at first as to discourage unnecessary explanations; besides, there could be no question of his going back that night. And the difficulty of the morning, which he had quite forgotten in the train, was not allowed to mar a moment of his day in town.

The time-table of that boy's day must speak for itself. It was already one o'clock, and he was naturally hungry, especially after the way his breakfast had been spoilt by Coverley's card. At 1.15 he was munching a sausage roll and sipping chocolate at a pastry-cook's in Oxford Street. The sausage roll, like the cup of chocolate, was soon followed by another; and a big Bath bun completed a debauch of which Dr. Bompas would undoubtedly have disapproved.

At 1.45, from the top of an Atlas omnibus in Baker Street, he espied a placard with "Collapse of Middlesex" in appalling capitals. And at the station he got down to learn the worst before going on to Lord's for nothing.

The worst was so hopelessly bad that Pocket wished himself nearer the theatres, and then it was that the terra-cotta pile of Madame Tussaud's thrust itself seductively upon his vision. He had not been there for years. He had often wanted to go again, and go alone. He remembered being taken by his sister when a little boy at Coverley's, but she had refused to go into the Chamber of Horrors, and he had been relieved at the time but sorry ever afterwards, because so many of the boys of those days had seen everything and seemed none the worse for the adventure. It was one of the things he had always wanted not so much to do as to have done. The very name of the Chamber of Horrors had frozen his infant blood when he first heard it on the lips of a criminological governess. On the brink of seventeen there was something of the budding criminologist about Pocket Upton himself; had not a real murder and Henry Dunbar formed his staple reading in the train? And yet the boy had other sensibilities which made him hesitate outside the building, and enter eventually with quite a nutter under the waistcoat.

A band in fantastic livery was playing away in the marble hall; but Pocket had no ear for their music, though he was fond enough of a band. And though history was one of his few strong points at school, the glittering galaxy of kings and queens appealed to him no more than the great writers at their little desks and the great cricketers in their unconvincing flannels. They were waxworks one and all. But when the extra sixpence had been paid at the inner turnstile, and he had passed down a dungeon stair into the dim vaults below, his imagination was at work upon the dreadful faces in the docks before he had brought his catalogue to bear on one of them.

Here were wretches whose vile deeds had long been familiar to the schoolboy through a work on his father's shelves called Annals of Our Time. He recalled bad nights when certain of those annals had kept him awake long after his attack; and here were the actual monsters, not scowling and ferocious as he had always pictured them, but far more horribly demure and plump. Here were immortal malefactors like the Mannings; here were Rush and Greenacre cheek by jowl, looking as though they had stepped out of Dickens in their obsolete raiment, looking anything but what they had been. Some wore the very clothes their quick bodies had filled; here and there were authentic tools of death, rusty pistols, phials of poison with the seals still bright, and a smug face smirking over all in self-conscious infamy. There was not enough of the waxwork about these creatures; in the poor light, and their own clothes, and the veritable dock in which many of them had heard their doom, they looked hideously human and alive. One, a little old man, sat not in the dock but on the drop itself, the noose dangling in front of him; and the schoolboy felt sorry for him, for his silver bristles, for the broad arrows on his poor legs, until he found out who it was. Then he shuddered. It was Charles Peace. He had first heard of Charles Peace from the nice governess aforesaid; and here under his nose were the old ruffian's revolver, and the strap that strapped it to his wrist, with the very spectacles he had wiped and worn. The hobbledehoy was almost as timorously entranced as he had been in infancy by untimely tale of crime. He stood gloating over the gruesome relics, over ropes which had hanged men whose trials he had read for himself in later days, and yet wondering with it all whether he would ever get these things out of his mind again. They filled it to overflowing. He might have had the horrid place to himself. Yet he had entered it with much amusement at the heels of a whole family in deep mourning, a bereaved family drowning their sorrow in a sea of gore, their pilot through the catalogue a conscientious orphan with a monotonous voice and a genius for mis-pronunciation. Pocket had soon ceased to see or hear him or any other being not made of wax. And it was only when he was trying to place a nice-looking murderer in a straw hat, who suddenly moved into a real sightseer like himself, that the unwholesome spell was broken.

Pocket was not sorry to be back in the adulterated sunshine and the comparatively fresh air of the Marylebone Road. He was ashamed to find that it was after four o'clock. Guy and Vivian Knaggs would be home from Westminster in another hour. Still it was no use getting there before them, and he might as well walk as not; it was pleasant to rub shoulders with flesh and blood once more, and to look in faces not made of wax in the devil's image. His way, which he knew of old, would naturally have led him past Miss Harbottle's door; but, as she was only to be his second string for the night, he preferred not to be seen by that old lady yet. Such was the tiny spring of an important action; it led the wanderer into Circus Road and a quite unforeseen temptation.

In the Circus Road there happens to be a highly respectable pawnbroker's shop; in the pawnbroker's window the chances are that you might still find a motley collection of umbrellas, mandolines, family Bibles, ornaments and clocks, strings of watches, trays of purses, opera-glasses, biscuit-boxes, photograph frames and cheap jewellery, all of which could not tempt you less than they did Pocket Upton the other June. There were only two things in the window that interested him at all, and they were not both temptations. One was an old rosewood camera, and Pocket was interested in cameras old and new; but the thing that tempted him was a little revolver at five-and-six, with what looked like a box of cartridges beside it, apparently thrown in for the price. A revolver to take back to school! A revolver to fire in picked places on the slow walks with a slow companion which were all the exercise this unfortunate fellow could take! A revolver and cartridges complete, so that one could try it now, in no time, with Guy and Vivian at the end of their garden in St. John's Wood Park! And all very likely for five bob if one bargained a bit!

Pocket took out his purse and saw what a hole the expenditure of any such sum would make. But what was that if it filled a gap in his life? Of coure it would have been breaking a school rule, but he was prepared to take the consequences if found out; it need not involve his notion of dishonour. Still, it must be recorded that the young or old as was conscientious enough to hesitate before making his fatal plunge into the pawnbroker's shop.

The young Westminsters had not come in when Pocket finally cast up in St. John's Wood Park. But their mother was at home, and she gave the boy a cup of tepid tea out of a silver tea-pot in the drawing-room. Mrs. Knaggs was a large lady who spoke her mind with much freedom, at all events to the young. She remarked how much Upton (so she addressed him) had altered; but her tone left Pocket in doubt as to whether any improvement was implied. She for one did not approve of his luncheon in Oxford Street, much less of the way he had spent a summer's afternoon; indeed, she rather wondered at his being allowed alone in London at all. Pocket, who could sometimes shine in conversation with his elders, at once reminded Mrs. Knaggs that her own Westminster boys were allowed alone in London every day of their lives. But Mrs. Knaggs said that was a very different thing, and that she thought Pocket's public school must be very different from Westminster. Pocket bridled, but behaved himself; he knew where he wanted to stay the night, and got as far towards inviting himself as to enlarge upon Mr. Coverley's misfortune and his own disappointment. Mrs. Knaggs in her turn did ask him where he meant to and even the conscientious Pocket caught himself declaring he had no idea. Then the boys were heard returning, and Mrs. Knaggs said of course he would stop to schoolroom supper, and Pocket thanked her as properly as though it were the invitation he made sure must follow. After all, Vivian Knaggs had stayed at Pocket's three weeks one Christmas, and Guy a fortnight at Easter; the boys themselves would think of that; it was not a matter to broach to them, or one to worry about, prematurely.

Vivian and Guy were respectively rather older and rather younger than Pocket, and they came in looking very spruce, the one in his Eton jacket, the other in tails, but both in shiny toppers that excited an unworthy prejudice in the wearer of the green tie with red spots. They seemed very glad to see him, however, and the stiffness was wearing off even before Pocket produced his revolver in the basement room where the two Westminsters prepared their lessons and had their evening meal.

The revolver melted the last particle of ice, though Vivian Knaggs pronounced it an old pin-firer, and Guy said he would not fire it for a thousand pounds. This only made Pocket the more eager to show what he and his revolver were made of, then and there in the garden, and the more confident that it never would be heard in the house.

"It would," answered Vivian, "and seen as well. No, if you want to have a shot let's stick up a target outside this window, and fire from just inside."

The window was a French one leading into the back garden; but, unhappily, Mrs. Knaggs's bedroom was only two floors higher, and it also looked out on the back; and Mrs. Knaggs herself was in her room and near her window when the report startled her, and not less because she little dreamt what it was until she looked out in time to see a cloud of smoke escaping from the schoolroom window, and Pocket examining the target, weapon in hand.

There was a great scene about it. Mrs. Knaggs shrieked a prohibition from aloft, and having pacified an incoherent cook upon the stairs, descended to extract a solemn promise which might well have ended the matter. Pocket was very contrite, indeed, drew his weapon's teeth with a promptitude that might have been his death, and offered it and them to be placed under lock and key until he left. But Mrs. Knaggs contented herself with promoting a solemn promise into a Sacred Word of Honour—which rather hurt poor Pocket—and with sending him a very straight message by Vivian after supper.

"The mater's awfully sorry," said Vivian, returning from a mission which Pocket had been obliged to instigate after all. "There's not a spare bed in the house."

Guy incontinently declared there was. A fraternal frown alone prevented him from going into particulars.

"A sofa would do me all right," suggested Pocket, who had long ago lost his last train, and would have preferred a bare plank where there were boys to fussy old Miss Harbottle's best bed. But Vivian Knaggs shook his head.

"The mater says she couldn't sleep with firearms in the house."

"I'll bury them in the garden if she likes."

"Then you smoke in the night, and at Coverley's you once walked in your sleep," pursued Vivian, who certainly seemed to have been urging the interloper's cause. "And the mater's afraid you might walk out of a window or set the house on fire."

"I shouldn't do either to-night," protested Pocket, with a grin. "I've not got anything to smoke, and I have got something to keep me quiet."

And with further information on both points the son of the house went upstairs again, only to return in quicker time with a more embarrassed gravity.

"She's awfully sorry," he said unconvincingly, "but she can't undertake the responsibility of putting you up with your asthma."

Oddly enough, for he was only too sensitive on some points, Pocket was not really hurt by his treatment at the hands of these people; he felt he had made rather a mistake, but not that he had been most inhumanly cast adrift at sixteen among the shoals and quicksands of London. Nor was this quite the case as yet; there was still old Miss Harbottle in Wellington Road. But to her he was not going until decency compelled him; he was going to have another game of bagatelle with Guy Knaggs first. It will be seen that with all his sensibilities the youngest Upton was a most casual and sanguine youth. He took a great deal for granted, prepared only for the best, and although inclined to worry over the irrevocable, took no thought for the morrow until he was obliged. He was sorry he had been so positive with Spearman on the subject of his friend's hospitality. He was sorry he had asked and been refused, rather sorry he had not caught that last train back from St. Pancras. Yet he left poor Miss Harbottle the best part of another hour to go to bed in; and that was neither the first nor the last of his erratic proceedings.

"What about your luggage?" asked the elder Knaggs, as he put on his hat to walk round with Pocket.

"Good Lord!" cried that worthy, standing still in the hall.

"Haven't you got any?"

"I left it at Madame Tussaud's!"

"Left your luggage there?"

"It was only a handbag. How long are they open?"

Young Knaggs looked in Whitaker and said they closed at ten. There was still time to recover the bag with a taxicab, but in that case it was not much use his going too. So they said goodbye at the Swiss Cottage, and the adventures of Pocket Upton began in earnest.

Old Miss Harbottle, his mother's great friend, would have none of him either! He stopped on the way to Baker Street to make sure. The garden gate was one that only opened by a catch and a cable manipulated indoors. The downstairs lights were out. The gate opened at last, a light shone through the front door, and the door opened a few inches on the chain. Pocket confronted a crevice of quilted dressing-gown and grey curls; but his mother's friend's mastiff was making night so hideous within, and trying so hard to get at his mother's son, that it was some time before he could exchange an intelligible word with the brute's mistress. It was not a satisfactory interchange then, for Miss Harbottle at first flatly refused to believe that this was Tony Upton, whom she had not seen since his preparatory schooldays, and she seemed inclined to doubt it to the end. Upton or no Upton, she could not take him in. She had no sheets aired, no fire to air them at, and the cook had just left. Miss Harbottle's cook had always just left, except when she was just leaving. The rejected visitor got an instant's fun out of the reflection as he returned to his palpitating taxicab.

His position was now quite serious. He had not many shillings in his purse. The only thing to do was to put up at Shaw's Hotel, Trafalgar Square; that was where his people always stayed, where every servant was supposed to know them all. He pushed on at once through the cool June night, and paid away three of his last shillings for the drive. Alas! not a bed to be had at Shaw's; it was the worst time of the year, they told him, and he supposed they meant the best. He also supposed there had been changes in the staff, for nobody seemed to know his name as well as he had been led to expect at home.

They were quite nice about it. They pointed out the big hotels opposite, and recommended more than one of the little ones in Craven Street. But the big hotels were all full to overflowing; and at the only little one he tried the boy lost his temper like a man on being requested to deposit six shillings before proceeding to his room. Pocket had not got it to deposit, and the galling reflection caused him to construe the demand as a deliberate reflection upon his outward respectability—as if he could not have borrowed the money from Dr. Bompas in the morning!

"I'll see you blowed," was his muttered reply, and he caught up his bag in a passion.

"All right, little man! I shouldn't be rude about it," said the dapper cashier. "If I couldn't pay my shot I should sleep in the Park, on a nice fine night like this."

"I shall!" shouted Pocket through his teeth, as though that would prevent the brute of a cashier from sleeping soundly in his bed. And it was his own idle and childish threat that set him presently wondering what else he was to do. He had the spirit of adventure, as we have seen.

He had the timorous, or let us say, the imaginative temperament, which lends to adventure its very salt. He wished to have done dangerous or heroic things, if not to have to do them. He had so little to boast about; his brothers, and so many other fellows of his own age, had so much. It would make a great yarn some day, how he had come up from school to see a doctor—and slept in the Park!

Meanwhile he had only a vague idea of his way there; he knew hardly anything of London except St. John's Wood and his present landmark of the Nelson column and the Landseer lions. He knew them from having stayed some time (under another doctor) as a child at Shaw's Hotel. But, I say! What would Bompas say to his sleeping out, and what sort of night could he expect in the open air?

He had an overcoat. It had been in his way all day; it would come in more than handy for the night. And it suddenly struck Pocket, with all the force of a forgotten novelty, that he had a revolver and cartridges as well.

That decided him. Not that he seriously thought himself the kind of person to use a revolver with resolution or effect; but it made him feel doughty and even truculent to find the means of heroic defence all ready to his hand. He began to plume himself on his providential purchase. He would sell his young life dearly if he fell among London thieves; in his death he would not be unhonoured at school or at home. Obituary phrases of a laudatory type sprang like tears to a mind still healthy enough to dash them away again, as though they had been real tears; but it was with all the nervous exaltation of the unsuspected desperado that he inquired his way of a colossal constable at the corner of Pall Mall and the Haymarket.

The man wanted to know if he meant Hyde Park Corner. "Yes," said Pocket, hastily, because his heart was in his mouth and the policeman looked as though he had seen it there. And he overshot the mark in the motor omnibus through being ashamed to ask again, only alighting at Albert Gate; but here there was quite a little stream of decent people to follow without further tremors into the indubitable Park.

He followed them across the drive and across Rotten Row, gaining confidence as he went. In a minute it was all delightful; his eyes were turned outward by all there was to see; and now his chief fear was lest some one or other of the several passers should stand in his path and ask what he was doing there. He was still afraid of speaking or being spoken to, but no longer unreasonably so. Detection as an escaped schoolboy was his one great dread; he felt he was doing something for which he might be expelled.

But nobody took any notice of him; this gradually encouraged him to take more notice of other people, when he found, not altogether to his surprise, that the majority of those passing through the Park at that late hour were hardly of his own class. So much the more infinitesimal were the chances of his being recognised or even suspected for what he was. There were young men in straw hats, there were red-coated soldiers, and there were girls. They all filled the schoolboy with their fascinating possibilities. They were Life. The boy's heart beat at what he heard and saw. The couples were hilarious and unrefined. One wench, almost under his nose, gave her soldier a slap with such a remark as Pocket had never heard from a woman's lips before. He turned away, tingling, and leant upon the parapet of a bridge he had been in the act of crossing, and thought of school and home and Mr. Coverley.

It was not really a bridge at all. It was only the eastern extremity of the Serpentine; but as the boy leant over the stone balustrade, and gazed upon the artificial flood, broadening out indefinitely in the darkness, it might have been the noblest river in the world. Its banks were muffled in a feather boa of trees, bedizened by a chain of many lights; the lights of a real bridge made a diadem in the distance; and between these sped the lamps of invisible vehicles, like fretful fireflies. And the still water gave back every glimmer with its own brilliance, unchallenged and undimmed by moon or star, for not a trace of either was in the sky; and yet it was the most wonderful sky the boy had ever seen—a black sky tinged with sullen rose, or a red sky seen through smoked glasses, he hardly knew which he would have called it. But he did know that warm and angry glow for the reflection of London's light and life; he could not forget he was in London for a moment. Her mighty machinery with its million wheels throbbed perpetually in his ears; and yet between the beats would come the quack of a wild duck near at hand, the splash of a leaping fish, the plaintive whistle of water-fowl: altogether such a chorus of incongruities as was not lost upon our very impressionable young vagabond. The booming strokes of eleven recalled him to a sense of time and his immediate needs. His great adventure was still before him; he pushed on, bag in hand, to select its scene. Another road he crossed, alive with the lamps of cyclists, and came presently upon a wide space intersected with broad footpaths from which he shrank; it was altogether too public here; he was approaching an exposed corner in an angle of lighted streets, with the Marble Arch at its apex, as a signboard made quite clear. He had come right across the Park; back over the grass, keeping rather more to the right, in the direction of those trees, was the best thing now.

It was here that he found the grass distinctly damp; this really was enough to deter an asthmatic, already beginning to feel asthmatical. Pocket Upton, however, belonged to the large class of people, weak and strong alike, who are more than loth to abandon a course of action once taken. It would have required a very severe attack to baulk him of his night out and its subsequent description to electrified ears. But when bad steering had brought him up at the bandstand, the deserted chairs seemed an ordained compromise between prudence and audacity, and he had climbed into the fenced enclosure when another enormous policeman rose up horribly in its midst.

"What are you doing here?" inquired this policeman, striding upon Pocket with inexorable tread.

"No harm, I hope," replied our hero humbly, but with unusual readiness.

"Nor no good either, I'll be bound!" said the policeman, standing over him.

"I was only going to sit down," protested Pocket, having satisfied his conscience that in the first place that was all he really had been going to do.

"There are plenty of places to sit down," rejoined the policeman. "You're not allowed in here. And unless you look sharp about it you won't have time to sit down at all."

"Why not?"

"The Park closes at twelve."

"Closes?"

"At twelve o'clock, and it's half-past eleven now." The boy's heart sank into his wet boots. Here was an end of all his dashing plans. He was certain he had heard or read of people sleeping in the Park; he had looked upon it as a vast dormitory of the houseless; that was the only reason he was there. The offensive clerk in the hotel had evidently entertained the same belief. This idiot of a policeman must be wrong. But he seemed quite clear about it.

"Did you think we were open all night?" he inquired with a grin.

"I did," said Pocket; and he was inspired to add, "I even thought a lot of loafers used to sleep here all night!"

The policeman chuckled aloud.

"They may if they get up the trees; that's about their only chance," said he.

"You search the whole place so thoroughly?"

"We keeps our eyes open," said the policeman significantly, and Pocket asked no more questions; he scaled the forbidden fence and made off with the alacrity of one who meant to go out before he was put out. Such was his then sincere and sound intention. But where next to turn, to what seat on the Embankment, or what arch in the slums, in his ignorance of London he had no idea.

Meanwhile, to increase the irony of his dilemma, now that he was bent on quitting the Park he found himself striking deeper and deeper into its heart. He skirted a building, left it behind and out of sight, and drifted before the wind of destiny between an upright iron fence on one hand and a restricted open space upon the other. He could no longer see a single light; but the ground rose abruptly across the fence, and was thick with shrubs. Men might have been lying behind those shrubs, and Pocket could not possibly have seen them from the path. Did the policeman mean to tell him that he or his comrades were going to climb every fence and look behind every bush in Hyde Park?

Pocket came to anchor with a new flutter at his heart. This upright fence was not meant for scaling; it was like a lot of area palings, as obvious and intentional an obstacle. And the whole place closed at twelve, did it? The flutter became a serious agitation as Pocket saw himself breaking the laws of the land as well as those of school, saw himself not only expelled but put in prison! Well, so much the better for his story so long as those penalties were not incurred; even if they were, so much the greater hero he!

No wonder his best friends called him disparaging names; he was living up to the hardest of them now, and he with asthma on him as it was! But the will was on him too, the obstinate and reckless will, and the way lay handy in the shape of a row of Park chairs which Pocket had just passed against the iron palings. He went back to them, mounted on the first chair, wedged his bag between two of the spikes, set foot on the back of the chair, and somehow found himself on the other side without rent or scratch. Then he listened; but not a step could he hear. So then the cunning dog put his handkerchief through the palings and wiped the grit from the chair on which he had stood. And they called him a conscientious ass at school!

But then none of these desperate deeds were against his conscience, and they had all been thrust on Pocket Upton by circumstances over which he had lost control when the last train went without him from St. Pancras. They did not prevent him from kneeling down behind the biggest bush that I he could find, before curling up underneath it; neither did his prayers prevent him from thinking—even on his knees—of his revolver, nor yet—by the force of untimely association—of the other revolvers in the Chamber of Horrors. He saw those waxen wretches huddled together in ghastly groups, but the thought of them haunted him less than it might have done in a feather bed; he had his own perils and adventures to consider now. One thing, however, did come of the remembrance; he detached the leather strap he wore as a watch-guard. And used it to strap a pin-fire revolver, loaded in every chamber, to his wrist instead.

That was the last but one of the silly boy's proceedings under the bush; the last of all was to drain the number-one draught prescribed by Bompas in the morning, and to fling away the phial. The stuff was sweet and sticky in the mouth, and Pocket felt a singular and most grateful warmth at his extremities as he curled up in his overcoat. It was precisely then that he heard a measured tread approaching, and held his breath until it had passed without a pause. Yet the danger was still audible when the boy dropped off, thinking no more about it, but of Mr. Coverley and Charles Peace and his own people down in Leicestershire.

HIS PEOPLE

It so happened that his people in Leicestershire were thinking of him. They had been talking about him at the very time of the boy's inconceivable meanderings in Hyde Park. And two of them were at it still.

On a terrace outside lighted windows a powerful young fellow, in a butterfly collar and a corded smoking jacket, was walking up and down with a tall girl not unlike him in the face; but their faces were only to be seen in glimpses as they passed the drawing-room windows, and at not less regular intervals when a red light in the sky, the source of which was concealed by the garden foliage, became positively brilliant. The air was sweet with the scent of honeysuckle and musk-roses and mown grass; midges fretted in and out of the open windows. But for the lurid lighting of the sky, with its Cyclopean suggestion of some mammoth forge, you were in the heart of England undefiled.

"It's no use our talking about Tony," the tall girl said. "I think you're frightfully down on him; we shall never agree."

"Not as long as you make a fool of the fellow," said the blunt young man.

"Tony's no fool," remarked Lettice Upton, irrelevantly enough.

"You know what I mean," snapped her brother Horace. "He's being absolutely spoilt, and you're at the bottom of it."

"I didn't give him asthma!"

"Don't be childish, Letty."

"But that's what's spoiling his life."

"I wasn't talking about his life. I don't believe it, either."

"You think he enjoys his bad nights?"

"I think he scores by them. He'd tell you himself that he never even thinks of getting up to first school now."

"Would you if you'd been sitting up half the night with asthma?"

"Perhaps not; but I don't believe that happens so often as you think."

"It happens often enough to justify him in making one good night pay for two or three bad ones."

"I don't call that playing the game. I call it shamming."

"Well, if it is, he makes up for it. They were doing Ancient Greek Geography in his form at early school last term. Tony tackled it in his spare time, and got most marks in the exam."

"Beastly young swot!" quoth his elder brother. "I'm glad he didn't buck to me about that."

"I don't think there's much danger of his bucking to you," said Lettice, smiling in the red light. She did not add as her obvious reason that Horace, like many another athletic young man, was quite incapable of sympathising with the non-athletic type. But he guessed that she meant something of the sort, and having sensibilities of his own, and a good heart somewhere in his mesh of muscles, he felt hurt. "I looked after him all right," said Horace, "the one term we were there together. So did Fred for the next year. But it's rather rough on Fred and myself, who were both something in the school at his age, to hear and see for ourselves that Tony's nobody even in the house!"

Lettice slipped a sly hand under the great biceps of her eldest brother.

"But don't you see, old boy, that it makes it the worse for Tony that you and Fred were what you were at school? They measure him by the standard you two set up; it's natural enough, but it isn't fair."

"He needn't be a flyer at games," said Horace, duly softened by a little flattery. "But he might be a tryer!"

"Wait till we get a little more breath into his body."

"A bag of oxygen wouldn't make him a cricketer."

"Yet he's so keen on cricket!"

"I wish he wasn't so keen; he thinks and talks more about it than Fred or I did when we were in the eleven, yet he never looked like making a player."

"I should say he thinks and talks more about most things; it's his nature, just as it's Fred's and yours to be men of action."

"Well, I'm glad he's not allowed to cumber the crease this season," said Horace, bowling his cigarette-end into the darkness with a distinct swerve in the air. "To have him called our 'pocket edition,' on the cricket- field of all places, is a bit too thick."

Lettice withdrew her sympathetic hand.

"He's as good a sportsman as either of you, at heart," she said warmly. "And I hope he may make you see it before this doctor's done with him!"

"This doctor!" jeered Horace, quick to echo her change of tone as well. "You mean the fool who wanted to send that kid round the world on his own?"

"He's no fool, Horace, and you know nothing whatever about him."

"No; but I know something about our Tony! If he took the least care of himself at home, there might be something to be said for letting him go; but he's the most casual young hound I ever struck."

"I know he's casual."

Lettice made the admission with reluctance; next moment she was sorry her sense of fairness had so misled her.

"Besides," said Horace, "he wouldn't be cured if he could. Think what he'd miss!"

"Oh, if you're coming back to that, there's no more to be said."

And the girl halted at the lighted windows.

"But I do come back to it. Isn't he up in town at this moment under this very doctor of yours?"

"He's not my doctor."

"But you first heard about him; you're the innovator of the family, Letty, so it's no use trying to score off me. Isn't Tony up in London to-night?"

"I believe he is."

"Then I'll tell you what he's doing at this moment," cried Horace, with egregious confidence, as he held his watch to the windows. "It's after eleven; he's in the act of struggling out of some theatre, where the atmosphere's so good for asthma!" Lettice left the gibe unanswered. It was founded on recent fact which she had been the first to deplore when Tony made no secret of it in the holidays; indeed, she was by no means blind to his many and obvious failings; but they interested her more than the equally obvious virtues of her other brothers, whose unmeasured objurgations drove her to the opposite extreme in special pleading. She tried to believe that there was more in her younger brother than in any of them, and would often speak up for him as though she had succeeded. It may have been merely a woman's weakness for the weak, but Lettice had taught herself to believe in Tony. And perhaps of all his people she was the only one who could have followed his vagaries of that night without thinking the worse of him.

But she had no more to say to Horace about the matter, and would have gone indoors without another word if Mr. Upton had not come out hastily at that moment. He had been looking for her everywhere, he declared with some asperity. Her mother could not sleep, and wished to see her; otherwise it was time they were all in bed, and what there was to talk about till all hours was more than he could fathom. So he saw the pair before him through the lighted rooms, a heavy man with a flaming neck and a smouldering eye. Horace would be heavy, too, when his bowling days were over. The girl was on finer lines; but she looked like a woman at her worst; tired, exasperated, and clearly older than her brother, but of other clay.

That young man smoked a last cigarette in his father's library, and unhesitatingly admitted the subject of dissension and dissent upon the terrace.

"I said he wasn't doing much good there," he added, "and I don't think he is. Letty stood up for him, as she always does."

"Do you mean that he's doing any harm?" asked Mr. Upton plainly.

"Not for a moment. I never said there was any harm in Tony. I—I sometimes wish there was more!"

"More manhood, I suppose you'd call it?"

Mr. Upton spoke with a disconcerting grimness.

"More go about him," said Horace. He could not say as much to his father as he had to Letty. That was evident. But he was not the boy to bolt from his guns.

"Yet you know how much he has to take all that out of him?" continued Mr. Upton, with severity.

"I know," said Horace hastily, "and of course that's really why he's doing no good; but I must say that doctor of his doesn't seem to be doing him any either."

Mr. Upton got excitedly to his feet, and Horace made up his mind to the downright snub that he deserved. But by a lucky accident Horace had turned the wrath that had been gathering against himself into quite another quarter.

"I agree with you there!" cried his father vehemently. "I don't believe in the man myself; but he was recommended by the surgeon who has done so much for your poor mother, so what could one do but give him a trial? The lad wasn't having a fair chance at school. This looked like one. But I dislike his going up to town so often, and I dislike the letters the man writes me about him. He'd have me take him away from school altogether, and pack him off to Australia in a sailing ship. But what's to be done with a boy like that when we get him back again? He'd be too old to go to another school, and too young for the University: no use at the works, and only another worry to us all."

Mr. Upton spoke from the full heart of an already worried man, not with intentional unkindness, but yet with that unimaginative want of sympathy which is often the instinctive attitude of the sound towards the unsound. He hated sickness, and seemed at present surrounded by it. His wife had taken ill the year before, had undergone a grave operation in the winter, and was still a great anxiety to him. But that was another and a far more serious matter; he had patience and sympathy enough with his wife. The case of the boy was very different. Himself a man of much bodily and mental vigour, Mr. Upton expected his own qualities of his own children; he had always resented their apparent absence in his youngest born. The others were good specimens; why should Tony be a weakling? Was he such a weakling as was made out? Mr. Upton was often sceptical on the point; but then he had always heard more about the asthma than he had seen for himself. If the boy was not down to breakfast in the holidays, he was supposed to have had a bad night; yet later in the day he would be as bright as anybody, at times indeed the brightest of the party. That, however, was usually when Lettice drew him out in the absence of the two athletes; he was another creature then, excitable, hilarious, and more capable of taking the busy man out of himself than any of his other children. But Lettice overdid matters; she made far too much of the boy and his complaint, and was inclined to encourage him in random remedies. Cigarettes at his age, even if said to be cigarettes for asthma, suggested a juvenile pose to the man who had never studied that disorder. The specialist in London seemed another mistake on the part of that managing Lettice, who had quite assumed the family lead of late. And altogether Mr. Upton, though he saw the matter from a different point of view, was not far from agreeing with his eldest son about his youngest.

And what chance was there for a boy whose own father thought he posed, whose brothers considered him a bit of a malingerer, and his schoolfellows "a conscientious ass," while his sister spoilt him for un enfant incompris? You may say it would have taken a miracle to make an ordinary decent fellow of him. Well, it was a night of strange happenings to the boy and his people; perhaps it was the one authentic type of miracle that capped all in the morning.

The father had gone to bed at midnight, after an extra allowance of whisky-and-water to take the extra worry off his mind; it did so for a few hours only to stretch him tragically awake in the early morning. The birds were singing down in Leicestershire as in Hyde Park. The morning sun was slanting over town and country, and the father's thoughts were with his tiresome son in town. Suddenly a shrill cry came from the adjoining room.

In a trice the wakeful man was at his sick wife's side, supporting her in bed as she sat up wildly staring, trembling in his arms.

"Tony!" she gasped. "My Tony!"

"I was just thinking of him!" he cried. "What about him, dear?"

"I saw him," she quavered. "I saw him plainer than I see you now. And I'm almost positive I heard—a shot!"

A GRIM SAMARITAN

Though he afterwards remembered a shout as well, it actually was the sound of a shot that brought the boy to his senses in Hyde Park. He opened his eyes on a dazzle of broad daylight and sparkling grass. The air was strangely keen for the amount of sunshine, the sunshine curiously rarefied, and the grass swept grey where it did not sparkle.

Pocket's first sensation was an empty stomach, and his next a heavy head into which the puzzle of his position entered by laborious steps. He was not in bed. He was not at school. He was not even under the shrub he now remembered in a mental flash which lit up all his adventures overnight. He was wandering ankle deep in the dew, towards a belt of poplars like birch-rods on the skyline, and a row of spiked palings right in front of his nose. He had walked in his sleep for the first time for years, and some one had fired a shot to wake him.

Slow as these automatic discoveries had seemed, they had been in reality so swift that the report was still ringing in his ears when he who must have made it sprang hideously into being across the palings. A hand darted through them and caught Pocket's wrist as in a vice. And he looked up over the spikes into a gnarled face tinged with fear and fury, and working spasmodically at the suppression of some incomprehensible emotion.

"Do you know what you did?" the man demanded in the end. The question seemed an odd one, but a very slight foreign accent, not to be reproduced phonetically, corresponded with the peculiarity of tense, reminding Pocket of the music-masters at his school. It was less easy to account for the tone employed, which was low in pitch and tremulous with passion. And the man stood tall and dominant, with a silver stubble on an iron jaw, and a weird cloak and hat that helped to invest him with the goblin dignity of a Spanish inquisitor; no wonder his eyes were like cold steel in quivering flesh.

"I must have been walking in my sleep," began Pocket, shakily; further explanations were cut very short.

"Sleep!" echoed the other, in bitter unbelief.

Pocket felt his prime quality impugned.

"Well? I can't help it! I've done it before to-day; you needn't believe me if you don't like! Do you mind letting go of my hand?"

"With that in it!"

The scornful tone made the boy look down, and there was the pistol he had strapped to his wrist, not only firm in his unconscious clasp, but his finger actually on the trigger.

"You don't mean to say I let it off?" cried Pocket, horrified.

"Feel the barrel."

The tall man had done so first. Pocket touched it with his left hand. The barrel was still warm.

"It was in my sleep," protested Pocket, in a wheezy murmur.

"I'm glad to hear it."

"I tell you it was!"

The tall man opened his lips impulsively, but shut them on a second impulse. The daggers in his eyes probed deeper into those of the boy, picking his brains, transfixing the secrets of his soul. No master's eye had ever delved so deep into his life; he felt as though the very worst of him at school was known in an instant to this dreadful stranger in the wilds of London. He writhed under the ordeal of that protracted scrutiny. He tugged to free his imprisoned wrist. His captor was meanwhile fumbling with a penknife in his unoccupied hand. A blade was slowly opened; the leather watch-guard was sliced through in a second; the revolver dropped harmlessly into the dew. The man swooped down and whipped it through the railings with a snarl of satisfaction.

"And now," said he, releasing Pocket, but standing by with his weapon, "I suppose you know that, apart from everything else, you had no right to spend the night in here at all?"

The boy, already suffering from his humiliating exertions, gasped out, "I'm not the only one!" He had just espied a recumbent figure through the palings; it was that of a dilapidated creature lying prone, a battered hat beside him, on the open grass beyond the path. The tall man merely redoubled his scrutiny of the face in front of, him, without so much as a glance behind.

"That," said he, "is the sort that staggers in as soon as the gates are open, and spends the day sleeping itself sober. But you are not that sort at all, and you have spent the night here contrary to the rules. Who are you, and what's the matter with you?"

"Asthma," wheezed Pocket, clinging to the palings in dire distress.

"So I thought. Yet you spend your night on the wet grass!"

"I had nowhere else to go."

"Have you come up from the country?"

"To see a doctor about it!" cried Pocket bitterly, and told the whole truth about himself in a series of stertorous exclamations. It scarcely lessened the austerity of the eyes that still ran him through and through; but the hard mouth did relax a little; the lined face looked less deeply slashed and furrowed, and it was a less inhuman voice that uttered the next words.

"Well, we must get you out of this, my young fellow! Come to these chairs."

Pocket crept along the palings towards the chairs by which he had climbed them. His breathing was pitiful now. The stranger accompanied him on the other side.

"If I lift one over, and lend you a hand, do you think you can manage it?"

"I did last night."

"Here, then. Wait a bit! Can you tell me where you slept?"

Pocket looked round and pointed.

"Behind that bush."

"Have you left nothing there?"

"Yes; my bag and hat!"

In his state it took him some time to go and fetch them; he was nearly suffocating when he came creeping back, his shoulders up to his ears.

"Stop! I see something else. Is that medicine-bottle yours? There—catching the sun."

"It was."

"Bring it."

"It's empty."

"Bring it!"

Pocket obeyed. The strange man was standing on a chair behind the palings, waiting to help him over, with a wary eye upon the path. But no third creature was in sight except the insensate sprawler in the dew. Pocket surmounted the obstacle, he knew not how; he was almost beside himself in the throes of his attack. Later, he feared he must have been lifted down like a child; but this was when he was getting his breath upon a seat. They had come some little distance very slowly, and Pocket had received such support from so muscular an arm as to lend colour to his humiliating suspicion.

His grim companion spoke first.

"Well, I'm sorry for you. But I feel for your doctor too. I am one myself."

Pocket ignored the somewhat pointed statement.

"I'll never forgive the brute!" he panted.

"Come, come! He didn't send you to sleep in the Park."

"But he took away the only thing that does me any good."

"What's that?"

"Cigarettes d'Auvergne."

"I never heard of them."

"They're the only thing to stop it, and he took away every one I had."

But even as he spoke Pocket remembered the cigarette he had produced from his bag, but lacked the moral courage to light, in the train. He had slipped it into one of his pockets, not back into the box. He felt for it feverishly. He gave a husky cheer as his fingers closed upon the palpable thing, and he drew forth a flattened cylinder the size of a cigarette and the colour of a cigar. The boy had to bite off both ends; the man was ready with the match. Pocket drank the crude smoke down like water, coughed horribly, drank deeper, coughed the tears into his eyes, and was comparatively cured.

"And your doctor forbids a sovereign remedy!" said his companion. "I cannot understand him, and I'm a doctor myself." His voice and look were deliberate even for him. "My name is Baumgartner," he added, and made a pause. "I don't suppose you know it?"

"I'm not sure I don't," replied Pocket, swelling with breath and gratitude; but in truth the name seemed vaguely familiar to him.

"A schoolboy in the country," observed Dr. Baumgartner, "is scarcely likely to have heard of me; but if you inquire here in London you will find that I am not unknown. I propose to carry you off to my house for breakfast, and a little rest. That is," added the doctor, with his first smile, "if you will trust yourself to me first and make your inquiries later."

Pocket scouted the notion of inquiries in an impulsive outburst; but even as he proceeded to mumble out his thanks he could not help feeling it would have been less embarrassing to know more exactly whom he was thanking and must needs accompany now. Dr. Baumgartner? Where was it he had come across that name? And when and where had anybody ever seen such a doctor as this unshaven old fellow in the cloak and hat of a conspirator by limelight?

But the schoolboy had still to learn the lesson of naked personality as the one human force; and he learnt it now unknown to himself. The gaunt grey man stood up in his absurd and rusty raiment, and Pocket thought, "How the chaps would rag him at school!" because the dreadful old hat and cloak suggested a caricature of a master's cap and gown. But there was no master at Pocket's school whom he would not sooner have disobeyed than this shabby stranger with the iron-bound jaw and the wintry smile; there was no eye on the staff that had ever made him quail as he had quailed that morning before these penetrating eyes of steel. Baumgartner said they must hurry, and Pocket had his asthma back in the first few yards. Baumgartner said they could buy more cigarettes on the way, and Pocket kept up, panting, at his side.

In the cab Baumgartner said, "Try sitting with your head between your knees." Pocket tried it like a lamb. They had encountered a young man or so hurrying into the Park with towels round the neck but no collar, an early cavalcade who never looked at them, and that was about all until the hansom had been hailed outside. During the drive, which seemed to Pocket interminable, his extraordinary attitude prevented him from seeing anything but his own boots, and those only dimly owing to the apron being shut and indeed pressing uncomfortably against his head. Yet when Dr. Baumgartner inquired whether that did not make him easier, he said it did. It was not all imagination either; the posture did relieve him; but it was none the less disagreeable to be driven through London by an utter stranger, and not to see the names of the streets or a single landmark. Pocket had not even heard the cabman's instructions where to drive; they had been given after he got in. His ear was more alert now. He noted the change from wood-paving to rough metal. Then more wood, and an indubitable omnibus blundering by; then more metal, in better repair; quieter streets, the tinkle of cans, the milkman's queer cry; and finally, "Next to the right and the fifth house on your left," in the voice with the almost imperceptibly foreign accent.

The fifth house on the left was exactly like the fourth and the sixth from the little Pocket saw of any of them. He was hurried up a tiled path, none too clean between swarthy and lack-lustre laurels; the steps had not been "done"; the door wore the nondescript complexion of prehistoric paint debased by the caprices of the London climate. One touch of colour the lad saw before this unpromising portal opened and shut upon him: he had already passed through a rank of pollard trees, sprouting emeralds in the morning sun, that seemed common to this side of the road, and effectually hid the other.

Within the doctor held up a finger and they both trod gently. The passage was dark and short. The stairs began abruptly on the right. Baumgartner led the way past a closed door on the left, into an unexpectedly bright and large room beyond it. "Sit down," said he, and shut the door softly behind him.

Pocket took observations from the edge of his chair. The room was full of walnut trivialities that looked aggressively obsolete in the sunshine that filled it and flooded a green little garden at the back of the house. Dr. Baumgartner had pulled up a blind and opened a window, and he stood looking out in thought while Pocket hurriedly completed his optical round. A set of walnut chairs were dreadfully upholstered in faded tapestry; but a deep, worn one looked comfortable enough, and a still more redeeming feature was the semi-grand piano. There were books, too, and in the far corner by the bow-window a glass door leading into a conservatory as minute as Pocket's study at school, and filled with geraniums. On the walls hung a series of battle engravings, one representing a bloody advance over ridged fields in murderously close formation, others the storming of heights and villages.

Baumgartner met his visitor's eyes with the faint cold smile that scarcely softened the hoary harshness of his visage.

"I was present at some of those engagements," said he. "They were not worse than disarming a man who has just fired a revolver in his sleep!"

He flung his cloak upon one of the walnut chairs, and Pocket heard the pistol inside it rattle against the back; but his attention was distracted before he had time to resent the forgotten fact of its forcible confiscation. Under his cloak the doctor had been carrying all this time, slung by a strap which the boy had noticed across his chest, a stereoscopic camera without a case. Pocket exclaimed upon it with the instructed interest of a keen photographer.

"Do you take photographs?" asked Baumgartner, a reciprocal note in his unemotional voice.

"Rather!" cried the schoolboy, with considerable enthusiasm. "It's the only thing I have to do instead of playing games. But I haven't got an instantaneous camera like that. I only wish I had!"

And he looked with longing eyes at the substantial oblong of wood and black morocco, and duplicate lenses like a pair of spectacles, which the doctor had set between them on one of the fussy little walnut tables.

THE GLASS EYE

Dr. Baumgartner produced a seasoned meerschaum, carved in the likeness of a most ferocious face, and put a pinch of dark tobacco through the turban into the bowl. "You see," said he, "I must have my smoke like you! I can't do without it either, though what is your misfortune is my own fault. So you are also a photographer!" he added, as the fumes of a mixture containing latakia spiced the morning air.

"I am only a beginner," responded Pocket, "but a very keen one."

"You don't merely press the button and let them do the rest?" suggested the doctor, smiling less coldly under the influence of his pipe.

"Rather not! I develop, print, tone, and all the rest of it; that's half the fun."

"Plates or films?" inquired Baumgartner, with an approving nod.

"Only plates, I'm afraid; you see, the apparatus is an old one of my father's."

And honest Pocket was beginning to blush for it, when the other made a gesture more eloquent and far more foreign than his speech.

"It's none the worse for that," said he. "So far we have much in common, for I always use plates myself. But what we put upon our plates, there's the difference, eh?"

"I should imagine so," said Pocket, smiling.

Dr. Baumgartner was smiling too, and still less coldly than before, but yet darkly to himself, and at the boy rather than with him.

"You take portraits of your friends, perhaps?"

"Yes; often."

"In the body, I presume?"

Pocket looked nonplussed.

"You only take them in the flesh?"

"Of course."

"Exactly! I take the spirit," said the doctor; "that's the difference."

Pocket watched the now wonderfully genial countenance of Baumgartner follow the brutal features of the meerschaum Turk through a melting cloud of smoke. The boy had been taken aback. But his bewilderment was of briefer duration than might have been the case with a less ardent photographer; for he took a technical interest in his hobby, and read the photographic year-books, nearly as ravenously as Wisden's Almanacke.

"I see," he said, lukewarmly. "You go in for psychic photography."

"Psychic," said Baumgartner; for the public schoolboy, one regrets to report, had pronounced the word to rhyme with sly-chick. The doctor added, with more disdain: "And you don't believe in it?"

"I didn't say so."

"But you looked and sounded it!"

"I don't set myself up as a believer or unbeliever," said the boy, always at his ease on a subject that attracted him. "But I do say I don't believe in the sort of thing I read somewhere last holidays. It was in a review of a book on that sort of photography. The chap seemed to have said you could get a negative of a spirit without exposing the plate at all; hide away your plate, never mind your lens, only conjure up your spirit and see what happens. I'll swear nothing ever happened like that! There may be ghosts, you may see them, and so may the camera, but not without focusing and exposing like you've got to do with ordinary flesh and blood!"

The youth had gone further and flown higher than he meant, under the stimulus of an encouragement impossible to have foreseen. And the doctor had come to his feet, waving eloquently with his pipe; his grey face beamed warmly; his eyes were lances tipped with fire.

"Well said, my young fellow!" cried he. "I agree with every syllable you have spoken."

"It's a question of photography, not of spiritualism," concluded Pocket, rounding off his argument in high excitement.

"I agree, I agree! All that is rubbish, pure moonshine; and you see it even at your age! But there's much more in it than that; you must see the rest as well, since you see so far so clearly." The boy blushed with pleasure, determined to see as far as anybody. "You admit there may be such things as ghosts, as you call them?" he was asked as by an equal.

"Certainly, sir."

"Visible shapes, in the likeness of man? As visible and yet as tangible as that sunbeam?"

"Rather!"

"You allow that the camera can see them if we can?"

Pocket allowed it like the man he was being made to feel; the concession gave him a generous glow. Promotion had come to him by giant leaps. He felt five years older in fewer minutes.

"Then," cried the doctor, with further flattery in his air of triumph, "then you admit everything! You may not see these images, but I may. I may not see them, but my lens may! Think how much that glass eye throws already upon the retina of a sensitised film that our living lenses fail to throw upon ours; think of all that escapes the eye but the camera catches. Take two crystal vases, fill one with one acid and the other with another; one comes out like water as we see it; the other, though not less limpid in our sight, like ink. The eye sees through it, but not the lens. The eye sees emptiness as though the acid itself were pure crystal; the lens flings an inky image on the plate. The trouble is that, while you can procure that acid at the nearest chemist's, no money and no power on earth can summon or procure at will the spirit which once was man."

His voice was vibrant and earnest as it had been when Pocket heard it first an hour earlier in the Park. It was even as passionate, but this was the passion of enthusiastic endeavour. If the man had a heart at all, it was in this wild question without a doubt. Even the schoolboy perceived this dimly. There was something else which had become clearer to him with each of these later remarks. Striking as they seemed to him, they were not wholly unfamiliar. The ring of novelty was wanting to his ear.

Suddenly he exclaimed, "I knew I knew your name!"

"You do know it, do you?"

Baumgartner spoke ungraciously, as though the announcement was discounted by the interruption it entailed.

"It was in connection with the very book I mentioned. I knew I had come across it somewhere."

"You read the correspondence that followed the review?"

"Some of it."

"My letter among others?"

"Yes! I remember every word of it now."

"Then you recall my view as to the alleged necessity of a medium's co-operation in these spirit-photographs?"

"You said it wasn't necessary, if I remember," replied Pocket somewhat tentatively, despite his boast.

"It was the pith and point of my contention! I mentioned the two moments at which I hold that a man's soul may be caught apart, may be cut off from his body by no other medium than a good sound lens in a light-tight camera. You cannot have forgotten them if you read my letter."

"One," said the boy, "was the moment of death."

"The moment of dissolution," the doctor corrected him. "But there is a far commoner moment than that, one that occurs constantly to us all, whereas dissolution comes but once."

Pocket believed he remembered the other instance too, but was not sure about it, the fact being that the whole momentous letter had struck him as too fantastic for serious consideration. That, however, he could not and dared not say; and he was not the less frightened of making a mistake with those inspired eyes burning fanatically into his.

"The other moment," the doctor said at last, with a pitying smile, "is when the soul returns to its prison after one of those flights which men call dreams. You know that theory of the dream?" Baumgartner asked abruptly. The answer was a nod as hasty, but the doctor seemed unconvinced, for he went on didactically: "You visit far countries in your dreams; your soul is the traveller. You speak to the absent or the dead; it is your soul again; and we dismiss the miracle as a dream! I fix the moment as that of the soul's return because its departure on these errands is imperceptible, but with its return we awake. The theory is that in the moment of waking the whole experience happens like the flash of an electric spark."

The boy murmured very earnestly that he saw; but he was more troubled than enlightened, and what he did see was that he had picked up a very eccentric acquaintance indeed. He was not a little scared by the man's hard face and molten eyes; but there was a fascination also that could not be lost upon an impressionable temperament, besides that force of will or character which had dominated the young mind from the first. He began to wish the interview at an end—to be able to talk about it as the extraordinary sequel of an extraordinary adventure—yet he would not have cut it short at this point if he could.

"I grant you," continued the doctor, "that the final flight of soul from body is infinitely the more precious from my point of view. But how is one to be in a position to intercept that? When beloved spirits pass it would be cold-blooded desecration; and public opinion has still to be educated up to psychical vivisection! I have myself tried in vain to initiate such education. I have applied for perfectly private admission to hospital deathbeds, even to the execution-shed in prisons. My applications have been peremptorily refused."

Pocket's thoughts went off at a gruesome tangent.

"You could see a man hanged!" he shuddered, and himself saw the little old effigy on the model drop in Marylebone Road.

"Why not?" asked the other in wide wonder. "But as I am not allowed," he continued in lighter key, "I have to do the best I can. If I cannot be in at the death, I may still by luck be in at a dream or two! And now you may guess why I wander with my camera where men come in to sleep in broad daylight. I prowl among them; a word awakens them; and then I take my chance."

"They're not all like that man this morning, then," remarked Pocket, looking back on the inanimate clod reclining in the dew.

The doctor deliberated with half-shut eyes that seemed to burn the brighter for their partial eclipse.

"This morning," he rejoined, "was like no other. I owe you some confidence in the matter. I had the chance of a lifetime this morning—thanks to you!"

"Thanks to me?" repeated Pocket. A flash enlightened him. "Do you mean to say I—you took me—walking—?"

"You shall see my meaning," replied Baumgartner, rising. "Wait one minute."

He was not gone longer. Pocket heard him on the other side of double doors in an alcove; but he had gone out into the passage to get there. Running water and the chink of porcelain were specially audible in his absence, but the boy was thinking of another sound. The doctor before leaving had discarded a black alpaca jacket, light as a pocket handkerchief, which had fallen so softly as to recall by contrast the noise made by the revolver in the pocket of the cloak. The lad was promptly seized with a strong desire to recover his property; he was within an ace of doing so, the cloak containing it being actually in his hands and only dropped as Baumgartner returned to announce that all was ready.

Sharp to the left, at the end of the passage, was a door which would simply have been a second way into the drawing-room had the double doors within been is use; these being shut, the space behind made a separate chamber which again reminded the schoolboy of his study, that smallest of small rooms. This one was as narrow, only twice the length. One end was monopolised by the door that admitted them, the other by a window from floor to ceiling. And this window was in two great sheets of ruby glass, so that Pocket looked down red-hot iron steps into a crimson garden, and therefrom to his companion dyed from head to foot like Mephistopheles.

"This is something like a dark-room!" exclaimed the lad as the door was shut and locked behind him. The folding doors were permanently barred by shelves and lockers; opposite was a long porcelain trough, pink as the doctor's shirt-sleeves in the strong red light; racks of negatives and stoppered bottles glimmered over brass taps stained to an angry copper.

Everything was perfection from a photographer's standpoint; the boy felt instantaneously spoilt for his darkened study and his jugs of water. All he had ever sighed for in the prosecution of his hobby was here in this little paradise of order and equipment. The actual work, he felt, would be a secondary consideration in such a workshop; the mere manipulation of such stoppered bottles as his host was handling now, the choice of graduated phials, the wealth of trays and dishes, would have been joy enough for him. He watched the favoured operator with a watering mouth. A crimson blind had been lowered to reduce the light; the doctor had turned up his shirt-cuffs; his wrists were muscular and furry, as it now seemed with a fiery fur, yet they trembled with excitement as he produced his plate. And Pocket remembered how extravagant an image was expected on that plain pink surface.

He did not know whether to expect it or not himself. It was difficult to believe in that sort of thing, difficult to disbelieve in this sort of man, who entertained no shadow of doubt himself, whose excitement and suspense were as infectious as everything else about him. Pocket had come into the dark-room wheezing almost as much as ever; he was not to be heard breathing as the plate was rocked to and fro as in raspberry-juice, and gradually the sky showed sharp and black. But the sky it was that puzzled Pocket first. It was broken by perpendicular objects like white torpedoes. He was photographer enough to know what these were almost at once; they were those poplars in the park. But how could Baumgartner have photographed Pocket with those poplars behind him when they had been behind Baumgartner all the time?

Pocket said to himself, "Where am I, by the way?" and bent lower to see. His ear touched the doctor's; it heard the doctor breathing as though he were the asthmatic; and now a human shape was visible, but not walking in its sleep, lying in it like the man in the wet grass. "When did you get me?" asked Pocket aloud. But the tense crimson face paid no attention; in the ruby light it was glistening as though with beads of blood.

"There! there! there!" croaked a voice, husky and yet staccato. Pocket could scarcely believe it was the voice of his host—the one gentle thing about him. "You saw the figure? Surely you saw something else, hovering over it? I did, I swear I did! But now we shall have to wait."

The plate had blackened all over, as though the uncanny thing had choked out its life. It was meticulously held under a tap, between fingers that most distinctly trembled now. Then he plunged it in the hyposulphite, and pulled up the blind. The sun shone again through the tall window, blood- red as before; grass and sky were as richly incarnadined. Baumgartner babbled while he waited for the fixing-bath to clear the plate. The chance of his life, he still pronounced it. "And I owe it to you, my young fellow!" This he said again and again, aloud but chiefly to himself. He picked up the plate at last and held it to the flaming window. He cried out in German to himself, a cry the schoolboy never forgot.

"Open the window!" he ordered. "It opens like a door."

Pocket did as he was told. The pure white sunlight struck him momentarily blind. Baumgartner had the plate under the tap again. Pocket thought him careless with it, thought the tap on too full; it was held up an instant to the naked sun, and then dashed to a hundred fragments in the porcelain trough.

Pocket knew better than to ask a question. He followed his leader back into the drawing-room, and watched him pick up his coat. It might have been a minute before their eyes met again; the doctor's were calm and cold and critical as in the earlier morning. It was another failure, he said, and nothing more. Breakfast would be ready soon; they would go upstairs; and if his young fellow felt equal to a warm bath, he thought as a physician it might do him good.

AN AWAKENING

It was a normal elderly gentleman, with certain simple habits, but no little distinction of address, who welcomed the schoolboy at his breakfast-table. The goblin inquisitor of Hyde Park had vanished with his hat and cloak. The excited empiric of the dark-room was a creature of that ruby light alone. Dr. Baumgartner was shaved and clad like other men, the iron-grey hair carefully brushed back from a lofty forehead, all traces of strong acids removed from his well-kept hands. There was a third person, and only a third, at table in the immature shape of a young lady whom the doctor introduced as his niece Miss Platts, and addressed as Phillida.

Pocket thought he had never heard of nobler atonement for unmitigable surname. He could not help thinking that this Phillida did not look the one to flout a fellow, after the fashion of the only other Phillida he had ever heard of, and then that it was beastly cheek to start thinking of her like that and by her Christian name. But he was of the age and temperament when thoughts will come of contact with young animals of the opposite sex. He looked at her sidelong from time to time, but all four eyes dropped directly they met; she seemed as shy and uninteresting as himself; her conversation was confined to table attentions to her uncle and his guest.

Pocket made more valiant attempts. A parlour billiard-table, standing against the wall, supplied an irresistible topic. "We have a full-size table at home," he said, and could have mutilated his tongue that instant. "I like a small one best," he assured the doctor, who shook his head and smiled.

"Honestly, sir, and snob-cricket better than the real thing! I'm no good at real games."

The statement was too true, but not the preference.

"That must be awkward for you, at an English public school," was the doctor's comment.

Pocket heaved an ingenuous sigh. It was hateful. He blamed the asthma as far as modesty would permit. He was modest enough in his breakfast-table talk, yet nervously egotistical, and apt to involve himself in lengthy explanations. He had two types of listener—the dry and the demure—to all he said.

"And they let you come up to London alone!" remarked Dr. Baumgartner when he got a chance.

"But it wasn't their fault that I—"

Pocket stopped at a glance from his host, and plunged into profuse particulars exonerating his house-master, but was cut short again. Evidently the niece was not to know where he had spent the night.

"I suppose there are a number of young men at your—establishment?" said the doctor, exchanging a glance with Miss Platts.

"There are over four hundred boys," replied Pocket, a little puzzled.

"And how many keepers do they require?"

A grin apologised for the word.

"There must be over thirty masters," returned Pocket more pointedly than before. He was not going to stand chaff about his public school from a mad German doctor.

"And they arm you for the battle of life with Latin and Greek, eh?"

"Not necessarily; there's a Modern Side. You can learn German if you like!" said Pocket, not without contempt.

"Do you?"

"I don't like," said the boy gratuitously.

"Then we must stick to your excellent King's English."

Pocket turned a trifle sulky. He felt he had not scored in this little passage. Then he reflected upon the essential and extraordinary kindness which had brought him to a decent breakfast-table that morning. That made him ashamed; nor could he have afforded to be too independent just yet, even had he been so disposed in his heart. His asthma was a beast that always growled in the background; he never knew when it would spring upon him with a roar. Breakfast pacified the brute; hot coffee always did; but the effects soon wore off, and the boy was oppressed again, yet deadly weary, long before it was time for him to go to Welbeck Street.

"Is there really nothing you can take?" asked Dr. Baumgartner, standing over him in the drawing-room, where Pocket sat hunched up in the big easy- chair.

"Nothing now, I'm afraid, unless I could get some of those cigarettes. And Dr. Bompas would kick up an awful row!"

"But it's inhuman. I'll go and get them myself. He should prescribe for such an emergency."

"He has," said Pocket. "I've got some stuff in my bag; but it's no use taking it now. It's meant to take in bed when you can have your sleep out."

And he was going into more elaborate details than Dr. Bompas had done, when the other doctor cut him short once more.

"But why not now? You can sleep to your heart's content in that chair; nobody will come in."

Pocket shook his head.

"I'm due in Welbeck Street at twelve."

"Well, I'll wake you at quarter to, and have a taxi ready at the door. That will give you a good two hours."

Pocket hesitated, remembering the blessed instantaneous effect of the first bottle under the bush.

"Would you promise to wake me, sir? You're not going out?"

"I shall be in again."

"Then it is a promise?"

Pocket would have liked it in black and white.

"Certainly, my young fellow! Is the stuff in your bag?"

It was, and the boy took it with much the same results as overnight. It tasted sweeter and acted quicker; that was the only difference. The skin seemed to tighten on his face. His fingers tingled at the ends It was not at all an unpleasant sensation, especially as the labour in his breast came to an end as if by magic. The faintly foreign accents of Dr. Baumgartner sounded unduly distant in his last words from the open door. It was scarcely shut before the morning's troubles ceased deliciously in the cosy chair.

Yet they seemed to begin again directly, and this was a horrid crop! Of course he was back in Hyde Park; but the sky must have rained red paint in his absence, or else the earth was red-hot and the sky reflected it. No! the grass was too wet for that. It might have been wet with blood. Everything was as red as beet-root, as wet and red and one's body weltering in it like the slain! Reddest of all was the old photographer, who turned into Mr. Spearman in cap and gown, who turned into various members of the Upton family, one making more inconsequent remarks than the other, touching wildly on photography and the flitting soul, and between them working the mad race up to such a pace and pitch that Pocket woke with a dreadful start to find Dr. Baumgartner standing over him once more in the perfectly pallid flesh.

"I've had a beast of a dream!" said Pocket, waking thoroughly. "I'm in a cold perspiration, and I thought it was cold blood! What time is it?"

"A quarter to six," said the doctor, who had invited the question by taking out his watch.

"A quarter to twelve, you mean!"

"No—six."

And the boy was shown the dial, but would not believe it until he had gaped at his own watch, which had stopped at half-past three. Then he bounded to his feet in a puerile passion, and there lay the little garden, a lake of sunlight as he remembered it, swallowed up entirely in the shadow of the house.

"You promised to wake me!" gasped Pocket, almost speechless. "You've broken your word, sir!"

"Only in your own interest," replied the other calmly.

"I believe you were waiting for me to wake—to catch my soul, or some rot!" cried the boy, with bitter rudeness; but he looked in vain for the stereoscopic or any other sort of camera, and Dr. Baumgartner only shrugged his shoulders as he opened an evening paper.

"I apologise for saying that," the boy resumed, with a dignity that sounded near to tears. "I know you meant it for the best—to make up for my bad night—you've been very kind to me, I know! But I was due in Welbeck Street at twelve o'clock, and now I shall have to bolt to catch the six-thirty from St. Pancras."

"You won't catch the six-thirty from St. Pancras," replied Baumgartner, scarcely looking up from his paper.

"I will unless I'm in some outlandish part of London!" cried Pocket, reflecting for the first time that he had no idea in what part of London he was. "I must catch it. It's the last train back to school. I'll get into an awful row if I don't!"

"You'll get into a worse one if you do," rejoined the doctor, looking over his paper, and not unfeelingly, at the boy.

"What about?"

Pocket held his breath instinctively as their eyes met. Baumgartner answered with increased compassion and restraint, a grey look on his grey face:

"Something that happened this morning. I fear you will be wanted here in town about it."

"Do tell me what, sir!"

"Can you face things, my young fellow?"

"Is it about my people—my mother?" the boy cried wildly, at her funeral in a flash.

"No—yourself."

"Then I can!"

The doctor overcame his final hesitation.

"Do you remember a man we left behind us on the grass?"

"Perfectly; the grass looked as wet as it felt just now in my dream."

"Exactly. Didn't it strike you as strange that he should be lying there in the wet grass?"

"I thought he was drunk."

"He was dead!"

Pocket was shocked; he was more than shocked, for he had never witnessed death before; but next moment the shock was uncontrollably mitigated by a sudden view of the tragic incident as yet another adventure of that adventurous night. No doubt one to retail in reverential tones, but a most thrilling adventure none the less. He only failed to see why it should affect him as much as the doctor suggested. True, he might be called as witness at the inquest; his very natural density was pierced with the awkward possibility of that. But then he had not even known the man was dead.

Had the doctor?

Yes.

Pocket wondered why he had not been told at the time, but asked another question first.

"What did he die of?"

"A bullet!"

"Suicide?"

"No."

"Not murder?"

"This paper says so."

"Does it say who did it?"

"It cannot."

"Can you?"

"Yes!"

"Tell me."

The doctor threw out both hands in a despairing gesture.

"Have I to tell you outright, my young fellow, that you did it yourself?"

BLOOD-GUILTY

His overwhelming horror was not alleviated by a moment's doubt. He marvelled rather that he had never guessed what he had done. The walking in his sleep, the shot that woke him, the first words of Dr. Baumgartner, his first swift action, and the warm pistol in his own unconscious hand: these burning memories spoke more eloquently than any words. They would have told their own tale at once, if only he had known the man was dead. Why had he been deceived? It was cruel, it was infamous, to have kept the truth from him for a single instant. Thus wildly did the stricken youth turn and rend his benefactor for the very benefaction of a day's rest in ignorance of his deed. The doctor defended himself firmly, frankly, with much patience and some cynicism. Pocket was reminded of the state he himself had been in at the time. He also might have been a dying man, he was assured, and could well believe on looking back. Baumgartner had actually opened his lips to tell him the truth, but had checked himself in sheer humanity. Again the boy could confirm the outward detail out of his own recollection. To have told him later in the morning, the doctor went on to say, with an emphasis not immediately understood, could have undone nothing. He acknowledged a grave responsibility, but rightly or wrongly he had put the living before the dead.

How had he known the man was dead? Baumgartner smiled at the question. He was not only a doctor, but an old soldier who had fought in one at least of the bloodiest battles in European history. He had seen too many men fall shot through the heart to be mistaken for a moment; but in point of fact he had confirmed his conviction by brief examination while Pocket was fetching his things from behind the bush. Pocket pressed for earlier details with a morbid appetite which was not gratified without reluctance, and out of a laconic interchange the deed was gradually reconstructed with appealing verisimilitude. It was Baumgartner who had first caught sight of the somnambulist, treading warily like the blind, yet waving the revolver as he went, as though any moment he might let it off. The moment came with a wretched reeling man who joined Baumgartner on the path, and would not be warned. The poor man had raised a drunken shout and been shot pointblank through the heart. The doctor described him as leaping backward from the levelled barrel, then into the air and down in the dew upon his face.

The boy buried his face and wept; but even in his anguish he now recalled the shout before the shot. The enforced description had been so vivid in the end that he beheld the scene as plainly as though he had been wide awake. Then he dwelt upon the dead man, looking nothing else as he now remembered him, and that sent him off at a final tangent.

He cried, looking up with a shudder for all his tears, "What about that negative you smashed? It was the poor dead man all the time!"

"It was," replied Baumgartner; "but it was never meant to be. I had you in focus when you fired. What I did was done instinctively, but with time to think I should have done just the same. You had given me the chance of a lifetime, though nothing has come of it so far. And that was another reason for saving you, ill as you were, from the immediate consequences of an innocent act."

Pocket was passionately honest, as his worst friends knew; he had an instinctive admiration for downright honesty in another. His young soul was torn with grief and pity for the dead; he was already haunted by the inevitable and complex consequences of his fatal misadventure, and yet he could dimly appreciate the candid declaration of one who had attempted to turn that tragedy to instantaneous and inconceivable account. It was the mistaken kindness to himself that he still found most difficult to forgive.

"It's got to come out," he groaned; "this will make it all the worse."

"You mean the delay?"

"Yes! Who's to tell them I didn't do it on purpose, and run away, and then think better of it?"

Baumgartner smiled.

"Surely I am," said he; but his smile went out with the words. "If only they believe me!" he added as though it was a new idea to him.

It was a terrifying one to Pocket.

"Why shouldn't they?" was his broken exclamation.

"I don't know. I never thought of it before. But what can I swear to, after all? I can swear you shot a man, but I can't swear you shot him in your sleep!"

"You said you saw I did!"

"So I did, my young fellow," replied the doctor, with a kinder smile; "at least I can swear that you were walking with your eyes shut, and I thought you were walking in your sleep. It's not quite the same thing. It is near it. But we are talking about my evidence on oath in a court of justice."

"Shall I be tried?" asked the schoolboy in a hoarse whisper.

"Perhaps only by the magistrate," replied the other, soothingly; "let us hope it will stop at that."

"But it must, it must!" cried Pocket wildly. "I'm absolutely innocent! You said so yourself a minute ago; you've only to swear it as a doctor? They can't do anything to me—they can't possibly!"

The doctor stood looking into the sunless garden with a troubled face.

"Dr. Baumgartner!"

"Yes, my young fellow?"

"They can't do anything to me, can they?"

Baumgartner returned to the fireside with his foreign shrug.

"It depends what you call anything," said he. "They cannot hang you; after what I should certainly have to say I doubt if they could even detain you in custody. But you would only be released on bail; the case would be sent for trial; it would get into every paper in England; your family could not stop it, your schoolfellows would devour it, you would find it difficult to live down both at home and at school. In years to come it will mean at best a certain smile at your expense! That is what they can do to you," concluded the doctor, apologetically. "You asked me to tell you. It is better to be candid. I hoped you would bear it like a man."

Pocket was not even bearing it like a manly boy; he had flung himself back into the big chair, and broken down for the first time utterly. One name became articulate through his sobs. "My mother!" he moaned. "It'll kill her! I know it will! Oh, that I should live to kill my mother too!"

"Mothers have more lives than that; they have more than most people," remarked Baumgartner sardonically.

"You don't understand! She has had a frightful illness, bad news of any kind has to be kept from her, and can you imagine worse news than this? She mustn't hear it!" cried the boy, leaping to feet with streaming eyes. "For God's sake, sir, help me to hush it up!"

"It's in the papers already," replied Baumgartner, with a forbearing shrug.

"But my part in it!"

"You said it had got to come out."

"I didn't realise all it meant—to her!"

"I thought you meant to make a clean breast of it?"

"So I did; but now I don't!" cried Pocket, vehemently. "Now I would give my own life, cheerfully, rather than let her know what I've done—than drag them all through that!"

"Do you mean what you say?"

Baumgartner appeared to be forming some conditional intention.

"Every syllable!" said Pocket.

"Because, you know," explained the doctor, "it is a case of now or never so far as going to Scotland Yard is concerned."

"Then it's never!"

"I must put it plainly to you. It's not too late to do whatever you decide, but you must decide now. I would still go with you to Scotland Yard, and the chances are that they would still accept the true story of to-day. I have told you what I believe to be the worst that can happen to you; it may be that rather more may happen to me for harbouring you all day as I have done. I hope not, but I took the law into my own hands, and I I am prepared to abide by the law if you so decide this minute."

"I have decided."

"Mind you, it would mean putting yourself unreservedly in my hands, at any rate for the present," said Baumgartner, impressively. "Better come to Scotland Yard this minute than go back to school and blab about the whole thing there!"

"I shouldn't do that."

"I'm not so sure," replied the acute doctor. "I believe I know you better than you know yourself; one learns more of a person in an hour like this than in a whole humdrum lifetime. I believe you would find it very difficult not to tell somebody."

Pocket admitted it with a natural outburst of his leading quality. In truth no previous act or word of Baumgartner's had inspired such confidence as this unerring piece of insight. It seemed to the boy a perfect miracle of discernment. He was not old enough to know that what he would have done, in his weakness, most grown-up men and women of his temperament would have done in theirs.

"Remember," resumed the doctor, "you would have the whole of to-day to account for; it's not as though you wouldn't have some very awkward questions to answer the moment you got back to school."

And again the lad marvelled at this intuition into public-school conditions on the part of one who could have no first-hand knowledge of those insular institutions. But this fresh display of understanding only confirmed him in his resolve.

"I trust you, sir," said he; "haven't you done enough for me to make me? I put myself, as you say, absolutely in your hands; and I'm grateful to you for all you've done and whatever you mean to do!"

"Even though it comes to hiding with us here in London?"

"No matter what it comes to," cried Pocket, strangely exalted now, "so long as my people never know!"

"They may think you dead." He thought of saying that he wished he was; but it would not have been true; even then it would have been a lie, and Pocket was not the boy to tell one if he knew it.

"That would be better than knowing what I have done," was what he said; and in his exaltation he believed no less.

"You quite see that you are taking a step which must be final?"

"It is final—absolutely—so far as I am concerned."

And it was meant to be, in all good faith; the very fulness and fairness of the doctor's warnings served but to strengthen that resolve. But Baumgartner, as if to let well or ill alone, dropped the matter with a clinching shrug; and presently he left his visitor, less wisely, to brood on it alone.

Pocket was a dab at brooding! That is the worst of your conscientious ass; he takes his decision like a man; he means to stick to it like a sportsman; but he cannot help wondering whether he has decided for the best, and what would have happened if he had decided otherwise, and what his world will say about him as it is.

This one went much further in the unique stress of his extraordinary position. He pictured his people dressing for dinner at home; he pictured his form sitting down to private-work in his form-master's hall; there was no end to his mental pictures, for they included one of himself on the scaffold in the broad-arrows of the little old waxwork at Madame Tassaud's! He could not help himself; his mind was crumbling with his dreadful deed and its awful possibilities. Now his heart bled honestly for the poor dead man, now for his own mother and sister, and now not less freely for himself. He had been so innocent in the whole matter; he had only been an innocent and rather sporting fool. And now one of these lives was ended by his hand, and all the rest would be darkened for ever after!

It was too great a burden for a boy to bear; but Pocket bore it far into the long June twilight, scarcely stirring in the big soft chair, yet never leaning back in it again. He sat hunched up as though once more battling for breath, but curiously enough his bodily distress had flown before that of the mind. Pocket would thankfully have changed them back again, for his brain was as clear as his bronchial tubes, its capacity for suffering undimmed by a single physical preoccupation. Between seven and eight the young lady of the house came in with candles and a kind of high-tea on a tray; she also brought a box of d'Auvergne Cigarettes and the latest evening paper, which her uncle thought that Mr. Upton would like to see. That was how the girl addressed the boy, and the style always made him feel, and wish to seem, something of a man. But his present effort in that direction was sadly perfunctory: he almost ejected little Miss Platts in his eagerness to shut the door on her and see the news.

It was neither unimportant nor at first sight reassuring. The dead man had been identified by the police, who knew him of old, and were reported as hopeful of obtaining a clue through his identity. The clue was the point that stuck like a burr in the boyish brain; his idea of a clue was one leading straight to himself; it took Dr. Baumgartner to explain the true value of the identity clause, and bid the boy eat his meal.

"Trust the police!" said he. "They're on a false scent already; they may try at that end till it turns their hair grey!"

Pocket disliked this tone; he had begun to think almost as reverentially of his victim as of a dead member of his own family. It appeared thus early, however, that in life the defunct had been by no means worthy of respect. Rowton Houses had been his only home, except when his undistinguished offences got him into gaol; the surreptitious practices of the professional mendicant, his sole means of livelihood. So much was to be read between the few brief lines in the stop-press column of the latest evening paper. Again it required Baumgartner to extract comfort from such items.

"At all events," said he, "you cannot reproach yourself with the destruction of a valuable life! The man was evidently the worthless creature that he looked. You talk about your undesirable aliens, but here in England you breed undesirables enough to manure the world! It's a public service to reduce their number."

This pitch of nauseous cynicism had not been reached at a bound; the doctor had been working up to it all the evening, and this was the climax of his cold-blooded consolation as the schoolboy mechanically undressed himself for bed. His host had accompanied him up two pairs of stairs, carrying candles, and his meerschaum pipe in aromatic blast. Pocket felt a new chill through his veins, but he was not revolted as he would have been at first. This extraordinary man had shown him still more extraordinary kindness; the die was cast for them to stand or fall together; and there was something about the gaunt old visionary, a confidential candour, a dry intellectual plausibility, which could not but stimulate respect for his ungodliest views. Whether they really were his views, or only a tortuous attempt at comfort, the sympathy underlying their expression was undoubted and indubitable. But the doctor spoke as though he meant every word, and the boy only longed to agree with him: his conscientious failure to do so declared itself in a series of incoherent expostulations to which Baumgartner himself gave articulate shape in order to demolish them in the next breath.

"You say his life was as much to him as yours to you? Is that it, my young fellow?"

Pocket acknowledged the interpretation, and watched the Turk's head wreathed in cool blue clouds.

"You might as well compare withered weed with budding flower!" cried the poetic doctor. "You have an honourable life before you; he had a disreputable one behind him. You were bred and nurtured in the lap of luxury; he finds it for the first time in his—"

But here even Baumgartner broke off abruptly. The boy was writhing in his bed; the man sat down on the end of it.

"You do such poor devils a service," said he, "in sending them to a world that cannot use them worse than this one. They are better under the ground than lying on it drenched and drunk!"

"It was a human life," groaned the boy, shutting his eyes in pain.

"Human life!" cried Baumgartner, leaping to his feet, his huge shadow guying him on the ceiling. "What is this human life, and who are you and I, that we set such store by it? The great men of this world never did; it's only the little people and the young who pule and whine about human life. The ancient Roman sacrificed his weaklings as on an altar; there are some of us in these days who would prescribe a Tarpeian Rock for modern decadence. So much in pious parenthesis! Napoleon thought nothing of your human life. Von Moltke, Bismarck, and our staff in Germany thought as little of it as Napoleon; the Empire of my countrymen was founded on a proper appreciation of the infinitesimal value of human life, and your British Empire will be lost through exaggerating its importance. Blood and Iron were our watchwords; they're on the tip of every Fleet Street pen to-day, but I speak of what I know. I've heard the Iron shriek without ceasing, like the wind, and I've felt the Blood like spray from a hot spring! I fought at Gravelotte; as a public schoolboy you probably never heard the name before this minute. I fought in the Prussian Guard. I saw you looking at the pictures downstairs. I was in that charge across those hellish ridges. Over two thousand of us fell dead in half an hour, but we gained the victory. More Germans were killed that day—that sweltering August afternoon—than English in your whole South African War that took you years! The flower of Germany fell at Gravelotte; that was human life with a vengeance! But an Empire rose out of my comrades' ashes. And that's all it's for, this human life of yours: for the master- builders to lay out in their wisdom on the upward road."

The schoolboy was carried away. In the sudden eloquence of this strange outburst, with its poetic frenzy, its ruthless idealism, its wild bloodthirsty nobility, the youthful listener lost sight of its irrelevancy, or rather it was the irrelevant features that flared up first in his brain. It was a childish question, but here was a very child, and he could not help asking the fierce old soldier whether he had escaped without a wound.

"Without a scratch," was the reply. "I come home. I leave the army. I ally my human life with one that is all but divine. My Queen is struck down dead at my side within a year. And you expect me to pity the veriest pawn in the game!"

The boy was never to forget these bitter speeches altogether; there was not a single sentence of them that he failed to recall at one time or another word for word. He would see a wild arm waving, wisps of smoke from a waving pipe, a core of nicotine in a curve of amber, and the Turk's face glistening in its heat like that of the hard old man himself. He would hear the cynical and scornful voice softening in a breath to the simple, tender, and domestic humanity of his race. The voice and the face were with him throughout that night of his own manifold misery; but the time had not come for so young a boy to realise that Dr. Baumgartner had begun to say one thing, and been carried away like his listener.

POINTS OF VIEW

On the following morning, the ominous Friday of this disastrous week, there was a letter for Mr. Upton on the breakfast-table down in Leicestershire. This circumstance was not so usual as it sounds, because Mr. Upton conducted all his correspondence from his office at the works. If you simply put the name of the village, as he did on his stationery, to the works it went; it was necessary to direct your letter to the hall if you wished it to be delivered there; and few there were who had anything to say to Mr. Upton, on paper, unless it was on business too. His youngest son, however, had furnished the more impressive address to Dr. Bompas, whose hurried hand it was that dealt the first blow.

It so happened that a letter from Dr. Bompas had been expected; this made the letter he wrote especially upsetting, and for the following reason. Mrs. Upton had been so shaken by her vivid dream on the Thursday morning, that her husband had telegraphed to Bompas, somewhat against his own judgment, to know how he found their son. The reply had been: "Better expecting him again to-day will write"—which prepared the family for still more reassuring accounts in the morning. Lettice felt relieved as the original discoverer of Dr. Bompas. Horace found his views confirmed as to the systematic exaggeration of a touch of asthma, and Fred was only prevented by absence from entirely agreeing with Horace. Mr. Upton thought no more about the matter. But poor Mrs. Upton lay upstairs looking forward to a letter which it was quite impossible to show her now that it had come.

Mr. Upton read it more than once without a word; and it was not his way to keep a family matter to himself at his own table; but on this occasion he triumphed over temperament with an extraordinary instinct for what was in the air.

"The most infernal letter I ever had in my life!" was his only comment as he thrust it in his pocket out of sight. Lettice, however, might have seen that her father was far more distressed than angry had not Horace promptly angered him by saying he was not surprised. The young fellow's face and the old one's neck were redder before the last was heard of that remark. A garbled paraphrase of the letter was eventually vouchsafed; the boy had made very little improvement, and was not likely to make more while he remained at a school where he was allowed to use any remedy he liked; in fact, until he was taken away from school, and placed under his own immediate control in town, Dr. Bompas declined to persevere with the case.

"Blighter!" said Horace impartially, as though now there were two of them. Such was, in fact, the sum of his observations to Lettice when their father had taken himself and his letter upstairs. Young Tony was not "playing the game"; but then he never did play it to the expert satisfaction of Fred and Horace.

Upstairs the husband gave a more elaborate version of his letter, and told a lie. He said he had destroyed the letter in his indignation. He had destroyed it, but solely to escape any question of his showing it to his wife. He said a happier thing by chance; he said that for two pins he would motor over to the school and see for himself how the boy really was; then perhaps he would be in a position to consider the entreaty which Mrs. Upton added to the specialist's demand, that his patient should be placed under his eye in town. Mr. Upton went so far, however, without much immediate intention of taking so strong a measure.

He wished to discuss the matter with Horace; he might be quite justified in his fears. He was sorry he had let them lead to words with his eldest son. There were aspects of the case, as it presented itself to his mind, which he could hardly thresh out with Lettice, and her mother must not know of his anxiety on any account. Horace, however, had gone off earlier than usual in his dudgeon.

Mr. Upton was not long in following him to the works.

It was a charming garden that he passed through on his way; it charmed its owner all the more from his having made it himself out of a few rolling meadows. The rhododendrons were at the climax of their June glory. The new red gravel (his own colouring to a shade) appealed to an eye which had never looked longer than necessary in the glass. Lawn-tennis courts were marked out snowily on a shaven lawn; the only eyesore the good man encountered was poor Pocket's snob-wickets painted on a buttress in the back premises; his own belching blast-furnaces, corroding and defiling acres and acres within a few hundred yards of his garden wall, were but another form of beauty to the sturdy Briton who had made them too.

Horace was called into the private office and speedily propitiated. "I was more anxious than I could tell you at the time," his father said; "the fact is, I concealed half the fellow's letter on account of Lettice. But it's a man's matter, and you ought to know."

Of course the letter had stated that the erratic patient had failed to keep his appointment on the morning of writing; but if it had drawn the line of information there, it is highly improbable that Mr. Upton would have exercised so wise a discretion at table and in his wife's room. It now appeared that as a busy professional man the outspoken Bompas had gone far out of his way to play Mahomet to his patient's mountain. Tony had told him where he hoped to stay in London, which Bompas particularly wished to know on account of some special prescription the boy was to try that night. On his failure to appear at the appointed time, the doctor had telephoned to the address in question, only to learn that the boy had not stayed there at all. He had been given another address with the same result, except that from the second house he gathered that the young gentleman had gone on to some hotel. Horace was left to imagine a professional opinion of such proceedings, and asked for his own on the facts as a man of the world.

"Exactly like young Tony!" quoth Horace, never afraid to say what he thought.

"What! Like a lad of sixteen to go and put up at some hotel?"

"Like Tony," repeated Horace significantly. "Trust him to do what nobody else ever did."

"But how could Spearman give him the chance?"

"Heaven knows! Fred and I never got it."

"I thought he was to stay at Coverley's?"

"So I heard."

"I don't like it! It's all wrong at his age," said Mr. Upton. He had his notions of life and its temptations, and he was blunt enough with his elder sons, yet it was not without some hesitation that he added: "You don't think there's any question of bad company, do you?"

And though Horace had "no use for" his so-called pocket edition, he answered without any hesitation at all: "Not for a moment, from what I know of Tony."

Mr. Upton was sorry he had said so much. He excused himself by mentioning his wife's dream, now family property, which had been on his mind all this time. Horace, however, had no hesitation in informing him that nobody nowadays believed in dreams.

"Well, I never have, certainly," said Mr. Upton. "But what can it be?"

"He probably went up to Lord's, and forgot all about his doctor."

"I hope not! You're too down on him, Horace."

"If there was nobody to put him up it was the game to go back to school."

"But he's said to have gone to some hotel."

"I don't suppose he did," said Horace. "I expect he got back somehow."

The question was still under discussion when a telegram from Mr. Spearman settled it. Where was Tony? He had not returned when due the day before, and his friends in London wired that they knew nothing about him.

"What friends?" cried Mr. Upton, in a fury. "Why the devil couldn't Spearman give their names or Bompas the addresses he talked about?"

Horace could only think of Mr. Coverley or "that Knaggs crowd." Neither he nor Fred had been at Coverley's school, and young Tony's friends were by no means theirs.

Mr. Upton thought Lettice would know, and was going to speak to her on the telephone when Horace reminded him of his own remark about its being "a man's matter"; it was beginning to look, even to Horace, like a serious one as well, and in his opinion it was much better that neither his mother nor his sister should know anything at all about it before it was absolutely necessary. Horace now quoted his mother's dream as the devil did Scripture, but adduced sounder arguments besides; he was speaking quite nicely of them both, for instance, when he declared that Lettice was wrapped up in Tony, and would be beside herself if she thought any evil had overtaken him. It would be simply impossible for her to hide her anxiety from the mother on whom she also waited hand and foot. Mr. Upton disagreed a little there; he had good reason to believe in Lettice's power of suppressing her own feelings; but for her own sake, and particularly in view of that discredited dream, he now decided to keep his daughter in the dark as long as his wife.

It was his first decision; his next was to motor over to the school, as he had fortunately told his wife he might, and have a word with Mr. Spearman, who deserved hanging for the whole thing! The mischief was done, however, and it was now a matter in which home and school authorities must act together. A clerk was instructed to telephone to the garage for the car to come straight to the works. And the ironmaster stood waiting at his office window in a fever of anxiety.

The grimy scene on which he looked had a constant charm for him, and yet to-day it almost added to the bitterness of his heart. His was the brain that had conceived those broad effects of smoke and flame, and blackened faces lit by the light of molten metal; his strong hand and the stout heart which had brought his conception into being. Those were his trucks bringing in his ore from his mines; that was his consequential little locomotive fussing in front of them. His men, dwellers in his cottages on the brow of that hill, which was also his, happened to be tapping one of his furnaces at the moment; that was his pig-iron running out into the moulds as magically as an electric advertisement writes itself upon the London sky at night. The sense of possession is the foible of many who have won all they have; the ironmaster almost looked upon the hot air dancing over the white-hot bars as his too. The whole sulphurous prospect, once a green pasture, had long been his to all intents and purposes, and no second soul would ever take his pride in it; to his children it would never be more than the means of livelihood; and how had it repaid even him for a life's devotion? With a house of sorrow in the next valley! With a stricken wife, and sons whose right hands kept their cunning for the cricket-field, and one of whom the very thought had become a sudden madness!

Yet he could think of nothing else, except his wife, even in the great green car that whisked him westward in a dancing cloud of dust; for he did not drive himself, and the rush through the iced fragrance of the summer's day was a mental stimulant that did its work only too well. Now it recalled the ailing infancy of the missing boy—bronchitis it had been in the early stages—and how his mother had taken him to Hastings three successive winters, and wrapped him up far too much. Old family jokes cropped up in a new light, dimming the eyes without an instant's warning. On one of those flittings south the solicitous mother had placed the uncomplaining child on a footwarmer, and forgotten him until a cascade of perspiration apprised her of the effect: poor Mr. Upton had never thought of the incident without laughter, until to-day. Without doubt she had coddled him, and all for this, and she herself too ill to hear a word about it!

His mind harked back to his wife. In her sad case there was no uncertainty. He thought of thirty years ago when he had seen her first. There had been drama and colour in their meeting; the most celebrated of the neighbouring packs had run a fox to earth on his works, indeed in his very slag-heap! The author of cancerous furnaces in the green heart of a grass country had never been a popular personage with the hunting folk; but he was master of the situation that memorable day. It was his terrier that went into the slag-heap like a ferret, and came out bloody with a moribund fox; his pocket-knife that shore through the brush, his hand that presented it across the wall to the only young lady in at the death. The men in pink looking over, the hunt servants with their work cut out on the other side, the tongue of molten slag sticking out of the furnace mouth—the momentary contact of the industrial and the sporting world—it was that strange and yet significant scene which had first endeared its dingy setting to the ironmaster's heart. But he had made the contact permanent by falling in love with the young lady of the brush and marrying her under all the guns of her countified kith and kin. And now she was a stricken invalid, and their youngest-born was God knew where!

Of course there were no tidings of him at the school, where the now distracted father spent a more explosive hour than he cared to think about as he flew on to town in the car. He was afraid he had been very rude to Mr. Spearman; but then Spearman had been rash enough to repudiate his obvious responsibility in the matter. It was not his fault that the boy went up to town so often to see his doctor and stay the night. He had his own opinion of that arrangement, but it had become his business to see it carried out. Mr. Upton got in a sharp thrust here, to which the house-master retorted that if a boy of seventeen could not be trusted to keep his word, he should like to know who could! Tony had promised him faithfully to return that same night, failing friends whom he had mentioned as certain to put him up; their names Mr. Upton was able to demand at last as though they were so much blood; and he could not have cursed them more freely if Spearman had been a layman like himself. But that was all the information forthcoming from this quarter; for, happening to ask what the head master thought of the affair, Mr. Upton was calmly informed that it had still to reach his ears; at which he stared, and then merely remarked that he was not surprised, but in such a tone that Spearman sprang up and led him straight into the presence.

Now the Benevolent Despot of this particular seat of learning was an astute pedagogue who could handle men as well as boys. He explained to Mr. Upton that the safe-keeping of the unit was the house-master's concern, but agreed it was time that he himself was made acquainted with the present case. He took it as seriously, too, as Mr. Upton could have wished, but quite as frankly from his own point of view as his two visitors did from each of theirs. He had no doubt the boy would turn up, but when he did it would be necessary for him to give a satisfactory account of his proceedings before he could be received back into the school.

"Bother the school!" cried Mr. Upton, diluting the anathema with difficulty. "Let me find my lad alive and well; then you can do what you like."

"But how do you propose to find him?" inquired the head master, with only a dry smile (which disappointed Spearman) by way of rejoinder.

"First I shall have a word with these infernal people who, on their own showing, refused the boy a bed. I'll give them a bit of my mind, I promise you! Then there's the hotel they seem to have driven him to; it may be the one we always stay at, or one they've recommended. If I can't hear anything of him there, I suppose there'll be nothing for it but to call in the police."

"My dear sir," exclaimed the head master, "you may as well call in the public at once! It will be in the papers before you know where you are; and that, I need hardly point out to you, is as undesirable from our point of view as I should have thought it would be from yours."

"It's more so from mine!" cried Mr. Upton, in fresh alarm and indignation. "You think about your school. I think about my wife and boy; it might kill her to hear about this before he's found. But if I don't go to the police, who am I to go to?" The head master leant back in his chair, and joined his finger-tips judicially.

"There was a man we had down here to investigate an extraordinary case of dishonesty, in which I was actually threatened with legal proceedings on behalf of a certain boy. But this man Thrush came down and solved the mystery within twenty-four hours, and saved the school a public scandal."

"He may save you another," said Mr. Upton, "if he can find my boy. What did you say the name was?"

"Thrush—Eugene Thrush—quite a remarkable man, and, I think, a gentleman," said the head master impressively. Further particulars, including an address in Glasshouse Street, were readily supplied from an advertisement in that day's Times, in which Mr. Thrush was described as an "inquiry agent," capable alike of "delicate investigations" and "confidential negotiations."

That was the very man for Mr. Upton, as he himself agreed. And he departed both on speaking terms with Mr. Spearman, who said a final word for his own behaviour in the matter, and grimly at one with the head master on the importance of keeping it out of the papers.

MR. EUGENE THRUSH

The remarkable Mr. Thrush was a duly qualified solicitor, who had never been the man for that orderly and circumscribed profession. The tide of events which had turned his talents into their present channel, was known to but few of his many boon companions, and much nonsense was talked about him and his first career. It was not the case (as anybody might have ascertained) that he had been struck off the rolls in connection with the first great scandal in which he was professionally concerned. Nor was there much more truth in the report that he drank, in the ordinary interpretation of the term.

It is true, however, that Mr. Thrush had a tall tumbler on his dressing- table, to help him shave for the evening of that fateful Friday. He was dressing for an early dinner before a first night. His dressing-room, in which he also slept in Spartan simplicity, was the original powder-closet of the panelled library out of which it led. There was a third room in which his man Mullins prepared breakfast and spent the day. But the whole was a glorified garret, at the top of such stairs as might have sent a nervous client back for an escort.

Mullins, with the expression of an undertaker's mute (a calling he had followed in his day), was laying out his master's clothes as mournfully as though his master were in them, instead of chatting genially as he shaved.

"I'm sorry to have missed your evidence, Mullins, but if we go into this case it's no use letting the police smell the competitive rat too soon. Inquests are not in my line, and they'd have wondered what the devil I was doing there, especially as you refrained from saying you were in my service."

"I had no call, sir."

"Quite right, Mullins! An ideal witness, I can see you were. So you'd only to describe the finding of the body?"

"That was all, sir."

"And your description was really largely founded on fact?"

Mullins stood like a funereal grenadier at his gentleman's shaving elbow. "I told the truth, sir, and nothing but the truth," said he, with sombre dignity.

"But not the whole truth, eh, Mullins! What about the little souvenirs you showed me yesterday?"

"There was no call to name them either, sir. The cheroot-end I must have picked up a hundred yards away, and even the medicine-cork wasn't on the actual scene of the murder."

"That's all right, Mullins. I don't see what they could possibly have to do with it, myself; and really, but for the fluke of your being the one to find the body, and picking the first-fruits for what they're worth, it's the last kind of case that I should dream of touching with a ten-foot pole. By the way, I suppose they won't require you at the adjourned inquest?"

"They may not require me, sir, but I should like to attend, if quite convenient," replied Mullins deferentially. "The police were very stingy with their evidence to-day; they've still to produce the fatal bullet, and I should like a sight of that, sir."

Mr. Thrush did not continue the conversation, possibly because he took as little real interest as he professed in the case which was being thrust upon him, but more obviously owing to the necessary care in shaving the corners of a delightfuly long and mobile mouth. Indeed, the whole face emerging from the lather, as a cast from its clay, would have delighted any eye but its own. It was fat and flabby as the rest of Eugene Thrush; there was quite a collection of chins to shave; and yet anybody but himself must have recognised the invincible freshness of complexion, the happy penetration of every glance, as an earnest of inexhaustible possibilities beneath the burden of the flesh. Great round spectacles, through which he stared like a wise fish in an aquarium, were caught precariously on a button of a nose which in itself might have prevented the superficial observer from taking him any more seriously than he took himself.

Mr. Upton, who arrived before Thrush was visible, was an essentially superficial and antipathetic observer of unfamiliar types; and being badly impressed by the forbidding staircase, he had determined on the landing to sound his man before trusting him. In the rank undergrowth of his prejudices there was no more luxuriant weed than an innate abhorrence of London and all Londoners, which neither the cause of his visit nor the murky mien of Mullins was calculated to abate. The library of books in solid bindings, many of them legal tomes, was the first reassuring feature; another was the large desk, made business-like with pigeon-holes and a telephone; but Mr. Upton was only beginning to recover confidence when Eugene Thrush shook it sadly at his first entry.

It might have been by his face, or his fat, or his evening clothes seen from the motorist's dusty tweeds, almost as much as by the misplaced joviality with which Thrush exclaimed: "I'm sorry to have kept you waiting, sir, and the worst of it is that I can't let you keep me!"

This touched a raw nerve in the ironmaster, as the kind of reception one had to come up to London to incur. "Then I'll clear out!" said he, and would have been as good as his word but for its instantaneous effect.

Thrush had pulled out a gold watch after a stare of kindly consternation.

"I really am rather rushed," said he; "but I can give you four minutes, if that's any good to you."

Now, at first sight, before a word was spoken, Mr. Upton would have said four hours or four days of that boiled salmon in spectacles would have been no good to him; but the precise term of minutes, together with a seemlier but not less decisive manner, had already quickened the business man's respect for another whose time was valuable. This is by no means to say that Thrush had won him over in a breath. But the following interchange took place rapidly.

"I understand you're a detective, Mr. Thrush?"

"Hardly that, Mr.—I've left your card in the other room."

"Upton is my name, sir."

"I don't aspire to the official designation, Mr. Upton, an inquiry agent is all I presume to call myself."

"But you do inquire into mysteries?"

"I've dabbled in them."

"As an amateur?"

"A paid amateur, I fear."

"I come on a serious matter, Mr. Thrush—a very serious matter to me!"

"Pardon me if I seem anything else for a moment; as it happens, you catch me dabbling, or rather meddling, in a serious case which is none of my business, but strictly a matter for the police, only it happens to have come my way by a fluke. I am not a policeman, but a private inquisitor. If you want anything or anybody ferreted out, that's my job and I should put it first."

"Mr. Thrush, that's exactly what I do want, if only you can do it for me! I had reason to fear, from what I heard this morning, that my youngest child, a boy of sixteen, had disappeared up here in London, or been decoyed away. And now there can be no doubt about it!"

So, in about one of the allotted minutes, Thrush was trusted on grounds which Mr. Upton could not easily have explained; but the time was up before he had concluded a briefly circumstantial report of the facts within his knowledge.

"When can I see you again?" he asked abruptly of Thrush.

"When? What do you mean, Mr. Upton?"

"The four minutes must be more than up."

"Go on, my dear sir, and don't throw good time after bad. I'm only dining with a man at his club. He can wait."

"Thank you, Mr. Thrush."

"More good time! How do you know the boy hasn't turned up at school or at home while you've been fizzing in a cloud of dust?"

"I was to have a wire at the hotel I always stop at; there's nothing there; but the first thing they told me was that my boy had been for a bed which they couldn't give him the night before last. I did let them have it! But it seems the manager was out, and his understrappers had recommended other hotels; they've just been telephoning to them all in turn, but at every one the poor boy seems to have fared the same. Then I've been in communication with these infernal people in St. John's Wood, and with the doctor, but none of them have heard anything. I thought I'd like to do what I could before coming to you, Mr. Thrush, but that's all I've done or know how to do. Something must have happened!"

"It begins to sound like it," said Thrush gravely.

"But there are happenings and happenings; it may be only a minor accident. One moment!"

And he returned to the powder-closet of its modish day, where Mullins was still pursuing his ostensibly menial avocation. What the master said was inaudible in the library, but the man hurried out in front of him, and was heard clattering down the evil stairs next minute.

"In less than an hour," explained Thrush, "he will be back with a list of the admissions at the principal hospitals for the last forty-eight hours. I don't say there's much in it; your boy had probably some letter or other means of easier indentification about him; but it's worth trying."

"It is, indeed!" murmured Mr. Upton, much impressed.

"And while he is trying it," exclaimed Eugene Thrush, lighting up as with a really great idea, "you'll greatly oblige me by having a whisky-and-soda in the first place."

"No, thank you! I haven't had a bite all day. It would fly to my head."

"But that's its job; that's where it's meant to fly," explained the convivial Mr. Thrush, preparing the potion with practised hand. Baited with a biscuit it was eventually swallowed, and a flagging giant refreshed by his surrender. It made him like his new acquaintance too well to bear the thought of detaining him any more.

"Go to your dinner, man, and let me waylay you later!"

"Thank you, I prefer to keep you now I've got you, Mr. Upton! My man begins his round by going to tell my pal I can't dine with him at all. Not a word, I beg! I'll have a bite with you instead when Mullins gets back, and in a taxi that won't be long."

"But do you think you can do anything?"

The question floated in pathetic evidence on a flood of inarticulate thanks.

"If you give me time, I hope so," was the measured answer. "But the needle in the hay is nothing to the lost unit in London, and it will take time. I'm not a magazine detective, Mr. Upton; if you want a sixpenny solution for soft problems, don't come to me!"

At an earlier stage the ironmaster would have raised his voice and repeated that this was a serious matter; even now he looked rather reproachfully at Eugene Thrush, who came back to business on the spot.

"I haven't asked you for a description of the boy, Mr. Upton, because it's not much good if we've got to keep the matter to ourselves. But is there anything distinctive about him besides the asthma?"

"Nothing; he was never an athlete, like my other boys."

"Come! I call that a distinction in itself," said Mr. Thrush, smiling down his own unathletic waistcoat. "But as a matter of fact, nothing could be better than the very complaint which no doubt unfits him for games."

"Nothing better, do you say?"

"Emphatically, from my point of view. It's harder to hide a man's asthma than to hide the man himself."

"I never thought of that."

It was impossible to tell whether Thrush had thought of it before that moment. The round glasses were levelled at Mr. Upton with an inscrutable stare of the marine eyes behind them.

"I suppose it has never affected his heart?" he inquired nonchalantly; but the nonchalance was a thought too deliberate for paternal perceptions quickened as were those of Mr. Upton.

"Is that why you sent round the hospitals, Mr. Thrush?"

"It was one reason, but honestly not the chief."

"I certainly never thought of his heart!"

"Nor do I think you need now, in the case of so young a boy," said Thrush earnestly. "On the other hand, I shouldn't be surprised if his asthma were to prove his best friend."

"It owes him something!"

"Do you know what he does for it?"

"Yes, I do," said Mr. Upton, remembering the annoying letter he seemed to have received some weeks before. "He smokes, against his doctor's orders."

"Do you mean tobacco?"

"No—some stuff for asthma."

"In cigarettes?"

"Yes."

"Do you know the name?"

"I have it here."

The offensive letter was not only produced, but offered for inspection after a precautionary glance. Thrush was on his feet to receive it in outstretched hand. Already he looked extraordinarily keen for his bulk, but the reading of the letter left him alive and alert to the last superfluous ounce.

"But this is magnificent!" he cried, with eyes as round as their glasses.

"I confess I don't see why."

"Cigarettes d'Auvergne!"

"Some French rubbish."

"The boy has evidently been dependent on them?"

"It looks like it."

"And this man Bompas made him give them all up?"

"So he has the impudence to say."

"Is it possible you don't see the importance of all this?"

Mr. Upton confessed incompetence unashamed.

"I never heard of these cigarettes before; they're an imported article; you can't get them everywhere, I'll swear! Your boy has got to rely on them; he's out of reach of the doctor who's forbidden them; he'll try to get them somewhere! If he's been trying in London, I'll find out where before I'm twenty-four hours older!"

"But how can you?" asked Mr. Upton, less impressed with the possibility than by this rapid if obvious piece of reasoning.

"A. V. M.!" replied Eugene Thrush, with cryptic smile.

"Who on earth is he?"

"Nobody; it's the principle on which I work."

"A. V. M.?"

"Otherwise the old nursery game of Animal, Vegetable, or Mineral."

Again Mr. Upton had to prevent himself by main force from declaring it all no laughing matter; but his silence was almost bellicose.

"You divide things into two," explained Thrush, "and go on so dividing them until you come down to the indivisible unit which is the answer to the riddle. Animal or Vegetable? Vegetable or Mineral? Northern or Southern Hemisphere? Ah! I thought your childhood was not so very much longer ago than mine."

Mr. Upton had shrugged an impatient recognition of the game.

"In this case it's Chemists Who Do Sell D'Auvergne Cigarettes and Chemists Who Don't. Then—Chemists Who Do and Did Yesterday, and Chemists Who Do but Didn't! But we can probably improve on the old game by playing both rounds at once."

"I confess I don't quite follow," said Mr. Upton, "though there seems some method in the madness."

"It's all the method I've got," rejoined Thrush frankly. "But you shall see it working, for unless I'm much mistaken this is Mullins back sooner than I expected."

Mullins it was, and with the negative information expected and desired, though the professional melancholy of his countenance might have been the precursor of the worst possible news. The hospitals on his rapid round had included Charing Cross, St. Thomas's, St. George's, and the Royal Free; but he had telephoned besides to St. Mary's and St. Bartholomew's. At none of these institutions had a young gentleman of the name of Upton, or of unknown name, been admitted in the last forty-eight hours. Mullins, however, looked as sympathetically depressed as though no news had lost its proverbial value; and he had one of those blue-black faces that lend themselves to the look, his chin being in perpetual mourning for the day before.

"Don't go, Mullins! I've another job for you," said Eugene Thrush. "Take the telephone directory and the London directory, and sit you down at my desk. Look up 'chemists' under 'trades'; there are pages of them. Work through the list with the telephone directory, and ring up every chemist who's on the telephone, beginning with the ones nearest in, to ask if he keeps d'Auvergne Cigarettes for asthma. Make a note of the first few who do; go round to them all in turn, and be back here at nine with a box from each. Complain to each of the difficulty of getting 'em elsewhere—say you wonder there's so little demand—and with any luck you should find out whether and to whom they've sold any since Wednesday evening."

"But surely that's the whole point?" suggested the ironmaster.

"It's the next point," said Thrush. "The first is to divide the chemists of London into the Animals who keep the cigarettes and the Vegetables who don't. I should really like to play the next round myself, but Mullins must do something while we're out."

"While we're out, Mr. Thrush?"

"My dear Mr. Upton, you're going to step across into the Cafe Royal with me, and have a square meal before you crack up!"

"And what about your theatre?" asked Mr. Upton, to whom resistance was a physical impossibility, when they had left the sombre Mullins entrenched behind telephone and directories.

"The theatre! I was only going out of curiosity to see the sort of tripe that any manager has the nerve to serve up on a Friday in June; but I'm not going to chuck the drama that's come to me!"

The ironmaster dined with his head in a whirl. It was a remarkably good dinner that Thrush ordered, if as inappropriate to the occasion as to his own weight. His guest, however, knew no more what he was eating or drinking than he knew the names of the people in diamonds and white waistcoats who stared at the distraught figure in the country clothes. It even escaped his observation that the obese Thrush was an unblushing gourmet with a cynical lust for Burgundy. The conscious repast of Mr. Upton consisted entirely of the conversation of Eugene Thrush, and of that conversation only such portions as exploited his professional theories, and those theories only as bearing on the case in hand. He was merely bored when Thrush tried to distract him with some account of the murder in which he himself was only interested because his myrmidon happened to have discovered the body. What was the murder of some ragamuffin in Hyde Park to a man from the country who had lost his son?

"I don't see how your theory can work there," he sighed, out of pure politeness, when Thrush paused to punish the wine.

"It should work all right," returned Thrush. "You take an absolutely worthless life; what do you do it for? It must be one of two motives: either you have a grudge against the fellow or his existence is a menace to you. Revenge or fear; he wants your money, or he's taken your wife! But what revenge can there be upon a poor devil without the price of a bed on his indescribable person? He hasn't anything to bless himself with, and he makes it a bit too hot for somebody who has, eh? So you whittle it down. And then perhaps by sheer luck you run your blade into the root of the matter."

Thrush gave up trying to take the other out of himself, since his boldest statements were allowed to pass unchallenged, unless they dealt with the one subject on the poor man's mind. The cessation of his voice, however, caused a twinge of conscience in the bad listener; he made a mental grab at the last phrase, and was astonished to find it germane to his own thoughts.

"That's the second time you've mentioned luck, Mr. Thrush!"

"When was the first?"

"You spoke of Friday as an unlucky day, as God knows this one is to me! Are you of a superstitious turn of mind?"

"Not seriously."

"You don't believe in dreams, for example?"

"That's another question," said Thrush, his spectacles twinkling to colossal rubies as he sipped his Santenay. "Why do you ask?"

"If you're a disbeliever it's no use my telling you."

"Perhaps I'm neither one thing nor the other."

"Have you ever known a mystery solved through a dream?"

"I've heard of one," said Thrush, with a significant stress upon the verb; "that's the famous old murder in the Red Barn a hundred years ago. The victim's mother dreamed three nights running that her missing daughter was buried in the Red Barn, and there she was all the time. There may have been other cases."

"Cases in which a parent has dreamt of an absent child, at the very time at which something terrible has happened to that child?"

"Any amount of those."

The father's voice had trembled with the question. Thrush put down his glass as he gave his answer, and his spectacled eyes fixed themselves in a more attentive stare.

"Do you think they're all coincidences?" demanded Mr. Upton hoarsely.

"Some of them may be, but certainly not all," was the reply. "That would be the greatest coincidence of the lot!"

"I hardly like to tell you why I ask," said Mr. Upton, much agitated; for he could be as emotional as most irascible men.

"You've been dreaming about the boy?"

"Not I; but my poor wife has; that was one reason why I daren't tell her he had disappeared."

"Why? What was the dream?"

"That she saw him—and heard a shot."

"A shot!"

Thrush looked as though he had heard one himself, but only until he had time to think.

"She says she did hear one," added Mr. Upton, "and that she wasn't dreaming at all."

"But when was this?"

"Between six and seven yesterday morning." This time Thrush did not move a muscle of his face; it only lit up like a Chinese lantern, and again he was quick to quench the inner flame; but now the coincidence was complete. Coincidences, however, had nothing to say to the A. V. M. system, neither was Eugene Thrush the man to jump to wild conclusions on the strength of one. He asked whether the boy was very fond of shooting in the holidays, as though that might have accounted for the dream, but his father was not aware that he had ever smelt powder in his life. He little dreamt what Thrush was driving at! The tone of subsequent inquiries concerning Mrs. Upton's health (already mentioned as the great reason for keeping the affair as long as possible a secret) sounded purely compassionate to an ear unconsciously aching for compassion.

"Then that accounts for it," said Thrush, when he had heard the whole sad story. There was the faintest ring of disappointment in his tone. "What do you mean?"

"That anybody as ill as that, more particularly a lady, is naturally fanciful, I'm afraid."

"Then you think it a mere delusion, after all?"

"My dear Mr. Upton, it would be presumption to express an opinion either way. I only say, don't think too much about that dream. And since you won't keep me company in my cups, we may as well rejoin the faithful Mullins."

They ran into Mullins, as it happened, in Glasshouse Street, and Mr. Upton for one would not have recognised him as the same being. His sepulchral face was alight with news—it was the transformation of the undertaker's mute into the wedding guest. And yet he had only one box of the d'Auvergne Cigarettes to show for his evening's work, and that chemist had declared it was the first he had sold for weeks.

Thrush ordered his man upstairs, and took his late guest's hand as soon as ever he dared.

"You need a good night's rest, my dear sir, and it's no use climbing to my masthead for nothing. Mullins and I will do best if you don't mind leaving us to ourselves for the night; but first thing tomorrow morning I shall be at your service again, and I hope there will be some progress to report."

Mullins was waiting for him with all the lights on, his solemn face still more strikingly illuminated.

"Look at this, sir, look at this! These are the d'Auvergne Cigarettes!"

"So I perceive."

"This stump is the stump of a d'Auvergne Cigarette."

"I hope you enjoyed it, Mullins."

"I didn't smoke it, sir!"

"Who did?"

"That's for you to say, sir; but it's one of the little things I collected near the scene of the murder, but took for a common cheroot, yesterday morning in Hyde Park."

"Near the actual place?"

Thrush had pounced upon the stump, and was holding it under the strongest of the electric lamps.

"Under a seat, sir, not above a hundred yards away!"

SECOND THOUGHTS

Pocket had been dreaming again. What else could he expect? Waking, he felt that he had got off cheaply; that he might have been through the nightmare of battle, as described by one who had, and depicted in the engravings downstairs, instead of on a mercifully hazy visit to the Chamber of Horrors at Madame Tussaud's. The trouble was that he had seen the one and not the other, and what he had seen continued to haunt him as he lay awake, but quite horribly when he fell back into a doze. There was nothing nebulous about the vile place then; it was as light and bright as the room in which he lay. The sinister figures in the panelled pens were swathed in white, as he had somewhere read that they always were at nights. Their evil faces were shrouded out of sight. But that only made their defiant, portly figures the more humanly inhuman and terrifying; it was as though they had all risen, in their winding-sheets, from their murderer's graves. Better by far their beastly faces, that you knew were wax! So he reasoned with himself, and screwed up his courage, and laid hands on one of the shorter figures that he could reach. It rocked stiffly in its place, a most palpable and reassuring waxwork. He unwound the cerements from the hollow and unyielding head; and the face was new to him; it had not been there the other afternoon. It was a young face like his own, as ill-mounted on high shoulders, with thickish lips ajar, and only a pair of intelligent eyes to redeem an apparent heaviness: one and all his own identical characteristics. And no wonder, for the last recruit to the waxen army of murderers was a faithful model of himself.

There was no awaking from this dream: the dreamer was not positive that he had been asleep. The veiled sunlight in his room was just what it had seemed in that deserted dungeon of swaddled malefactors. The boy shuddered till the bed shook under him. But after that he still lay on, facing himself as he had seen himself, and his deed as others must see it soon or late. Not the actual accident in the Park; but this hiding in the heart of London, this skulking among strangers, this leaving his own people to mourn him as the dead!

The thought of them drew scalding tears. Never had they seemed so dear to him before. It was not only Lettice and their parents. Fred and Horace, how good they had been to him at school, and how proud he had been of them! What would they think of him if he went on skulking like this? What would they have done in his place? Anything but lie low like that, thought Pocket, and resolved forthwith to play the game as preached and practised by his brothers. It was strange that he should have been so dense about so plain a duty overnight; this morning he saw it as sharp as an image in perfect focus on the ground-glass screen…To think that a mad photographer should have talked him into an attitude as mad as his own! This morning he saw the common sense of the situation as well as its right and wrong. Nothing would happen to him if he gave himself up, but anything might if he waited till he was caught. As for the consequences to his poor mother, surely in the end suspense and uncertainty would eat deeper into the slender cord of her life than the shock of the truth would cut.

Having made up his mind, however, as to the only thing to do, the boy behaved characteristically in not hastening to do it. The ordeal in front of him, beginning in certain conflict with Baumgartner, and ending in a blaze of wretched notoriety, was a severe one to face; meanwhile he lay in such peace and safety as it was only human to prolong a little. That night, for all his moral innocence, he might lie in prison; let him make the most of a good bed while he had one, especially as he was still mysteriously free from asthma. The last consideration took his mind off the ethical dilemma for quite a little time.

He remembered the doctor at home telling him that he himself had suffered from chronic asthma, but had lost it after a carriage accident in which he was nearly killed.

"My accident may have done the same for me," thought Pocket—and was bitterly ashamed next moment to catch himself thinking complacently of any aspect of his deed. Its other aspects were a sufficient punishment.

To get up, and raise the green linen blind, flooding with sunshine the plain upstairs room to which Baumgartner had conducted his guest, was to conjure uncomfortable visions of the eccentric doctor, with his ferocious meerschaum, his bloodthirsty battle-talk, and all his arguments in favour of the course which Pocket had now determined to abandon. The boy fully realised that he had been given his chance, and had refused it. And of all the interviews before him, that with Dr. Baumgartner was the one that he most dreaded, and would have given most to escape.

Could he escape it? That was an idea; others came of it. If he did escape, and did give himself up for what he had done, there was no reason why he should involve Baumgartner in that voluntary confession. Suppose he hailed the first cab he saw, and drove over to St. John's Wood to borrow money (they could scarcely refuse him that), and then took the first train home to tell his father everything in the first instance, that father would never hear of his incriminating a stranger who had befriended him according to his lights. He himself need never say where he had spent the twenty-four hours after the tragedy, even if he were ever to know. And so far he had no notion, thanks to the ridiculous posture prescribed by Baumgartner in the cab; he could only suppose the motive had been to keep him out of sight, the benefit to his breathing a mere pretext; and yet it was a curious result that after a day and a night he should still be in total ignorance of his whereabouts.

He opened his window and looked out; but it was a back window, and the sunny little strip of garden below was one of many in a row. Old discoloured walls divided them from each other and from the gardens of a parallel block of bigger houses, whose slates and chimneys towered above the intervening trees. The street in front of those houses was completely hidden, but the hum of its traffic travelled pleasantly to the ear, and there were other reassuring sights and sounds. In one of the contiguous gardens a very small boy was wheeling a doll's perambulator; on the other side, where the fine, warm gravel reminded Pocket of the carroty kind at home, a man was mowing an equally trim lawn. Pocket listened to the murmur of the machine, and watched the green spray playing over the revolving knives, and savoured the curiously countrified smell of cut grass; the combined effect was a still stronger reminiscence of his father's garden, where his own old pony pulled the machine in leather shoes.

Because such associations filled his eyes again, there seemed no end to them. Somebody was playing the piano near some open window, and playing almost as well as Lettice did, and playing one of her things! Pocket could not bear to listen or look out any longer, and he dressed as quietly as he could. He had almost resolved to slip out without a word, whatever else he did, if the opportunity offered. It simply never occurred to him, until he made the discovery, that anybody would dare to lock him in his room!

Yet they had done it; that infernal old German doctor had had the cheek to do it; and the effect on the boy, who so expressed the situation to himself, was rather remarkable. A wholly ineffectual tug or two told him he was on the wrong side of the door for applying mere bodily strength, that either he must raise an ignominious shout for freedom or else achieve it for himself by way of the window. Unathletic as he always had been, he was sportsman enough not to hesitate an instant between the two alternatives; and on again looking out of the window, saw his way down at a glance.

Immediately underneath was another window, opening on a leaded balcony over the bow-window in the drawing-room. To shift his bedstead with the least possible noise, to tie a sheet to it, and to slide down the sheet till he had but a few feet to drop into the balcony, was the work of a very few minutes to one as excitedly determined as Pocket had become on finding himself a prisoner. Thought they would lock him in, did they? They would just find out their mistake! It was exactly the same mood in which he had scaled the upright palings in defiance of the policeman who said he might not sleep in the Park.

The balcony window was open, the room within empty. It was obviously Baumgartner's bedroom. There was a camp bedstead worthy of an old campaigner, a large roll-top desk, and a waste-paper basket which argued either a voluminous correspondence or imperfect domestic service; it would have furnished scent for no short paper-chase. Otherwise the room was tidy enough, and so eloquent of Baumgartner himself, in its uncompromising severity, that Pocket breathed more freely on the landing. And in the hall he felt absolutely safe, for he had gained it without the creaking of a stair, and there on the pegs hung his hat, but neither the cloak nor the weird wide-awake affected by his host.

Baumgartner out. That was a bit of luck; and it was just like Pocket to lose a moment in taking advantage of it; but the truth was that he had made an interesting discovery. It was in that house the piano was being played. He heard it through the drawing-room door; he had heard it on the balcony up above; it had never stopped once, so silent had he been. It was that Phillida, with the large dark eyes, and she was playing something that Lettice sometimes played, and very nearly, though naturally not quite, as well. Pocket would have said that it was Mendelssohn, or Chopin, "or something," for his love of music was greater than his knowledge. But it was not exactly the music that detained him; he was thinking more of the musician, who had shown him kindness, after all. It would be only decent to thank her before he went, and the doctor himself through his niece. If she knew he had been locked in, and he had to tell her how he had made his escape and yet not a sound—well, she would not think the less of him at all events, and so they would part for ever. Or perhaps not for ever! The juvenile instinct for romance was not to be stifled at such a stimulating moment. The girl would be sorry for him when she knew all; she might know enough to be sorry for him as it was; in any case it was the game to say goodbye.

The girl sprang from the music-stool in extraordinary excitement. Her large eyes were larger than ever, as it were with fear, and yet they blazed at the intruder. Pocket could not understand it, unless she already knew the truth.

"I'm so sorry for starting you," he apologised. "I just came in to say goodbye."

And he held out a hand which she never seemed to see.

"To say goodbye!" she gasped.

"Yes, I've got to go. I'm afraid the doctor's out?"

"Yes, he is. Won't you wait?"

"I'm afraid I can't."

She was shrinking from him, shrinking round towards the door. He stood aside, to let her bolt if that was her desire. And then she in turn took her stand, back to the door.

"He'll be very sorry to miss you," she said more firmly, and with a smile.

"And I'm very sorry to miss him," said Pocket, unconscientiously enough for anybody. "He's been most awfully good to me, and I wish you'd tell him how grateful I am."

"I'm afraid he won't believe me," the girl said dryly, "if he finds you gone."

"I must go—really I must. I shall get into an awful row as it is. Do you mind giving him one other message?"

"As many as you like."

"Well, you might tell him from me that I'll give myself away, but I'll never give him! He'll know what I mean."

"Is that all?"

She was keeping him very cleverly, putting in her word always at the last moment, and again refusing to see his hand; but again it was the boy who helped to waste his own golden opportunity, this time through an indefensible bit of boyish braggadocio.

"No; you may tell the doctor that if he wanted to detain me he went the worst way about it by locking me into my room!"

She looked mystified at first, and then astounded.

"How did you get out?"

"How do you suppose?"

"I never heard anything!"

"I took care you shouldn't."

And he described the successful adventure with pardonable unction in the end. After that he insisted on saying goodbye. And the young girl stood up to him like a little heroine.

"I'm very sorry, but I can't let you go, Mr. Upton."

"Can't let me?"

"I really am sorry—but you must wait to see my uncle."

He stood aghast before the determined girl. She was obviously older than himself, yet she was only a slip of a girl, and if he forced his way past—but he was not the fellow to do it—and that maddened him, because he felt she knew it.

"Oh, very well!" he cried, sarcastically. "If you won't let me out that way, I'll go this!"

And he turned towards the tiny conservatory, which led down into the garden; but she was on him, and there was no hesitation about her; she held him firmly by the hand.

"If you do I'll blow a police-whistle!" she said. "We have one—it won't take an instant. You shan't come out the front way, and you'll be stopped if you climb the wall!"

"But why? Do you take me for a lunatic, or what?" he gasped out bitterly.

"Never mind what I take you for!"

"You're treating me as though I were one!"

"You've got to stay and see my uncle."

"I shan't! Let me go, I tell you! You shall you shall! I hate your uncle, and you too!" But that was only half true, even then while he was struggling almost as passionately as though the girl had been another boy. He could not strike her; but that was the only line he drew, for she would grapple with him, and release himself he must. Over went walnut whatnots, and out came mutterings that made him hotter than ever for very shame. But he did not hate her even for what she made him say; all his hatred and all his fear were of the dreadful doctor whose will she was obeying; and both were at their highest pitch when the door burst open, and in he sprang to part them with a look. But it was a look that hurt more than word or blow; never had poor Pocket endured or imagined such a steady, silent downpour of indignation and contempt. It turned his hatred almost in a moment to hatred of himself; his fear it only increased.

"Leave us, Phillida," said Baumgartner at last. Phillida was in tears, and Pocket had been hanging his head; but now he sprang towards her.

"Forgive me!" he choked, and held the door open for her, and shut it after her with all the gallantry the poor lad had left.

ON PAROLE

"So," said Dr. Baumgartner, "you not only try to play me false, but you seize the first opportunity when my back is turned! Not only do you break your promise, but you break it with brutal violence to a young lady who has shown you nothing but kindness!"

Pocket might have replied with justice that the young lady had brought the violence upon herself; but that would have made him out a greater cad than ever, in his own eyes at any rate. He preferred to defend his honour as best he could, which was chiefly by claiming the right to change his mind about what was after all his own affair. But that was precisely what Baumgartner would not allow for a moment; it was just as much his affair as accessory after the fact, and in accordance with their mutual and final agreement overnight. Pocket could only rejoin that he had never meant to give the doctor away at all.

"I daresay not!" said Baumgartner sardonically. "It would have been dragged out of you all the same. I told you so yesterday, and you agreed with me. I put it most plainly to you as a case of then or never so far as owning up was concerned. You made your own bed with your eyes open, and I left you last night under the impression that you were going to lie on it like a man."

"Then why did you lock me in?" cried Pocket, pouncing on the one point on which he did not already feel grievously in the wrong. The doctor flattered him with a slight delay before replying.

"There were so many reasons," he said, with a sigh; "you mustn't forget that you walk in your sleep, for one of them. We might have had you falling downstairs in the middle of the night; but I own that I was more prepared for the kind of relapse which appears to have overtaken you. I was afraid you had more on your soul than you could keep to yourself without my assistance, and that you would get brooding over what has happened until it drove you to make a clean breast of the whole thing. I tell you it's no good brooding or looking back; take one more look ahead, and what do you see if you have your way? Humiliating notoriety for yourself, calamitous consequences in your own family, certain punishment for me!"

"The consequences at home," groaned Pocket, "will be bad enough whatever we do. I can't bear to think of them! If only they had taken Bompas's advice, and sent me round the world in the Seringapatam! I should have been at sea by this time, and out of harm's way for the next three months."

"The Seringapatam?" repeated the doctor. "I never heard of her."

"You wouldn't; she's only a sailing vessel, but she carries passengers and a doctor, a friend of Dr. Bompas's, who wanted to send me with him for a voyage round the world. But my people wouldn't let me go. She sails this very day, and touches nowhere till she gets to Melbourne. If I could only raise the passage-money, or even stow away on board, I could go out in her still, and that would be the last of me for years and years!"

It was not the last of him in his own mind; suddenly as the thought had come, and mad as it was, it flashed into the far future in the boy's brain; and he saw himself making his fortune in a far land, turning it up in a single nugget, and coming home to tell of his adventures, bearded like the pard, another "dead man come to life," after about as many years as the dream took seconds to fashion. And Baumgartner looked on as though following the same wild train of thought, as though it did not seem so wild to him, but extremely interesting; so that Pocket was quite disappointed when he shook his head.

"A stowaway with an attack of asthma! I think I see my poor young fellow! Why, they'd hear you wheezing in the hold, and you'd gasp out your whole story before you were in the Bay of Biscay! No, no, my fellow; you've taken your line, and you must stick to it, and stop with me till we can think of something better than a long sea voyage. If you say you won't, I say I'll make you—to save you from yourself—to save us both."

There was no mistaking the absolute intention in this threat; it was fixed and final, and the boy accepted it as he accepted his oppressor's power to make good his words. It was true that he might have escaped already; the nearer he had been to it, the less chance was he likely to be given again. So reasoned Pocket from the face and voice now dominating him more powerfully than ever; but it is an interesting fact that his conclusion neither cowed nor depressed him as it might have done. There was actually an element of relief in his discomfiture. He had done his best to do his duty. It was not his fault that responsibility had been wrested from his shoulders, and an evil hour delayed. And yet there was a certain, an immediate, a creature comfort in such delay, which was all the greater because unsought by him; it was a comfort that he had both ways, as the saying is, and from all points of view but that of his poor people wondering what had become of him.

"If only they knew!" he cried; "then I shouldn't care. Let me write to one of them! My mother needn't know; but I must write to one of the others, and at least let them know I am alive and well. My sister would keep my secret; she'd play the game all right, I promise you! And I'd play any game you like if only you let me write a line to her!"

The doctor would not hear of it at first. Eventually he said he should have to inspect the letter before it went; and this proved the thin edge of consent. In the end it was arranged that Pocket should write what he liked to his sister only, and that Baumgartner should read and enclose it in a covering letter, so that everybody need not know it was a letter from the missing boy. Baumgartner was to have it posted from St. Martin's-le- Grand, to destroy all trace of a locality which he now refused point-blank to disclose even to the writer. And in return for the whole concession the schoolboy was to give his solemn word and sacred promise on the following points.

He was not to set foot outside the house without Baumgartner, nor to show himself for a moment at the windows back or front.

On no account was he to confide in the doctor's niece Phillida, to give her the slightest inkling of his connection with the latest of London mysteries, or even of the scene, or any of the circumstances of his first meeting with Baumgartner.

"You are bound to see something of each other; the less you say about yourself the better."

"But what can she think?"

"What she likes, my young fellow! I am a medical man; medical men may bring patients to their houses even when they have ceased to practise in the ordinary way. It is no business of hers, and what she chooses to think is no affair of ours. She has seen you very ill, remember, and she had your doctor's orders not to let you out of the house in his absence."

"She obeyed them like a little brick!" muttered Pocket, with a wistful heaviness.

"She did what she was told; think no more about it," said the doctor. "Give me your hand on these your promises, and die on your feet rather than break one of them! Now I trust you, my young fellow; you will play the game, as you call it, even as the poor lads in these pictures played it at Gravelotte, and die like them rather than go back an inch. Look at this one here. No, not the one with the ridges, but here where we come to bayonets and the sword. See the poor devils of the Prussian Guard! See the sheet-lightning pouring into us from the walls of St. Privat! Look at that fellow with his head bound up, and this one with no head to bind. That's meant for our colonel on the white horse. See him hounding us on to hell! And there's a drummer drumming as though we could hear a single beat! Our very colours were blown to ribbons, you see, and we ourselves to shreds; but the shreds hung together, my young fellow, and so will you and I in our day of battle!" Baumgartner might have known his boy for years, so sure was his touch upon the strings of a responsive nature, to strike the chords of a generous enthusiasm, and to wake the echoes of noble deeds. Pocket attacked his letter with the heart of a soldier, hardened and yet uplifted for the fight; it was only when he found himself writing down vague words, which nevertheless brought his innocent deed home to him as nothing had done before, that the artificial frost broke up, and real tears ran with his ink. He begged Lettice not to think too hardly of him, still less to be anxious about him, or to make anybody else; they must not fret for him, he wrote more than once, without seeing the humour of the injunction. He was better than he had been for years, and in the best of hands. But something terrible had happened; something he could not help, but would bitterly repent all his days, especially as it might prevent him from ever seeing any of them again. It was this monstrous remark, and others to which it led, that were literally blotted with the writer's tears. But just then he saw himself in all vivid sincerity as an outcast who could never show himself at home or at school again. And it required the spell of Baumgartner's presence to make the prospect such as could be borne with the least degree of visible manhood.

Be it remembered that he was not a man at all, but a boy in many ways younger than most boys of sixteen and three quarters, albeit older in some few. He was old in imagination, but young in common sense. One may be imaginative and still have a level head, but it is least likely in one's teens. The particular temperament does not need a label; but none who know it when they see it, and who see it here, will be surprised to learn that this emotional writer for one was enormously relieved and lightened in spirit when he had got his letter off his mind and hands.

True to his warning, Dr. Baumgartner began to glance at it with a kindly gravity; it was with something else that he shook his head over the second leaf.

"This is not for me to read!" said he. "I'd rather run the risk of trusting your discretion."

No words could have enslaved poor Pocket more completely; he clasped the hand that proceeded to write the covering note, and then the address, all openly before his eyes. And while the doctor was gone to the nearest messenger office to despatch the missive to the General Post Office, ostensibly to catch a particular post, his prisoner would not have decamped for a hundred pounds, and the doctor knew it.

Phillida did not appear at dinner, but at supper she did, and Pocket was only less uncomfortable in her absence, which he felt he had caused, than when they were both at table and he unable to say another word to express his sorrow for the unseemly scene of the forenoon. She spoke to him once or twice as though nothing of the kind had happened, but he could scarcely look her in the face. Otherwise both meals interested him; they were German in their order, a light supper following the substantial middle-day repast; but it appeared that they both came from an Italian restaurant, and the English boy was much taken with the pagoda-like apparatus in which the dishes arrived smoking hot in tiers. It provided a further train of speculation when he remembered that he had never seen a servant in the house, and that the steps had struck him as dirty, and the doctor's waste- paper basket as very full. Pocket determined to make his own bed next morning. He had meanwhile an unpleasing suspicion that the young girl was clearing away, for the doctor took him back into the drawing-room after supper; and later, when they returned for a game of billiards on the toy board, which they placed between them on the dining-table, both Phillida and the fragments had disappeared.

The little billiards were a bond and a distraction. They brought out Baumgartner's simple side, and they emphasised the schoolboy's simplicity. Both played a strenuous game, the doctor a most deliberate one; his brows would knit, his mouth shut, his eyes calculate, and his hand obey, as though his cue were a surgical instrument cutting deep between life and death. It was a curious glimpse of disproportionate concentration; even the Turk's head was only lit to be laid aside as an obstruction. Pocket's one chance was to hit hard and trust to the fortune that accrues on a small table. Both played to win, and the boy forgot everything when he actually succeeded in the last game. They had played very late for him, and he slept without stirring until Baumgartner came to his room about eight o'clock next morning.

Now Pocket had not seen a newspaper all Friday, but it was the first thing he did see on the Saturday morning, for the doctor was waving one like a flag to wake him.

"Trust your vermin press to get hold of the wrong end of the stick!" he cried, with fierce amusement; "it only remains to be seen whether they succeed in putting your precious police on the wrong tack too. Really, it's almost worth being at the bottom of a popular mystery to watch the smartest men in this country making fools of themselves!"

"May I see?" asked Pocket; he had winced at more than one of these remarks.

"Certainly," replied Baumgartner; "here's the journalistic wonder of the age, and there you are in its most important column. I brought it up for you to see."

The boy bit his lips as he read. His deed had been promoted to leaded type and the highest rank in headlines. It appeared, in the first place, that no arrest had yet been made; but it was confidently asserted (by the omniscient butt of Teutonic sallies) that the police, wisely guided by the hint in yesterday's issue (which Pocket had not seen), were already in possession of a most important clue. In subsequent paragraphs of pregnant brevity the real homicide was informed that his fatal act could only be the work of a totally different and equally definite hand. Pocket gathered that there had been a certain commonplace tragedy, in a street called Holland Walk, in the previous month of March. A licensed messenger named Charlton had been found shot under circumstances so plainly indicative of suicide that a coroner's jury had actually returned a verdict to that effect. There appeared, however, to have been an element of doubt in the case. This the scribe of the leaded type sought to remove by begging the question from beginning to end. It had not been a case of suicide at all, he declared, but as wilful a murder as the one in Hyde Park, to which it bore a close and sinister resemblance. Both victims had been shot through the heart in the early hours of the morning; both belonged to one neighbourhood, and to the same dilapidated fringe of the community. A pothouse acquaintanceship was alleged between them; but the suggestion was that the link lay a good deal deeper than that, and that the two dead men were known to the police, who were busy searching for a third party of equal notoriety in connection with both murders.

"But we know he had nothing to do with the second one," said the boy, looking up at last. "It wasn't a murder, either; neither was the first, according to the coroner's jury, who surely ought to know."

"One would have thought so," said Baumgartner, with his sardonic smile; "but the yellow pressman knows better still, apparently."

"Do you suppose there's a word of truth in what he says? I don't mean about Charlton or—or poor Holdaway," said Pocket, wincing over his victim's name, which he had just gleaned from the paper. "But do you think the police are really after anybody?"

"I don't know," said Baumgartner. "What does it matter?"

"It would matter a great deal if they arrested somebody for what I did!"

The boy was no longer looking up; and his voice trembled.

"It would alter the whole thing," he mumbled significantly.

"I don't see it," returned the doctor, with grim good-nature. "The little wonder of the English reading world has nearly unearthed another mare's nest, as two of its readers know full well. No real harm can come of this typical farrago. Let it lead to an arrest! There are only two living souls who can't account for their time at that of this unfortunate affair."

Pocket realised this; but it was put in a way that gave him goose-skin under the clothes. He was always seeing his accident in some new light, always encountering some new possibility, or natural consequence of his silence, which had not occurred to him before. But he was learning to keep his feelings under control, to set his face and his teeth against the regular reactions of his coward conscience and his fickle will. And once again did Dr. Baumgartner atone for an unintentional minor by striking a rousing chord on the very heart-strings of the boy.

"Eight o'clock!" cried the magician, with a glance at his watch and an ear towards the open window. "The postman's knock from door to door down every street in town—house to house from one end of your British Islands to the other! A certain letter is without doubt being delivered at this very moment— eh, my poor young fellow?"

HUNTING WITH THE HOUNDS

Eugene Thrush was a regular reader of the journal on which Dr. Baumgartner heaped heavy satire, its feats of compression, its genius for headlines, and the delicious expediency of all its views, which enabled its editorial column to face all ways and bow where it listed, in the universal joint of popularity, were points of irresistible appeal to a catholic and convivial sense of humour. He read the paper with his early cup of tea, and seldom without a fat internal chuckle between the sheets.

That Saturday morning, however, Mr. Thrush was not only up before the paper came, but for once he took its opinion seriously on a serious matter. It said exactly what he wished to think about the Hyde Park murder: that the murderer would prove to be the author of a similar crime, committed in the previous month of March, when the Upton boy must have been safe at school. If that were so, it was manifestly absurd to connect the lad with a mystery which merely happened to synchronise with that of his own disappearance—absurd, even if he were shown to have been somewhere near the scene of the murder, somewhere about the time of its perpetration.

That much, though no more, had, however, been fairly established overnight. It was a conclusion to which Mullins, with the facile conviction of his class, had jumped on the slender evidence of the asthma cigarette alone; but before midnight Thrush himself had been forced to admit its extreme probability. There was a medicine cork as well as an asthma cigarette; the medicine cork had been found very much nearer the body; in fact, just across the pathway, under a shrub on the other side of the fence. It was Mullins, who had made both discoveries, who also craved permission to ring up Dr. Bompas, late at night, to ask if there was any particular chemist to whom he sent his patients with their prescriptions. Dr. Bompas was not at home, which perhaps was just as well but his man gave the name of Harben, in Oxford Street. Harbens, rung up in their turn, found that they certainly had made up one of the doctor's prescriptions on the Wednesday, for a young Mr. Upton, and, within half an hour, had positively identified the cork found by Mullins in Hyde Park. It was still sticky with the very stuff which had put poor Pocket asleep.

Yet Thrush could not or would not conceive any actual connection between a harmless schoolboy and an apparently cold-blooded crime. He resisted the idea on more grounds than he felt disposed to urge in argument with his now strangely animated factotum. It was still a wide jump to a detestable conclusion, but he confined his criticism to the width of the jump. The cork and the cigarette might be stepping-stones, but at least one more was wanted to justify the slightest suspicion against the missing boy. Let it be shown that he had carried firearms on the Wednesday night, and Thrush undertook to join his satellite on the other side; but his mental bias may be gauged from the fact that he made no mention of the boy's mother's dream.

Mullins found him not only up, shaved and booted, but already an enthusiastic convert to the startling theory of a sensation journalist, and consequently an irritable observer of the saturnine countenance which darkened to a tinge of distinct amusement over the leaded type.

"So you don't think there's much in it, Mullins?"

"I shouldn't say there was anything at all, sir."

"Yet I suppose you remember the very similar occurrence in Holland Walk?"

"Oh yes, sir, but it was a case of suicide."

"I don't agree."

"But surely, sir, the jury brought it in suicide?"

"The coroner's jury did—in spite of the coroner—but it may come before another jury yet, Mullins! I remember the case perfectly; the medical evidence was that the shot had been fired at arm's length. That isn't the range at which we usually bring ourselves down! Then there was nothing to show that the man ever possessed a pistol, or even the price of one; he was so stony it would have gone up the spout long before. The very same point crops up in the case of this poor boy. Who says he ever had a revolver in his life? His father tells me explicitly that he never had; I happened to ask the question," added Thrush, without explaining in what connection.

"Well, sir," said Mullins, with respect enough in his tone, "you talk about jumping to conclusions, but it strikes me the gentleman who write for the papers could give me some yards and a licking, sir!"

This was a sprightly speech for Mullins; but it was delivered with the very faintest of deferential smiles, and Mr. Thrush shook his spectacles without one at all.

"The gentlemen on this paper have a knack of lighting on the truth, however," he remarked; "it may be by fair means, or it may be by foul, but they have a way of getting there before the others start."

Mullins remarked with quiet confidence that they were not going to do it this time. His position was, briefly, that he could not bring himself to believe in two separate mysteries, at one and the same time and place, with no sort of connection between them.

"That would be too much of a coincidence," said Mullins, sententiously.

Thrush looked at him for a moment.

"But life's one long collection of coincidences! That's what I'm always telling you; the mistake is to look on them as anything else. Don't you call it a bit of a coincidence that both these men should meet their death at the very hour of the morning when you're on your way over here from Netting Hill, and in much the same degree of latitude, which you've got to cross somewhere or other on your way? Yet who has the nerve to say you must have gone through Holland Walk that other morning, and been mixed up in that affair because you are in this?"

"I don't admit I'm mixed up in anything," replied Mullins, with some warmth.

"I mean as a witness of sorts. I was merely reducing your argument to the absurd, Mullins; you didn't take me literally, did you? It's no use talking when we both seem to have made up our minds; but I'm always ready to unmake mine if you show me that young Mr. Upton carried a pistol, Mullins! Now I should like my breakfast, Mullins, and you must be roaring inside for yours. The man who's been knocking up chemists all night is the man to whom breakfast is due; get your own and then mine, and after that you can tell me how you got on."

Anything more genial than the garrulous banter of Eugene Thrush, at his best, it was impossible to encounter or incur; he had been, however, for a few minutes at his worst, and it was difficult to see why the pendulum should have swung so suddenly to the other extreme. Mullins went about his business with his usual sleek solemnity. But Thrush was yet another man the moment he was alone. His face was a sunny background for ideas, misgivings, and half-formed plans, one after the other, whirling like clouds across a crimson sky. But the sky was clear whenever Mullins was in the room. And at the breakfast-table there was not a cloud.

"To come back to those chemists, and this shop-to-shop canvassing," resumed Thrush, as Mullins poured out his tea; "how many have you done, and how many have we still to do between us?"

Mullins produced a pocket-book that did him credit, and consulted notes as neat.

"Rung up when you were out at dinner—seventeen. Kept Cigarettes d'Auvergne—one. That was Thornycroft's in Shaftesbury Avenue, where I'd just been when I met you down below in the street. In the night I knocked up other eight-and-twenty, all either in the neighbourhood of Trafalgar Square or else on the line of the Park."

"Poor devils! I suppose you urged a pretty bad case?"

"A matter of life or death."

"Well?"

"Three more kept them, not counting Harbens: one in Knightsbridge, one in New Bond Street, and one a little way down the Brompton Road."

"Much demand in any of those quarters?"

"Only in the Brompton Road; a literary gentleman has a box regularly every week, and two in the autumn. Pringle, his name is."

"I know him; so he's as breathless as his own yarns, is he?" murmured Thrush, to his buttered egg. "But has one of these apothecaries sold a box of d'Auvergnes since Wednesday afternoon?"

"Two have," said Mullins, "but one was to Mr. Pringle."

Thrush levelled inquiring spectacles.

"How did you worm that out, Mullins?"

"By changing my tune a bit, sir. I started asking if they knew anybody who could recommend the cigarettes from personal experience, as we were only trying them on hearsay."

"Very smart of you, Mullins! And one wheezy novelist is the only consumer?"

"That's right, sir, but the man in Knights-bridge sold a box on Thursday to a doctor."

"Did you get the name?"

"Bone-Gardner, I think it was a Dr. Otto Bone-Gardner."

"Baumgartner, I expect you mean!" cried Thrush, straightening a wry face to spell the name. "I've heard of an Otto Baumgartner, though I can't say when or where. What's his address?"

"He couldn't tell me, sir; or else he wouldn't. Suppose he thought I'd be turning the doctor out next. Old customer, I understood he was."

"For d'Auvergne Cigarettes?"

"I didn't inquire."

"My good fellow, that's the whole point! I'll go myself and ask for the asthma cigarettes that Dr. Baumgartner always has; if they say he never had them before, that'll be talking. His being a doctor looks well. But I'm certain I know his name; you might look it up in Who's Who, and read out what they say."

And Mullins did so with due docility, albeit with queer gulps at barbaric mouthfuls such as the list of battle-fields on which Dr. Baumgartner had fought in his martial youth; the various Universities whereat he had studied psychology and theology in an evident reaction of later life; even the titles of his subsequent publications, which contained some long English words, but were given in German too. A copious contribution concluded with the information that photography and billiards were the doctor's recreations, and that he belonged to a polysyllabically unpronounceable Berlin club, and to one in St. James's which Mullins more culpably miscalled the Parthenian.

"Parthenon!" said Thrush, as though he had bitten on a nerve. "But what about his address?"

"There's no getting hold of that address," said Mullins, demoralised and perspiring. "It's not given here either."

"Well, the chemist or the directory will supply that if we want it, but I'm afraid he sounds a wheezy old bird. The author of 'Peripatetic Psychology' deserves to have asthma all his nights, and 'After this Life' smacks of the usual Schopenhauer and Lager. No, we won't build on Dr. Baumgartner, Mullins; but we'll go through the chemists of London with a small tooth-comb, from here to the four-mile radius."

Thrush had finished breakfast, and Mullins was beginning to clear away, when a stormy step was heard upon the stairs, and in burst Mr. Upton with a panic-stricken face. He was colourless almost to the neck, but he denied that he had any news, though not without a pregnant glance at Mullins, and fell to abusing London and the Londoners, but City men above all others, till Thrush and he should be alone together. The incidental diatribe was no mere padding, either; it was the sincere utterance of a passionately provincial soul. Nobody in all London, he declared, and apparently without excepting Mr. Thrush, cared a twopenny curse what became of his poor boy. In view of the fact that the present company alone knew of his disappearance, and not so very many more of the boy's existence, this was an extravagantly sweeping statement. But the distracted man had a particular instance to bear him out; he had been to see his boy's friends' father, "a swine called Knaggs," that very morning at his house in St. John's Wood.

"Rather early, wasn't it?" suggested Thrush, whose manner was more softly sympathetic than it had been the night before. The change was slight, and yet marked. He was more solicitous.

"Early!" cried Mr. Upton. "Haven't I lost my boy, and wasn't it these Cockney cads who turned him adrift in London? I ought to have gone to them last night. I wish I had, when my blood was up after your dinner; for I don't mind telling you now, Mr. Thrush, that in spite of your hospitality I was none too pleased at your anxiety to get rid of me afterwards. It made me feel like doing a little bit for the boy on my own; but I'd called once on my way into town, and only seen a servant then, so I thought I'd make sure of putting salt on somebody by waiting till this morning."

The visitor paused to look harder than ever at Mullins, and Thrush seized the opportunity to offer an apology for his abrupt behaviour in the street.

"I confess I showed indecent haste," said he; "but Mullins and I had our night's work cut out, and he at any rate has not had his boots off since you saw him."

"Hasn't he?" cried Mr. Upton, in remorseful recognition of an unsuspected devotion; "then I'll say what I've got to say in front of him, for you're both my friends, and I'll unsay all I said just now. Bear with my temper, both of you, if you can, for I feel beside myself about the boy! It was all I could do to keep my hands off that smug little lump of London inhumanity! Kept me waiting while he finished his breakfast, he did, and then came in polishing a hat as sleek as himself, and saying 'Rather early!'—just as you set me off by saying yourself a minute ago."

"But he seems to have told you something, Mr. Upton?"

"Has he not! He began by telling me he was sorry for me, confound him! I could have made him sorrier for himself! He was sorry for me, but what could he do? London was a large place, and 'we Londoners' were busy men. I told him so were some of us in the iron-trade, but not too busy to keep an eye on boys who were friends of our boys. He said London life was different; and I said so I could see. They never had spare beds at a moment's notice, much less for boys who might set fire to the house or—or shoot themselves—"

His two hearers uttered a simultaneous exclamation, and Mr. Upton stood glancing piteously from one to the other, as though his lad's death- warrant were written in their faces. Eugene Thrush, however, looked so genuinely distressed that the less legible handwriting on the face of Mullins also attracted less attention.

"Had he anything to shoot himself with?" inquired Thrush, in a curiously gentle voice.

Mr. Upton nodded violently as he moistened his lips.

"He had, after all!" he croaked. "Little as I dreamt it yesterday, my unhappy boy, who had never to my knowledge pulled a trigger in his life before, was going about London with a loaded revolver in his pocket!"

"Had he brought it from school?" asked Thrush, with a covert frown at the transfigured Mullins.

Mr. Upton repeated what he had heard through the young Westminsters, with their father's opinion of pawnbrokers' shops as resorts for young schoolboys, of young schoolboys who frequented them, and of parents and guardians who gave them the chance. How the two gentlemen had parted without fisticuffs became the latest mystery to Eugene Thrush, whose only comment was that it behoved him all the more to do something to redeem the capital in the other's eyes.

"Now we know why my poor wife heard a shot!" was the only rejoinder, in a voice not too broken to make Mullins prick up his ears; it was the first he had heard about the dream.

"I wouldn't say that, Mr. Upton. We know no more than we knew before. Yet I will own now," exclaimed Thrush, catching Mullins's bright eye, "that the coincidence will be tremendous if there's nothing in it!"

But only half the coincidence was present in the father's mind; no thought of the murder had yet entered it in connection with his boy; and to hear so emphatic an echo to his foreboding was more than his fretted nerves could stand. In the same breath he pounced on Thrush for a pessimist—apologised—and humbly entreated him to take a more hopeful view.

"There may have been an accident, Thrush, but not necessarily a fatal one!"

An accident! Thrush had never thought of that explanation of the public mystery; but evidently Mullins had, judging by his almost fiendish grins and nods behind the poor father's back. Thrush looked at both men with the troubled frown of a strenuously reasoning being—looked and frowned again—frowned and reasoned afresh. And then, all in an instant, the trouble lifted from his face; light had come to him in an almost blinding flash, such as might well obscure the quality of the light; enough for Eugene Thrush that it lit him back to his mystery every bit as brightly as it lit him onward to its solution.

He was even man enough to refrain from reflecting it automatically in his face, as he put a number of apparently irrelevant questions to Mr. Upton about the missing boy. What was his character? what its chief points? Was he a boy with the moral courage of his acts? Would he face their consequences like a man?

"I never knew him tell a lie in his life," said Mr. Upton, "either to save his own skin or any thing else; and it was a case of their young skins when they got into trouble with me! Poor Tony was the most conscientious of them all, and I hear that's what they say of him at school."

Thrush put one or two further questions, and then said he had a clue, though a very slight one, which he was rather in a hurry to follow up himself; and this time the ironmaster went off quietly of his own accord, with a dejected undertaking to be at his hotel when he was wanted.

"I don't like the look of our friend," remarked Thrush, looking hard at Mullins when at last they were alone. "He shapes none too well for the strain he's got to bear; if he cracks up there'll be a double tragedy, if not a triple one, in that family. We must catch our hare quickly, Mullins, or we may catch him too late."

Mullins turned on the disagreeable grin that Thrush had so resented a few minutes before; he took no notice of it now.

"You'll find your man," said Mullins significantly, "the very moment that I find mine, Mr. Thrush."

"Meaning they're the same person?"

"To be sure."

"That this lad is the actual slayer of the man Holdaway?"

"Surely, sir, it's as plain as a pikestaff now?"

"Not to me, Mullins—not to me."

Thrush was twinkling behind his great round goggles.

"Then who do you think has done it, sir?" inquired Mullins, in deferential derision.

"Ah! that's another matter, my man; but I can tell you whom I hope to get arrested within another hour!"

Mullins looked as though he could hardly believe his ears; his jaw, black as a crape hat-band this morning, fell in front of his grimy collar.

"You're actually thinking of arresting some one else?"

"I am—with your permission, Mullins."

"Tell me who it is, sir, for Heaven's sake!"

And with his fattest smile Thrush whispered into an ear that recoiled from his words as though they had been so many drops of boiling oil.

BOY AND GIRL

Pocket Upton was able to relieve his soul of one load that morning. Dr. Baumgartner had left the schoolboy to his soap and water, taking the newspaper with him; but apparently Pocket had followed him down in quicker time than the other anticipated. At any rate the little lady of the house was all alone in the dining-room, where Pocket found her boiling eggs on the gas-fire, and had her to himself for several seconds of which he wasted none. There was neither grace nor tact in what he said, and his manner was naturally at its worst, but the penitential torrent came from his heart, and was only stemmed by the doctor's hasty arrival on the scene. Miss Platts had not been given time to say a word, but now she asked Mr. Upton how many minutes he liked his egg boiled, and would not let him do it himself, but smiled when he told her it was "done to a shake." Dr. Baumgartner, on the other hand, scowled upon them both until observation or reflection had convinced him that no promises had been broken and no confidences exchanged.

The callow pair saw something more of each other during the morning; for Pocket hotly resented being distrusted, and showed it by making up to the young girl under the doctor's nose. He talked to her about books in the other room. He had the impertinence to invite her into the dining-room for a game of billiards, but the sense next moment to include her uncle in an amended form of more becoming suggestion. Baumgartner eventually countenanced a game, but spent most of the time with his back to the players and his eye on the street. The boy and girl got on very well now; they seemed frankly glad of each other, though he caught her more than once with a large and furtive eye on him. But she seemed to enjoy her baptism of schoolboy slang. And it was only when she began to question him about his special vocabulary, that Baumgartner looked on for a little, and put in his word.

"You see he still believes in his public school," said he to Phillida, in a tone which reminded their visitor of his first breakfast in the house.

"I should think I did!" cried Pocket, and did a little loyal boasting about the best of schools, and the best house in that school, until memory took him by the throat and filled his eyes. It was twelve o'clock, and a summer's Saturday. School was over for the week. Only your verses to do in your own time, and get signed by Spearman before you went up to dormitory on Saturday night; but meanwhile, Saturday afternoon! A match on the Upper, where you could lie on your rug and watch the game you couldn't play; call-over at the match; ices and lemon-drinks in a tent on the field; and for Saturday supper anything you liked to buy, cooked for you in the kitchen and put piping hot at your place in hall, not even for the asking, but merely by writing your name plainly on the eggs and leaving them on the slab outside! It was not these simple luxuries that Pocket missed so sorely; it was the whole full life of ups and downs, and no yesterdays and no to-morrows, that he had lost for ever since last Saturday. The heavy midday meal came in smoking from the Italian restaurant, and Pocket was himself again, as a boy will be; after all, they knew about him at home by this time, their worst fears were allayed, and in the end it would all come right. In the end he would be sitting in his own old place at home, instead of with strangers in an unknown street; telling them everything, instead of holding his peace; and watching even Fred and Horace listening to every word—much as Dr. Baumgartner was listening to something now.

What was it? Phillida was listening, too, and watching her uncle as she listened. Pocket did both in his turn.

It was the voice of newspaper hawkers, shouting in couples, coming nearer with their shouts. Dr. Baumgartner jumped up from the table, and ran outside without his hat.

His promise alone prevented Pocket from following and outstripping the doctor. He knew what the shouting was about before he could have sworn to a single raucous word. But Phillida could not know, and she resumed at once where they had left off before breakfast.

"Of course I forgive you," she whispered. "It was I began it!"

"Began what?"

"Our row yesterday."

Phillida had a demure twinkle, after all; but it was lost on Pocket now. "I'd forgotten all about it," he said with superfluous candour, his ear still on the street.

"I haven't."

Her voice made him remember better. "I hope to goodness I didn't hurt you?"

"Of course you didn't."

"But you must have thought me mad!"

There was a slight but most significant pause.

"Well, I never shall again."

"Then you did!" he gasped. Their eyes had met sharply; both young faces were flooded with light, and it was much the same light. There was no nonsense about it, but there was indignant horror on his side, and indignant shame on hers.

"You really are at school?" she whispered, not increduously, but as one seeking assurance in so many words; and in a flash he saw what she had thought, what she had been deliberately made to think, that his beloved school was not a school at all, but an Ayslum!

But at that moment Dr. Baumgartner was heard bargaining at the gate with one raucous voice, while the other went on roaring huskily, "Park murder—arrest! 'Rest o' de Park murderer! Park murder—Park murder—arrest!" And Pocket sprang up from the table in a state that swept his last thoughts clean from his mind.

The girl said something; he did not hear what. He was white and trembling, in pitiable case even to eyes that could only see skin-deep; but the doctor's step came beating like a drum to him, and he was solidly seated when the doctor entered—without any paper at all.

"It's that murder the papers are all exploiting," he explained benignly. "They were shouting out something about an arrest; you would hear them, I daresay. But it's the usual swindle; the police are merely hoping to effect an arrest. I threatened to send for them unless the scoundrel took his paper back!"

He was in his lightest mood of sardonic gaiety. The sins of the vendors recalled those of "your vermin press itself"; the association was wilfully unfair, the favourite phrase a studied insult; but the English boy was either dense or indifferent, and Phillida's great eyes were in some other world. Baumgartner subjected them both to a jealous scrutiny, and suddenly cried out upon his own bad memory. It appeared there was a concert at the Albert Hall, where "the most popular and handsome pair in England" (the inverted commas were in the doctor's sneer) were being welcomed on their return from the ends of the earth. He had intended going to hear what they could do; but Phillida should go instead; she was not past the ballad stage.

And Phillida rose submissively, with unreal thanks which could not conceal her recognition of the impromptu pretext for getting rid of her; her uncle called a taxicab, and with harsh hilarity turned her off the premises in the frock she had been wearing all day.

"And now," said he, returning with a scowl, "what the devil were you two talking about while my back was turned?"

"Yesterday," replied Pocket, more than ready for him, though his heart beat fast.

"What about yesterday?"

"Our scuffle in the other room."

"Is that all?"

"No—I found out something; she didn't tell me."

"What did you find out?"

"That you let her think me mad!" cried Pocket, in monstrous earnest. He might have laughed at himself, could he have seen his own reproachful face. But he could have killed Baumgartner for laughing at him; it did not occur to him that the laugh was partly one of pure relief.

"Why, my young fellow, how else can I account for you?"

"You said she would think I was a patient."

"Exactly! A mental case."

"You had no business to make me out mad," persisted Pocket, with dogged valour.

"Pardon me! I had all the business in the world; and I beg that you'll continue to foster the illusion as thoroughly as you did yesterday when I was out. It's no good shaking your head at me; listen to reason," continued Baumgartner, with an adroit change of tone. "And try, my good young fellow, do try to think of somebody besides yourself; have some consideration for my niece, if you have none for me."

Pocket was mystified, but still more incensed; for he felt himself being again put gently but clearly in the wrong.

"And I should like to know," he cried, "what good it does her to think she's associating with a lunatic?"

"She would probably prefer the idea to that of a murderer," was the suave reply. "I speak only of ideas; otherwise I should not make use of such an expression, even in jest. It's as ugly as it's ridiculous in your case. Yet you heard for yourself that others are applying the horrid term in all sobriety."

"I heard more than that," returned Pocket. "They've arrested somebody!"

"I thought I told you there was no truth in that?"

But Baumgartner had winced for once, and the boy had seen it, and his retort was a precocious inspiration.

"That was only to avoid a scene at table, Dr. Baumgartner!"

"Well, my young fellow," said the doctor, after one of his wise pauses, "and what if it was?"

"I can't sit here and let an innocent man lie in prison."

"He won't lie long."

"It's absolutely wicked to let them keep him at all."

"Nor will they, longer than another hour or two."

"Well, if they do, you know what I shall do!"

Pocket had never displayed such determination, nor incurred quite the same measure or quality of wrath that Baumgartner poured upon him without a word for the next few moments. It was a devouring gaze of sudden and implacable animosity. The ruthless lips were shut out of sight, yet working as though the teeth were being ground behind them; the crow's footed face flushed up, and the crow's feet were no more; it was as though age was swallowed in that flood of speechless passion till the whole man was no older than the fiery eyes that blazed upon the boy. And yet the most menacing thing of all was the complete control with which the doctor broke this pregnant silence.

"You say that. I say otherwise. You had better find a book in the other room till you know your own mind again."

"I know it now, unless they release that man," said Pocket, through his teeth, although they chattered.

"Give them a chance, and give yourself one! It will be time to think of clearing other people when they fail to clear themselves. Have more patience! Think of your own friends, and give them time too."

If the last allusion was to the lad's letter, due in Leicestershire that morning, it was as happy as all Baumgartner's last words. If he meant himself to be included among Pocket's friends, there was food for thought in the suggestion that a man of the doctor's obvious capacity was not idle in the boy's best interests. Pocket was made to feel rather ashamed of himself, as usual; but he could not forget the concentrated fury of the look which had not been weakened by infuriate words; and the recollection remained as an excuse, as well as a menace, in his mind. He had time enough to think it over. Dr. Baumgartner smoked his meerschaum in the gathering shade at the back of the house. The schoolboy sulked for some time in the big chair, but eventually took the doctor at his word about a book.

If it be ever true that a man may be known by his books, it was certainly so to some extent in the case of Dr. Otto Baumgartner. His library was singularly small for an intellectual man who wrote himself, and a majority of the volumes were in languages which no public schoolboy could be expected to read; but of the English books many were on military subjects, some few anthropological; there were photographic year-books and Psychical Research Reports by the foot or yard, and there was an odd assortment of second-hand books which had probably been labelled "occult" in their last bookseller's list. Boismont on "Hallucinations" was one of these; it was the book for Pocket. He took the little red volume down, and read a long chapter on somnambulism in the big chair. In a way it comforted him. It was something to find that he was far from being the only harmless creature who had committed a diabolical deed in his sleep; here among several cases was one of another boy who had made an equally innocent and yet determined attempt on his own father. But there was something peculiar in poor Pocket's case, something that distinguished it from any of those cited in the book, and he was still ferreting for its absolute fellow when Phillida came in long before he expected her. Boismont had made the time fly wonderfully, in spite of everything; the girl, too, appeared to have been taken out of herself, and talked about her concert as any other young girl might have done, both to Pocket and her uncle, who glided in at once from the garden. The doctor, however, was himself in mellower mood; and they were having tea, for all the world like any ordinary trio, the girl still making talk about sundry songs, the man quizzing them and her, and the boy standing up for one that his sister sang at home, when a metallic tattoo put a dramatic stop to the conversation.

The two young people, but not their elder, were startled quite out of their almost inadvertent tranquillity; and the knocker was not still before Pocket realised that it was the first time he had heard it. No letters were delivered at that house; not a soul had he seen or heard at the door before. Even in his excitement, however, with its stunning recrudescence of every reality, its instantaneous visions of his people or the police, there was room for a measure of disgust when the girl got up, at an ungallant nod from the German, to go to the door.

"It's a huge fat man," whispered Phillida, on her return to the big room at the back of the house. "Here's his card."

"Thrush!" muttered Baumgartner as though he knew the name, and he glowered at the two young faces on which it made no impression whatever. It was plain how he hated leaving them together; but for once it must be done, and done quickly—with both doors open and the visitor's very movements audible on the steps. To the door the doctor must go, and went, shutting that one pointedly behind him.

The young creatures, looking in each other's eyes, listened for raised voices and the slam of prompt expulsion; but the voices were pitched too low to reach their ears in words, and were only interrupted by the sound of footsteps in the hall, and the perfectly passive closing of an outer and an inner door in quick succession.

"He's taken him into the dining-room," murmured Phillida. "Who can it be?"

"Hasn't he any friends?"

"None who ever come here; none of that name anywhere, I feel sure." Her great eyes, without leaving his for an instant, filled with thought as a blank screen takes a shadow. "I wonder if it's about that!" she whispered.

"What?"

"What they were calling out with the newspapers while we were at table."

There was a pause. The look in her eyes had changed. It was purely penetrating now.

"Why should it be?" asked Pocket, his own eyes falling.

"It's no use asking me, Mr. Upton."

"But I don't understand the question."

"Is that true?"

"No," he muttered; "it isn't."

She was leaning over to him; he felt it, without looking up.

"Mr. Upton," she said, speaking quickly in the undertone they were both instinctively adopting, "you know now what I thought about you at first. I won't say what made me; but that was what I thought, but could hardly believe, and never will again. It makes it all the more a mystery, your being here. I can't ask my uncle—he tells me nothing—but there's something I can and must ask you."

Pocket hung his head. He knew what was coming. It came.

"My uncle brought you here, Mr. Upton, on the very morning that thing happened they were calling out about to-day. In the Park. It is to the Park he goes so often in the early morning with his camera! How can I say what I want to say? But, if you think, you will see that everything points to it; especially the way he ran out for that paper—and hid the truth when he came in!"

Pocket looked up at last.

"I know the truth."

"About the arrest?"

"Yes; it was quite obvious, and he admitted it when you'd gone."

"Why not before?"

"I couldn't tax him about it in front of you," he muttered, looking up and down quickly, unable to face her fierce excitement.

"Do tell me what it is you both know about this dreadful case!"

"I can't," the boy said hoarsely; "don't ask me."

"Then you know who did it. I can see you do."

There was a new anguish even in her whisper; he could hear what she thought.

"It was nobody you care about," he mumbled, hoarser than before, and his head lower.

"You don't mean—"

She stopped aghast.

"I can't say another word—and you won't say another to me!" he added, a bitter break in his muffled voice. He longed to tell her it had been an accident, to tell her all; but he had given his word to Baumgartner not to confide in her, and he did not think that he had broken it yet.

"You don't know me," she whispered, and for a moment her hand lay warm in his; "trust me! I'm your friend in spite of all you've said—or done!"

Dr. Baumgartner might have been ten minutes getting rid of the intruder; before that he had been first amazed and then relieved to hear the piano in the drawing-room; and that was all his anxious ear had heard of either boy or girl during his absence. Yet the boy was not standing over the piano, as he might have been, for Phillida was trying to recall one of the concert songs he said his sister sang. Pocket, however, was staring out into the garden with a troubled face, which he turned abruptly, aggressively, and yet apprehensively to meet the doctor's.

But the doctor no longer looked suspiciously from him to Phillida, but stood beaming on them both, and rubbing his hands as though he had done something very clever indeed.

BEFORE THE STORM

Sunday in London has got itself a bad name among those who occasionally spend one at their hotel, and miss the band, their letters, and the theatre at night; but at Dr. Baumgartner's there was little to distinguish the seventh day from the other six. The passover of the postman, that boon to residents and grievance of the traveller, was a normal condition in the dingy house of no address. More motor-horns were heard in the distance, and less heavy traffic; the sound of church bells came as well through the open windows; then the street-door shut, and there was a long period without Phillida, until it opened and shut again, and in she peeped with her parasol and Prayer-book, as though they were all quite ordinary people without a guilty secret among them!

Such was the Sunday morning. It was fine and warm. Dr. Baumgartner pottered about his untidy little garden, a sun-trap again as Pocket had seen it first; the Turk's head perspired from internal and external heat, but its rich yellow, shading into richer auburn, clashed rather with a red geranium which the doctor wore jauntily in the button-hole of his black alpaca jacket.

It was Phillida who had given him the flower at breakfast. She grew what she could in the neglected garden; the plants in the miniature conservatory were also hers, though the doctor took a perfunctory interest in them, obviously on her account. It was obvious at least to Pocket Upton. He saw all these things, and what they meant. He was not without his little gifts of observation and deduction. He noticed the difference in Baumgartner's voice when he addressed his niece, the humane kindling of the inexorable eyes, and to-day he thought he saw a reciprocal softening on the part of Phillida. There had been none to see yesterday or the day before. It was her uncle whom the girl had seemed unable to forgive for the unseemly scuffle of Friday morning. But now it was as though memory and common fairness had set years of kindness against these days of unendurable mystery, and bidden her endure them with a better grace. If she felt she had been disloyal to him, she could not have made sweeter amends than she did by many an unobtrusive little office. And she exchanged no more confidences with poor Pocket.

Yet these two were together most of the day; all three were; and it was a strangely peaceful day, a day of natural hush, and the cessation of life's hostilities, such as is sometimes almost pointedly bestowed before or after a time of strain. It was a day on which Pocket certainly drew his spiritual breath more freely than on any other since the dire catastrophe. There were few fresh clouds; perhaps the only one before evening was the removal of the book on hallucinations in which Pocket had become interested on the Saturday afternoon. It was no longer lying about the room as he had left it. There was a gap in its place in the shelf. The book had been taken away from him; it made him feel as though he were back again at his very first dame's school.

And the church bells sent him back to the school he was at now! They were more mellow and sedate then the chapel bells there, that rang you down the hill at the double if you were late and not too asthmatical; and Pocket saw and heard himself puffing up the opposite hill to take his place for chapel call-over in the school quad. The fellows would be forming in squads there now, all in their Sunday tails or Eton jackets as the case might be; of course Pocket was in tails, though still rather proud of them. The masters, in their silk hoods or their rabbit-skins were prominent in his mind's eye. Then came the cool and spacious chapel, with its marble pulpit and its brazen candelabra, and rows of chastened chapel faces, that he knew better than his own, giving a swing to chants which ran in his head at the very thought. How real it all was to him, and how unreal this Sunday morning, in the sunny room with the battle engravings over the book-cases, and the walnut chairs in front of them, and Dr. Baumgartner in and out in his alpaca coat! After chapel he would have gone for a walk with Blundell minor, most probably, or else written his letter home and got it over. And that chapter would have ended with cold boiled beef and apple-pie with cloves in it at Spearman's.

The Italian restaurant which sent in Dr. Baumgartner's meals certainly provided richer fare than that. There was a top-floor of soup in the portable contrivance, and before the meat a risotto, which the doctor praised without a single patriotic reservation.

"Italy is a country where one can live," said he. "Not that you must understand me to be altogether down on your own fatherland, my young fellow; there is something to be said for London, especially on a Sunday. No organs from my dear Italy, none of those so-called German bands which we in Germany would not tolerate for a moment; no postman every hour of the day, and no gaolbirds crying false news down the streets."

Pocket looked for a grim twinkle in the speaker's eye, but found it fixed on Phillida, who had not looked up. Instinct prompted Pocket to say something quickly; that he had not seen a postman there, was the actual remark.

"That is because I conduct my correspondence at my club," explained the doctor. "I give out no other address; then you only get your letters when you want them."

"Do you often go there?" the boy ventured to inquire, devoutly wishing he would go that afternoon.

"Not when I have visitors," replied Baumgartner, with a smiling bow. "And I look upon my patients in that light," he added, with benevolent but futile hypocrisy, embarrassing enough to Phillida, but not more so than if she had still believed it to be the truth.

Silence ensued until they were all in the other room; then the niece took refuge at her piano, and this time Pocket hung over her for an hour or more. He went through her music, and asked for everything that Lettice played or sang. Phillida would not sing to him, but she had the makings of a pianist. The boy's enthusiasm for the things he knew made her play then as well as ever he had heard them played. Even the doctor, dozing in the big chair with eyes that were never quite shut, murmured his approval more than once; he loved his Mendelssohn and Schubert, and had nothing to say against the Sousas and others that the boy picked out as well, and mentioned with ingenuous fervour in the same breath. Pocket would have sung himself if the doctor had not been there, for he had a bit of a voice when he was free from asthma; and once or twice he stopped listening to wonder at himself. Could he be the boy who had killed a man, however innocently, three days before! Could it be he whom the police might come and carry off to prison at any moment? Was it true that he might never see his own people any more? Such questions appalled and stunned him; he could neither answer them nor realise their full import. They turned the old man in the chair, who alone could answer them, back into the goblin he had seemed at first. Yet they did give a certain shameful zest and excitement even to this quiet hour of motley music in his presence.

Besides, there was always one comfort to remember now: his letter home. Of course Lettice would show it to their father; of course something would be done at once. Shame and sorrow for the accident would be his for ever; but as for his present situation, there were moments when Pocket felt rather like a story-book cabin-boy luxuriously marooned, and already in communication with the mainland.

He wondered what steps had been taken so far. No doubt his father had come straight up to town; it was a moving thought that he might be within a mile of that very room at that very moment. Would all the known circumstances of his disappearance be published broadcast in the papers? Pocket felt he would have red ears all his life if that were done; and yet it had hurt him a little to gather from Baumgartner that so far there was nothing in the papers to say he had so much as disappeared. That fact must have been known since Thursday or Friday. Once it did cross his mind that to keep it from his mother they would have to keep it out of the papers. Well, as long as she did not know!

He pictured the blinds down in her room; it was the hour of her afternoon rest. If he were at home, he would be going about quietly. Lettice would be reading or writing in the morning-room, most probably. Father would be gloating over his rhododendrons with a strong cigar; in his last letter the boy had heard how beautiful they were. Horace might be with him, smoking a cigarette, if he and Fred were not playing tennis. Their pocket edition had not to look very far ahead to see himself smoking proper cigarettes with the others, to hear his own voice telling them of his own experience—of this very hour at Dr. Baumgartner's. Even Fred and Horace would have to listen to that! Pocket looked at the long lean figure in the chair, at the eyelids never quite closed, and so imparting at once a softening and a sinister effect. He noted the drooping geranium in his buttonhole, and grey ash from the Turk's head sprinkling the black alpaca coat. It brought the very phrases of a graphic portrait almost to his lips.

Yet if anybody had told the boy he was beginning to gloat over the silver lining to the cloud that he was under, and that it was not silver at all but one of the baser metals of the human heart, how indignantly he would have denied it at first, how humbly seen it in the end!

When Phillida went off to make the tea her uncle sought his room and sponge, but did not neglect to take Pocket with him. Pocket was for going higher up to his own room; but Baumgartner said that would only make more work, in a tone precluding argument. It struck Pocket that the doctor really needed sleep, and was irritable after a continuous struggle against it. If so, it served him right for not trusting a fellow—and for putting Boismont in the waste-paper basket, by Jove!

There was no mistaking the red book there; it was one of the first things Pocket noticed, while the doctor was stooping over his basin in the opposite corner; and the schoolboy's strongest point, be it remembered, was a stubborn tenacity of his own devices. He made a dive at the waste-paper basket, meaning to ask afterwards if the doctor minded his reading that book. But the question never was asked; the book was still in the basket when the doctor had finished drying his face; and the boy was staring and swaying as though he had seen the dead.

"Why, what's the matter with my young fellow?" inquired Baumgartner, solicitously.

"Nothing! I'll be all right soon," muttered Pocket, wiping his forehead and then his hand.

"You look faint. Here's my sponge. No, lie flat down there first!"

But Pocket was not going to lie down on that bed.

"I do feel seedy," he said, in a stronger voice with a new note in it, "but I'm not going to faint. I'm quite well able to go upstairs. I'd rather lie down on my own bed, if you don't mind."

His own bed! The irony struck him even as he said the words. He was none the less glad to sit down on it; and so sitting he made his first close examination of two or three tiny squares of paper which he had picked out of the basket in the doctor's room instead of Boismont's book on hallucinations. There had been no hallucination about those scraps of paper; they were fragments of the boy's own letter to his sister, which Dr. Baumgartner had never posted at all.

A LIKELY STORY

At that moment help was as far away as it had been near the day before, when Eugene Thrush was closeted in the doctor's dining-room; for not only had Mr. Upton decamped for Leicestershire, without a word of warning to anybody, on the Saturday afternoon, but Thrush himself had followed by the only Sunday train.

A bell was ringing for evening service when he landed in a market town which reversed the natural order by dozing all summer and waking up for the hunting season. And now the famous grass country was lying in its beauty-sleep, under a gay counterpane of buttercups and daisies, and leafy coverts, with but one blot in the sky-line, in the shape of a permanent plume of sluggish smoke. But the works lay hidden, and the hall came first; and Thrush, having ascertained that this was it, abandoned the decrepit vessel he had boarded at the station, and entered the grounds on foot.

A tall girl, pacing the walks with a terribly anxious face, was encountered and accosted before he reached the house.

"I believe Mr. Upton lives here. Can you tell me if he's at home? I want to see him about something."

Lettice flushed and shrank.

"I know who you are! Have you found my brother?"

"No; not yet," said Thrush, after a pause. "But you take my breath away, my dear young lady! How could you be so sure of me? Is it no longer to be kept a secret, and is that why your father bolted out of town without a word?"

"It's still a secret," whispered Lettice, as though the shrubs had ears, "only I'm in it. Nobody else is— nobody fresh—but I guessed, and my mother was beginning to suspect. My father never stays away a Sunday unless he's out of England altogether; she couldn't understand it, and was worrying so about him that I wired begging him to come back if only for the night. So it's all my fault, Mr. Thrush; and I know everything but what you've come down to tell us!"

"That's next to nothing," he shrugged. "It's neither good nor bad. But if you can find your father I'll tell you both exactly what I have found out."

In common with all his sex, he liked and trusted Lettice at sight, without bestowing on her a passing thought as a person capable of provoking any warmer feeling. She was the perfect sister—that he felt as instinctively as everybody else—and a woman to trust into the bargain. It would be cruel and quite unnecessary to hide anything from that fine and unselfish face. So he let her lead him to a little artificial cave, lined and pungent with pitch-pine, over against the rhododendrons, while she went to fetch her father quietly from the house.

The ironmaster amplified the excuses already made for him; he had rushed for the first train after getting his daughter's telegram, leaving but a line for Thrush with his telephone number, in the hopes that he would use it whether he had anything to report or not.

"As you didn't," added Mr. Upton, in a still aggrieved voice, "I've been trying again and again to ring you up instead; but of course you were never there, nor your man Mullins either. I was coming back by the last train, however, and should have been with you late to-night."

"Did you leave the motor behind?"

"Yes; it'll be there to meet me at St. Pancras."

"It may have to do more than that," said Thrush, spreading his full breadth on the pitch-pine seat. "I've found out something; how much or how little it's too soon to tell; but I wasn't going to discuss it through a dozen country exchanges as long as you wanted the thing a dead secret, Mr. Upton, and that's why I didn't ring you up. As for your last train, I'd have waited to meet it in town, only that wouldn't have given me time to say what I've got to say before one or other of us may have to rush off somewhere else by another last train."

"Do for God's sake say what you've got to say!" cried Mr. Upton.

"Well, I've seen a man who thinks he may have seen the boy!"

"Alive?"

"And perfectly well—but for his asthma—on Thursday."

The ironmaster thanked God in a dreadful voice; it was Lettice who calmed him, not he her. Her eyes only shone a little, but his were blinded by the first ray of light.

"Where was it?" he asked, when he could ask anything.

"I'll tell you in a minute. I want first to be convinced that it really was your son. Did the boy take any special interest in Australia?"

"Rather!" cried Lettice, the sister of three boys.

"What kind of interest?"

"He wanted to go out there. It had just been talked about." She looked at her father. "I wouldn't let him go," he said. "Why?"

"I want to know just how it came to be talked about."

"A fool of a doctor in town recommended it."

Lettice winced, but Thrush nodded as though that tallied.

"Did he recommend any particular vessel?"

"Yes, a sailing ship—the Seringapatam— an old East Indiaman they've turned into a kind of floating hospital. I wouldn't hear of the beastly tub."

"Do you know when she was to sail?"

"I did know," said Lettice. "I believe it was just about now."

"She sailed yesterday," said Thrush, impressively; "and your brother, if it was your brother, talked a good deal about her to this man. He told him all about your having always been in favour of it, Miss Upton, and his father not. I'm bound to say it sounds as though it may have been the boy."

Thrush seemed to be keeping something back; but the prime and absorbing question of identity prevented the others from noticing this.

"It must have been!" cried Mr. Upton. "Who was the man, and where exactly did he see him?"

"First on Thursday morning, and last on Thursday night. But perhaps I'd better tell you about my informant, since we've only his word for Thursday, and only his suspicions as to what has happened since. In the first place he's a semi-public man, though I don't suppose you know his name. It's Baumgartner—Dr. Otto Baumgartner—a German scientist of some distinction."

The ironmaster made a remark which did him little credit, and Thrush continued with some pride: "There was some luck in it, of course, for he was the very first man I struck who'd bought d'Auvergne Cigarettes since Wednesday; but I was on his doorstep well within twenty-four hours of hearing that your son was missing; and you may chalk that up to A. V. M.! I might have been with him some hours sooner still, but I preferred to spend them getting to know something about my man. I tried his nearest shops; perfect mines! One was a chemist, who didn't know him by sight, and had never heard of the cigarettes, but remembered being asked for them by an elderly gentleman last Thursday morning! That absolutely confirmed my first suspicion that Baumgartner himself was not the asthmatic; if he had been, the nearest chemist would have known all about him. Yet he had gone to the nearest chemist first!"

"The nearest butcher was next door; but he was so short about Baumgartner that I scented a true-green vegetarian. It was a false scent, Mr. Upton; not to mention the baker and the candlestick-maker, there's a little restaurant in the same row, which was about the fifth place where I began by asking if they knew where a Dr. Baumgartner lived in that neighbourhood. The little Italian boss was all over me on the spot! The worthy doctor proved to be his most regular customer, having all his meals sent in hot from the restaurant in quite the Italian manner. I don't suppose you see how very valuable this was to me.

Germans love Italy, the little man explained; but I said that was the one point on which I should never yield to Germany—and I thought I was going to be kissed across the counter! It seems the good doctor lives alone with his niece (not always even her), and keeps no servants and never entertains. Yet on Friday, for the first time since the arrangement was made, the old chap went to the restaurant himself to complain of short commons; there had not been enough for them to eat on the Thursday night!"

"Had they been alone?" asked Mr. Upton, with a puzzled face.

"That's the whole point! My little Florentine understood they were, but I deduced one extra, and then conceived a course that may astonish you. It was the bold course; but it nearly always pays. I lunched at my leisure (an excellent Chianti my little friend keeps) and afterwards went round and saw the doctor himself. The niece opened the door—I wish I'd seen more of her—but she fetched her uncle at once and I begged for an interview on an urgent matter. He consented in a way that, I must say, impressed me very favourably; and the moment we were alone I said, 'I want to know, Doctor, who you bought those asthma cigarettes for last Thursday!' "

"That took him aback, but not unduly; so then I added, 'I'm an inquiry agent with a very delicate case in hand, and if you'll tell me it may solve at heart-breaking a mystery as I've ever handled.' Is was treating him like a gentleman, but I believe in that; there's no shorter cut to whether a man is one or not."

"Well, his face had lit up, and a very fine face it is; it hadn't blackened for the fifth of a second; but I had a disappointment in store. 'I'd tell you his name with all my heart,' he said, 'only I don't really know it myself. He said it was John Green—but his handkerchiefs were marked "A. A. U." ' "

"Tony's initials!" cried Tony's father.

"But it never was Tony under a false name," his sister vowed. "That settles it for me, Mr. Thrush."

"Not even if he'd got into some scrape or adventure, Miss Upton?"

"He would never give a name that wasn't his."

"Suppose he felt he had disgraced his name?"

"My brother Tony wouldn't do it!"

"He might feel he had?"

"He might," the father agreed, "even if he'd done no such thing; in fact, he's just the kind of boy who would take an exaggerated view of some things." His mind went back to his last talk with Horace on the subject.

"Or he might feel he was about to do something, shall we say, unworthy of you all?" Thrush made the suggestion with much delicacy.

"Then I don't think he'd do it," declared loyal Lettice.

"Let us hear what you think he did," said Mr. Upton.

"It's not what I think; it's what this man Baumgartner thinks, and his story that you ought to hear."

And that which they now heard at second-hand was in fact a wonderfully true version—up to a point—of poor Pocket's condition and adventures—with the sleep-walking and the shooting left out—from the early morning of his meeting with Baumgartner until the late afternoon of that day.

Baumgartner had actually described the boy's long sleep in his chair; it was with the conversation when he awoke that the creative work began in earnest.

"That's a good man!" said Mr. Upton, with unimaginable irony. "I'd like to take him by the hand—and those infernal Knaggses by the scruff of their dirty necks—and that old hag Harbottle by the hair!"

"I think of dear darling Tony," said Lettice, in acute distress; "lying out all night with asthma—it was enough to kill him—or to send him out of his mind."

"I wonder if it could have done that," remarked Thrush, in a tone of serious speculation which he was instantly called upon to explain.

"What are you keeping back?" cried Lettice, the first to see that he had been keeping something all this time.

"Only something he'd kept back from them," replied Thrush, with just a little less than his usual aplomb. "It was a surprise he sprang on them after waking; it will probably surprise you still more, Mr. Upton. You may not believe it. I'm not certain that I do myself. In the morning he had spoken of the Australian voyage as though you'd opposed it, but withdrawn your opposition—one moment, if you don't mind! In the evening he suddenly explained that he was actually sailing in the Seringapatam, that his baggage was already on board, and he must get aboard himself that night!"

"I don't believe it, Thrush."

"No more do I, father, for a single instant. Tony, of all people!"

Thrush looked from one to the other with a somewhat disingenuous eye. "I don't say I altogether accept it myself; that's why I kept it to the end," he explained. "But we must balance the possibilities against the improbabilities, never losing sight of the one incontestable fact that the boy has undoubtedly disappeared. And here's a man, a well-known man, who makes no secret of the fact that he found him wandering in the Park, in the early morning, breathless and dazed, and drove him home to his own house, where the boy spent the day; they took a hansom, the doctor tells me, than which no statement is more quickly and easily checked. Are we to believe this apparently unimpeachable and disinterested witness, or are we not? He was most explicit about everything, offering to show me exactly where he found the boy, and never the least bit vague or unsatisfactory in any way. If you are prepared to believe him, if only for the sake of argument, you may care to hear Dr. Baumgartner's theory as to what has happened."

Lettice shook her head in scorn, but Mr. Upton observed, "Well, we may as well hear what the fellow had to say to you; we must be grateful to him for taking pity on our boy, and he was the last who saw him; he may have seen something that we shouldn't guess."

"Exactly!" exclaimed Eugene Thrush; "he saw, or at any rate he now thinks he saw, enough to build up a pretty definite theory on the foundation of fact supplied by me. He didn't know the boy had come up to see a doctor and been refused a lodging for the night; he understood he had come up to join his ship, and suspected he had been on a sort of mild spree—if Miss Upton will forgive me!" And he turned deferential lenses on the indignant girl.

"I don't forgive the suggestion," said she; "but it isn't yours, Mr. Thrush, so please go on."

"It's an idea that Dr. Baumgartner continues to hold in spite of all I was able to tell him, and we mustn't forget, as Mr. Upton says, that he was the last to see your brother. Briefly, he believes the boy did meet with some misadventure that night in town; that he had been ill-treated or intimidated by some unscrupulous person or persons; perhaps threatened with blackmail; at any rate imbued with the conviction that he is not more sinned against than sinning. That, I think, is only what one expects of these very conscientious characters, particularly in youth; he was taking something or somebody a thousandfold more seriously than a grown man would have done. Afraid to go back to school for fear of expulsion, ashamed to show his face at home! What's to be done? He thinks of the ship about to sail, the ship he hoped to sail in, and in his desperation he determines to sail in her still—even if he has to stow away!"

"My God!" cried Mr. Upton, "he's just the one to think of it. His head was full of those trashy adventure stories!"

But Lettice shook hers quietly.

"To think of it, but not to do it," said she, with a quiet conviction that rather nettled Mr. Thrush.

"But really, Miss Upton, he must have done something, you know! And he actually talked to Dr. Baumgartner about this; not of doing it himself, but of stowaways in general, à propos of his voyage; and how many pounds of biscuit and how many ounces of water would carry one alive into blue water. There's another thing, by the way! He told Baumgartner the ship touched nowhere between the East India Docks and Melbourne; he would be out of the world for three whole months."

"And she only sailed yesterday?" cried Mr. Upton, coming furiously to his feet. "And you let her get through the Straits of Dover and out to sea while you came down here to tell me this by inches?"

Thrush blinked blandly through his port-hole glasses.

"I'm letting her go as far as Plymouth," said he, "where one or both of us will board her tomorrow if she's up to time!"

"You said she didn't touch anywhere between the docks and Melbourne?"

"No; your son said that, Mr. Upton, and it was his one mistake. They don't usually touch, but a son of one of the owners happens to have gone round in the ship to Plymouth for the trip. I got it first from an old boatswain of the line who's caretaker at the office, and the only man there, of course, yesterday afternoon; but I've since bearded one of the partners at his place down the river, and had the statement confirmed and amplified. One or two pasengers are only going aboard at Plymouth, so she certainly won't sail again before to-morrow noon, even if she's there by then. You will be in ample time to board her—and I've got a sort of search-warrant from the partner I saw—if you go down by the 12.15 from Paddington to-night."

The ironmaster asked no more questions; that was good enough for him, he said, and went off to tell a last lie to his wife, with the increasing confidence of one gradually mastering the difficulties of an uncongenial game. He felt also that a happy issue was in sight, and after that he could tell the truth and liberate his soul. He was pathetically sanguine of the solution vicariously propounded by Eugene Thrush, and prepared to rejoice in a discovery which would have filled him with dismay and chagrin if he had not been subconsciously prepared for something worse. It never occurred to Mr. Upton to question the man's own belief in the theory he had advanced; but Lettice did so the moment she had the visitor to herself in the smoking-room, where it fell to her to do certain honours vice Horace, luckily engaged at the works. "And do you believe this astounding theory, Mr. Thrush?"

Thrush eyed her over his tumbler's rim, but completed his draught before replying.

"It's not my province to believe or to disbelieve, Miss Upton; my job is to prove things one way or the other."

"Then I'll tell you just one thing for your guidance: my brother is absolutely incapable of the conduct you ascribe to him between you."

Thrush did not look as though he were being guided by anybody or anything, beyond the dictates of his own appetites, as he sat by the window of the restaurant car, guzzling new potatoes and such Burgundy as could be had in a train. But he was noticeably less garrulous than usual, and his companion also had very little to say until the train was held up inexplicably outside Willesden, when he began to fume.

"I never knew such a thing on this line before," he complained; "it's all the harder luck, for I never was on such an errand before, and it'll just make the difference to me."

"You'll have time," said Thrush, consulting his watch as the train showed signs of life at last.

"Not for what I want to do," said Mr. Upton firmly. "I want to shake that man's hand, and to hear from his own lips about my boy!"

"I'm not sure that you'll find him at home," Thrush said, after a contemplative pause.

"I'll take my chance of that."

"He said something about their both going out of town to-day—meaning niece and self. I heard her playing just before I left, and that seemed to remind him of it."

"Well, Thrush, I mean to risk it."

"And losing the train?"

"I can motor down to Plymouth; there's plenty of time. I might take him with me, as well as you?"

"Better," said Thrush, after another slight pause. "I'd rather you didn't count on me for that trip, Mr. Upton."

"Not count on you"?

"One of us will be quite enough."

"Have you some other case to shove in front of mine, then?" cried the ironmaster, touched on the old raw spot.

"I shouldn't put it like that, Mr. Upton."

"All right! I'll take your man Mullins instead; but I'll try my luck at that German doctor's first," he growled, determined to have his own way in something.

"I'm afraid you can't have Mullins," said Thrush, gently.

"Want him yourself do you?"

"I do; but I'm afraid neither of us can have him just now, Mr. Upton."

"Why not? Where is he."

Thrush leant across as they swam into the lighted terminus.

"In prison."

"In prison! Your man Mullins?"

"Yes, Mr. Upton, he's the man they arrested yesterday on suspicion of complicity in this Hyde Park affair!"

MALINGERING

Pocket had put the fragments of his poor letter together again, and was still poring over those few detached and mutilated words, which were the very ones his tears had blotted, when there came a warning chink of tea-things on the stairs. He was just able to thrust the pieces back into his pocket, and to fling himself at full length on the bed, before Dr. Baumgartner entered with a tray.

"There, my young fellow! This will make a man of you! Then we shall see you yourself again by supper-time."

"I'm not coming down again," said Pocket. "Don't force me, please"

"Force you?" Baumgartner cocked a keen eye at the open window. "What a tyrant you would make me out! On the contrary, I think you show your wisdom in remaining quiet. Perhaps you would be quieter still with the window shut—so—and fastened to prevent it rattling. I will open it when I come up again. There shall not be a sound in the house to disturb you."

And he took to tiptoes there and then, gliding about with a smiling stealth that set Pocket shivering on the bed; he shivered the more when an admirable doctor's hand, cool and smooth as steel, was laid upon his forehead.

"A little fever, I'm afraid! I should get right into bed, if I were you. It's nothing to be alarmed about, much less astonished; you have been through so much, my poor young fellow."

"I have indeed!" cried Pocket, with unguarded bitterness.

And Baumgartner paused between the foot of the bed and the door.

"But there's one consolation for you," he said at length, in a sibilant whisper. "They've had that letter of yours at home quite a long time now—ever since yesterday morning, haven't they?"

The bed shook under Pocket when the door was shut—he only hoped it was not before. Up to the last minute, he felt quite sure that Dr. Baumgartner, suspicious as he was, had suspected nothing of the discovery downstairs behind his back. If he himself had betrayed anything it was in the last few seconds, when it had been all that he could do to keep from screaming out his knowledge of the other's trickery. To play such a trick upon a broken-hearted boy! To have the heart to play it! No wonder he felt feverish to that wicked hand; the wonder was that he had actually lain there listening to the smooth impostor gratuitously revelling in his imposition!

Rage and disappointment seized him by turns, and both together; at first they bit deeper even than the fear of Baumgartner—a fear felt from the beginning, and naturally redoubled now. Disappointment had the sharper tooth: his letter had ever gone, not one of his people knew a thing about him yet, his tears had not drawn theirs, they had not hung in anxious conclave on his words! Not that he had recognised any such subtle consolations as factors in his temporary and comparative peace of mind; now that they were gone, he could not have said what it was he missed; he only knew that he could least forgive Baumgartner for this sudden sense of cruel and crushing disappointment.

The phase passed, for the boy had the temperament that sees the other side eventually, and of course there was something to be said for the doctor's stratagem. He could understand it, after all; the motive was not malevolent; it was to relieve his mind and keep him quiet. The plan had succeeded perfectly, and nobody was really any the worse off. His people would have known he was alive and well on the Friday; but that was all, and they had no reason yet to assume his death. No; even Pocket came to see that his letter had been more of a relief to write than it could have been to read; that, indeed, it could only have aggravated the anxiety and suspense at home. Yet there was in him some fibre which the deliberate deception had fretted and frayed beyond reason or forgiveness. He saw all there was to be said about it; he could imagine Baumgartner himself putting the case with irresistible logic, with characteristic plausibility, and all the mesmeric wisdom of a benevolent serpent; but for once, the boy felt, he would not be taken in. It was not coming to that, however, for he had quite decided not to betray his knowledge of the fraud—if only he had not already done so!

His fears on that score were largely allayed by Baumgartner's manner when at length he returned with another tray; for nothing could have been more considerate and sympathetic, and even fatherly, than the doctor's behaviour then. Pocket had never touched his tea; he was very gently chidden for that. Obstinately he declared he did not want any supper either: it was true he did not want to want any, or another bite of that man's bread, but he was sorry as soon as the words were out. It was against his reasoned policy to show temper, and he was beginning to feel very hungry besides. The doctor said, "You'll think better of that, my young fellow," which turned a mere remark into more than half an absolute resolution. The second tray was set with a lighted candle on a chair by the bedside. The boy eyed it wistfully with set teeth, and Baumgartner eyed the boy.

"Is there anything you could fancy, my young fellow?"

"Nothing to eat."

"Is there any book?"

"Yes," said Pocket, without a moment's premeditation. "There's the book I was reading yesterday."

"What was that?"

"Some Frenchman on hallucinations."

"So you were reading that book!" remarked the doctor, with detestable aplomb. "I wondered who had taken it down. It is a poor book. I have destroyed it."

"I'm sorry," said Pocket, and tried to look it rather than revolted.

"I am not," rejoined Baumgartner. "Even if it were a good book, it is no book for you at the present time. It is morbid to dwell on what is done and over."

"If it is over," murmured the boy.

"It is over!" said Baumgartner, fiercely.

"Well," said Pocket, "I'm glad I read what he'd got to say about somnambulism."

"Why?"

Pocket did not say it was a satisfaction to have done anything in spite of such a despot as his questioner. But he did say it was a comfort to know that others besides himself had committed terrible deeds in their sleep.

"But," he added, "they always seem to have dreamt the dreadful thing as well. Now, the funny thing is that I remember nothing until the shot woke me and I found myself where you saw me."

"I'm glad you find it funny!"

The sneer seemed strangely unworthy of a keen intelligence; the increased asperity of Baumgartner's manner, and his whole conduct about a harmless book, altogether inexplicable.

"You know what I mean," replied the boy, with spirit.

"Yes, I know what you mean! You mean to go out of your mind, and to do your best to drive me out of mine, for the sake of a technically human life less precious than the average dog's!"

And, much as it puzzled him, there was certainly something more human about this sudden outburst than in anything Dr. Baumgartner had said since the scene between them in the bedroom below. He even slammed the door behind him when he went. But Pocket preferred that novel exhibition, for its very heat and violence, to the sleek and calculated solicitude of the doctor's final visit, with pipe and candle, when the one by the bedside had burnt down almost to the socket.

"My young fellow!" he exclaimed in unctuous distress. "Not a bite eaten in all these hours! Do you know that it's nearly midnight?"

"I'm not hungry," replied Pocket, lying gloriously for once. "I told you I wasn't well."

"You'll be worse if you don't force yourself to eat."

"I can't help that."

"Well, well!" said the doctor, instead of the objurgation that seemed to tremble for an instant on his lips. He replaced between them the oval hook of clear amber enclosing the thin round one of black nicotine, and he puffed until the cruel carved face was hotter and more infuriate than ever, under the swirling smoke of mimic battle. To the boy it was all but a living face, and a vile one, capable of nameless atrocities; and the hard-frozen face of Baumgartner was capable of looking on.

"Well, well! If I am to have you ill on my hands it's my own fault. I take the responsibility for everything that has happened since the very first moment we met. Remember that, my young fellow! I took the law into my own hands, and you I took into my own house for better or worse. You were worse then, remember, and yet I took you in! Is it not strange that your asthma has entirely left you under my roof? Does it not lead you to believe in me, my young fellow—to trust me perhaps more than you have done?"

It did not. Pocket was not going to lie about that; he held his tongue stubbornly instead. He still believed in his own explanation, derived from one of his many doctors, and moreover already mentioned to this one, of the sudden cessation of his chronic complaint. He hated Baumgartner for forgetting that, and pretending for a moment to take any credit to himself. That again was not worthy of so cool and keen a brain, much less of the candid character with which Pocket had supposed himself to be dealing. The very young are pathetically apt to see their own virtues in those whom they trust at all; but the schoolboy's faith in Dr. Baumgartner had been shattered to its base; and now (as sure a symptom of his youth) he could see no virtue at all.

"You must trust me again," said Baumgartner, as though he knew what he had forfeited. "I know what will do you good."

"What?" asked Pocket, out of mere incredulous curiosity.

"Fresh air; some exercise; a glimpse of the beautiful town we live in, before another soul is about, before the sun itself is up!"

Pocket hardly knew what made him shudder at the proposition. It might have been the poignant picture of that other early morning, which came before him in a scorching flash. But there was something also in the way the doctor was bending over him in bed, holding his pipe nearer still, so that the two dreadful faces seemed of equal size. And Baumgartner's had become a dreadful face in the boy's eyes now; there was none among those cruel waxworks to match it in cold intellectual cruelty; and its smile—its new and strange smile it must have been that made him shudder and shake his head.

"But, my young fellow," urged the doctor, "it will do you so much good. And not a soul will see us so early, early in the morning!"

Again that insinuating smile inspired a horror of which the boy himself could have offered no satisfactory explanation, especially as there was much to commend the proposal to his mind. But his face was white enough as he moved it from side to side on the pillow.

"I tell you I'm ill," he whimpered. "How can I go out with you, when you see I can't eat a bite?"

Baumgartner gave it up for the night. He was coming back in the early, early lovely summer's morning; then they would see, would they not? Pocket had a last wave from the hideous meerschaum head, and a nod from the other. He was alone for the night. And he meant to be alone next morning when the doctor took his early walk; let him prowl by himself. Pocket was not going with him. He had never been more determined about anything than that. It was an animal instinct of fear and deep revulsion, an impulse quite distinct from a further determination to slip away in his turn as soon as the coast was clear. On this course he was equally decided, but on other and more palpable grounds. Baumgartner had broken his side of their treaty, so the treaty was torn up with the letter which had never gone. And Pocket was going instead of his letter—going straight to his people to tell them all, and have that poor innocent man set free before the day was out.

The night's immunity was meanwhile doubly precious; but it had been secured, or rather its continuance could only be assured, at a price which he wondered even now if he could pay. He was a growing, hungry boy, no longer ailing in wind or limb. Distress of mind was his one remaining ill; the rest was sham; and distress of mind did not prevent him from feeling ravenous after fasting ten or eleven hours. Here was food still within his reach, even at his side; but he felt committed to his declaration that he could not eat. If the tray were still untouched in the morning, surely there could be no further question of his going out with Baumgartner; but there was an "if." The boy was not used to being very stern with himself; his strongest point was not self-denial. Much of his moral stamina had been expended in nightly tussles for mere breath; he had grit enough there. But his temperament was self-indulgent, and that he triumphed over positive pangs only shows the power of that rival instinct not to accompany the doctor a yard from his door.

Yet it meant more hours with the food beside him than he could endure lying still. He got up, inch by inch, for he knew who lay underneath; and he opened the window, which Baumgartner had broken his promise to open, by even slower and more laborious degrees. He leant out as he had done that first morning, it might have been a month ago; and this scene must have challenged comparison with that, had his mind been even as free from dread and terror as it had been then. But all he saw was the few remaining lighted windows in the backs of those other houses; he could not have sworn there was a moon. The moon poured no beam of comfort on his aching head; but the lighted windows were as the open eyes of honest men, who would not see him come to harm; and the last rumble in the streets was a faint but cheering chorus for lonely ears.

Once a motor-horn blew a solo near at hand, and Pocket half recognised its note; but he did not connect it with quite another set of sounds, which grew but gradually on his ear out of the bowels of the house. Somebody was knocking and ringing at the doctor's door, not furiously, but with considerable pertinacity. Pocket was thrilled to the marrow just at first, and flew from the open window to the landing outside his door. The house was in perfect darkness, and still as death in the patient intervals between each measured attempt to rouse the inmates without disturbing the street. It came to Pocket that it must be Baumgartner himself, gone out for something without his key; and the boy was about to run down and let him in, when he distinctly heard the retreat of feet down the front steps, and then a chuckle on the next landing as the doctor closed his bedroom door.

Who could it have been? Baumgartner's chuckle suggested the police; but in that case it was the boy upstairs who was going to have the last laugh, though a grim one, and very terribly at his own expense. He could not close an eye for thinking of it, and listening for another knocking and ringing down below. But nothing happened until the doctor returned between five and six, still with his meerschaum pipe, still in his alpaca jacket, but wearing also the goblin hat and cloak of their first meeting, to renew and intensify the animal fear that glued the boy to his bed.

"It is a pity," said Baumgartner, standing at the window which Pocket had left open. "The air is like champagne at this hour, and not a cloud in the sky! It would do you more good than lying there. It is you who are making yourself ill. If I thought you were doing it on purpose "—and his eyes blazed—"I'd feed you like a fowl!"

"It's so likely that I should do it on purpose," muttered Pocket, with schoolboy sarcasm. His eyes, however, were purposely closed, and they had missed the old daggers in Baumgartner's.

"You know best," said the doctor. "But you are missing the morning of your life! Not a cloud in the sky, only the golden rain in my little garden. I suppose you have not learnt what the golden rain is at your public school? You English call it laburnum; but we Germans have more imagination, thank God!"

Pocket did not open his eyes again till he had gone; next instant he had the door open too, as the doctor's step was creaking down the lower flight of stairs. Once more Pocket ventured out upon the landing, not quite to the banisters; he trusted to his ears as before. They told him the doctor had gone into his dark-room. His heart sank. It was only for a moment. The dark-room door shut sharply. The steps came creaking back along the hall, went grating out upon the doorstep. There was another sharp shutting. Food at last!

It was neither very nice nor half enough for a famishing lad, that plate of cold mixed meats from the restaurant, with a hard stale roll to eke them out. But Pocket felt he had a fresh start in life when he had eaten every crumb and emptied his water-bottle. Nor was he without plan or purpose any longer; he was only doubtful whether to knock at Phillida's door and shout goodbye, or to leave her a note explaining all. Baumgartner would be out for hours; he always was, on these early jaunts of his; there would almost be time to wait and say goodbye properly when the girl came down. She would hardly hinder him a second time, and he longed to see her and speak to her again, especially if that was to be the end between them. He did not mean it to be the end, by any means; but any nonsense that might have been gathering in the schoolboy's head was, at this point, more than rudely dispelled by the discovery that Dr. Baumgartner had removed his clothes!

Pocket swore an oath that would have shocked him in a schoolfellow; it was a practice he indeed abhorred, but decent words would not meet such a case. It was to be met by action, however, just as that locked door had been met, and the policeman's prohibition in the Park. He knew where his clothes must be. He slipped his overcoat, which he was using as a dressing-gown, over his pyjamas, and ran right downstairs as Dr. Baumgartner had done not many minutes before him. His clothes were in the dark-room. But the dark-room door had a Yale lock; there was no forcing it by foot or shoulder, though Pocket in his passion tried both. So round he went without a moment's hesitation to the dark-room window by way of the little conservatory. The blind was drawn. That mattered nothing. He went back for a plant-pot, and smashed both it and a sheet of ruby glass with one vicious blow.

Entry was simple after that; he had only to be careful not to cut his hands or feet. Inside, he removed the broken glass, closed the window, and let the blind down as he had found it, without looking twice at his clothes. There they were for him to carry upstairs at his leisure. They were not his only property in that room either. His revolver was there somewhere under lock and key. He might want it, waking, if Dr. Baumgartner came back before his time.

It was easily located; of the lockers, built in with the shelves on the folding doors, only one was actually locked, and the revolver was not in the others. Pocket went to his waistcoat for one of those knives beloved of schoolboys, with the hook for extracting stones from hoofs, among other superfluous implements. Pocket had never used this one, had often felt inclined to wrench it off because it was hard to open and in the way of the other tools. But he used it now with as little hesitation as he had done the other damage, with almost a lust for breakage; and there was his revolver, safe and sound as his clothes.

It had been honoured with a place beside a rack of special negatives; at least, there were other racks, in the other lockers, not locked up like that; and there was no other treasure that Pocket could see. He had his hand on his own treasure, was in the act of taking it, trembling a little, but more elated, as he stood in a ruby flood only partially diluted by the broken window behind the blind.

At that moment there came such a thunder of knuckles on the door beside him that the revolver caught in the rack of negatives, and brought the whole lot crashing about his toes.

ON THE TRACK OF THE TRUTH

The unseen knuckles renewed their assault upon the dark-room door; and Pocket wavered between its Yale lock, which opened on this side with a mere twist of the handle, and the broken red window behind the drawn red blind. Escape that way was easy enough; and if ever one could take the streets in pyjamas and overcoat, with the rest of one's clothes in a bundle under one's arm, it was before six o'clock in the morning. But it was not a course that vanity encouraged in an excited schoolboy with romantic instincts and a revolver which he perceived at a glance to be still loaded in most of its chambers. Pocket was not one of nature's heroes, but he had an overwhelming desire to behave like one, and time to feel how he should despise himself all his life if he bolted by the window instead of opening the door. So he did open it, trembling but determined. And there stood Phillida in her dressing-gown, her dark hair tumbling over her shoulders.

"It's you!" she cried, taking the exclamation out of his mouth.

"Yes," he said, with a gust of relief; "did you think it was thieves?"

"Isn't it?" she demanded, pointing to the broken window visible through the blind. Then she saw his revolver, and drew back an inch.

"He took this from me," said Pocket. "I had a right to it. Take it if you will!"

And he offered it, in the best romantic manner, by the barrel. But Phillida was too angry to look at revolvers.

"You had no business to break in to get it," she told him, with considerable severity.

"I didn't! I broke in for my clothes; he took them, too, this morning before he went out. They're what I broke in for, and I'd a perfect right; you know I had! And while I'm about it I thought I might as well have this thing too. I knew it was in here somewhere. It was in there. And I'm glad I got it, and so should you be, because you and I are in the house of one of the greatest villains alive!"

The words tumbled over each other with quite hereditary heat. They were all out in a few seconds, and the boy left panting with his indignation, the girl's eyes flashing hers.

"I begin to think my uncle was right," said she. "This is the act of what he said you were, if anything could be."

"He lied to you, and he's been lying to me!"

"He may have been justified."

"You wait till you hear all he's done! I don't mean taking my revolver from me; he was justified in that, if you like, after what I'd done with it. He may even have been justified in taking away my clothes, if he couldn't trust me to keep my word and stay in this awful house. But that isn't the worst. He encouraged me to write a letter home, to my own poor people who may think me dead—"

"Well?"

There was more sympathy in her voice, more anxiety; but his was breaking with his great grief and grievance.

"He took it out himself, to send it to the General Post Office to catch the country post. So he said; and I was so grateful to him! On Saturday morning he said they must have got it; he kept on saying so, and you don't know how thankful I was every time! But yesterday afternoon I found scraps of my letter in the waste-paper basket in his room; he'd never posted it at all!"

Phillida looked shocked and distressed enough at this; her liquid eyes filled with sympathy as they gazed upon the wretched youth.

"I'm a fool to blub about it—but—but that was the Limit!" he croaked, and worked the poor word till it came distinctly.

"It was cruel," she allowed. "It must seem so, at any rate; it does to me; but then I understand so little. I can't think why he's hiding you, or why you let yourself be hidden."

"But you must know what I've done; you must guess?"

The revolver was still in his hand; he gave it a guilty glance, and she looked from it to him without recoiling.

"Of course I guessed on Saturday." There was a studious absence of horror in her tone. "Yet I couldn't believe it, unless it was an accident. And if it was an accident—"

"It was one!" he choked. "It was the most absolute accident that ever happened; he saw it; he can tell you; but he never told me till hours afterwards. I was nearly dead with asthma; he brought me here, he was frightfully good to me, I'm grateful enough for all that. But he should have told me before the accident became a crime! When he did tell me I lost my head, and begged him to keep me here, and afterwards when I came to my senses he wouldn't let me go. I needn't remind you of that morning! After that I promised to stay on, and I'd have kept all my promises if only my letter had gone to my poor people!"

He told her what a guarded letter it had been, only written to let them know he was alive, and that with the doctor's expressed approval. But now he had learnt his lesson, and he was going to play the game. It was more than ever the game with that poor fellow lying in prison for what he had never done. And so the whole story would be in to-morrow's papers, with the single exception of Dr. Baumgartner's name.

"Nothing shall make me give that," said Pocket valiantly; "on your account, if not on his!"

Phillida encouraged his new resolution without comment on this last assurance. She had stooped, and was picking up the unbroken negatives and putting them back in the rack; he followed her example, and collected the broken bits, while she put the rack back in its place, and certain splinters in theirs, until the locker shut without showing much damage. Pocket was left with the fragmentary negatives on his hands.

"I should throw those away," said Phillida. "And now, by the time you're ready to go, I'll have a cup of tea ready for you."

They faced each other in the rosy light, now doubly diluted by the open door, and Pocket did not move. He wanted to say something first, and he was too shy to say it. Shyness had come upon him all at once; hitherto they had both been like young castaways, finely regardless of appearances, he of his bare feet and throat, she of her dressing-gown and her bedroom slippers. She was unconscious or careless still, as with a brother; but he had become the very embodiment of mauvaise honte, an awful example of the awkward age; and it was all the fault of what he suddenly felt he simply must say.

"But—but I don't want to leave you!" he blurted out at last.

"But I want you to," she returned promptly and firmly, though not without a faint smile.

It was leaving her with a villain that he minded; but he could not get that out, except thus bluntly, nor could he denounce the doctor now as he had done when his blood was up. Besides, the man was a different man to his niece; all that redeemed him went out to her. Pocket did not think he was peculiar there; in fact, he thought romantically enough about the girl, with her dark hair all over her pink dressing-gown, and ivory insteps peeping out of those soft slippers especially when the vision was lost for ever, and he upstairs making himself as presentable as he could in a few minutes. But it seemed she was busy in the same way, and she took longer over it. He found the breakfast things on the table, the kettle on the gas-stove, but no Phillida to make the tea. He could not help wishing she would be quick; if he was going, the sooner he went the better, but he was terribly divided in his desires. He hated the thought of deserting a comrade, who was also a girl, and such a girl! He could only face it with the fixed intention of coming back to the rescue of his heroine, he the hero of their joint romance. But for his own immediate freedom he was already unheroically eager. And yet he could deliberately fit the broken negatives together, on the white tablecloth, partly to pass the time, partly out of a boyish bravado which involved little real risk; for the doctor had not yet been gone an hour; and a loaded revolver is a loaded revolver, be it brandished by man or boy.

The piecing of the plates was like a children's puzzle, only easier, because the pieces were not many. One of the reconstructed negatives was of painful interest; it reminded Pocket of the fatal one smashed to atoms by Baumgartner in the pink porcelain trough. There were trees again, only leafless, and larger, and there was a larger figure sprawling on a bench. Pocket felt he must have a print of this; he remembered having seen printing-frames and tubes of sensitised paper in the other room; and hardly had he filled his frame and placed it in position, than Phillida ran down stairs, and he told her what he had done.

"I wish you hadn't," she said nervously, as she made mechanical preparations with pot and kettle. "It would only make matters worse if my uncle came in now."

"But he wasn't back on Friday before ten or eleven."

"You never know!"

Pocket spoke out with a truculence which his brothers had inherited, but not he, valiantly as he might try to follow a family example.

"I don't care! I can't help it if he does come. I'll tell him exactly what I've done, and why, and exactly what I'm going to do next. I give him leave to stop me if he can."

"I'm afraid he won't wait for that. But I wish you had waited for his leave before printing his negative."

Pocket jumped up from table, and ran to the printing-frame in the sunny room at the back. He had been reminded of it only just in time. It was a rather dark print that he first examined, one half at a time, and then extracted from the frame. It was meshed with white veils, showing the joins of the broken plate. But it had been an excellent negative originally. And it was still good enough to hold Pocket rooted to the carpet in the sunny room, until Phillida came in after him, and stood looking over his shoulder.

"I know that place!" said she at once. "It's Holland Walk, in Kensington."

He turned to her quickly.

"The place where there was a suicide or something not long ago?"

"The very place!" exclaimed the girl, looking up from the darkening print.

"I remember my uncle would take me to see it next day. He's always so interested in mysteries. I'm sure that's the very spot he showed me as the one where it must have happened."

"Did he take the photograph then?"

"No; he hadn't his camera with him."

"Then this is the suicide, or whatever it was!" cried Pocket, in uncontrollable excitement. "It's not only the place; it's the thing itself. Look at that man on the bench!"

The girl took a long look nearer the window.

"How horrible!" she shuddered. "His head looks as though it were falling off! He might be dying."

"Dying or dead," said Pocket, "at the very second the plate was exposed!"

She looked at him in blank horror. His own horror was no less apparent, but it was more understanding. He had Baumgartner's own confession of his attempts to secure admission to hospital death-beds, even to executions; he expounded Baumgartner on the whole subject, briefly, clumsily, inaccurately enough, and yet with a certain graphic power which brought those incredible theories home to his companion as forcibly as Baumgartner himself had brought them home to Pocket. It was the first she had ever heard of them. But then he had never discussed his photography with her, never showed her plate or print. That it was not merely a hobby, that he was an inventor, a pioneer, she had always felt, without dreaming in what direction or to what extent. Even now she seemed unable to grasp the full significance of the print from the broken negative; and when she would have examined it afresh, there was nothing to see; the June sunshine had done its work, and blotted out the repulsive picture even as she held it in her hands.

"Then what do you think?" she asked at last; her voice was thin and strained with formless terrors.

"I think that Dr. Baumgartner has the strangest power of any human being I ever heard of; he can make you do anything he likes, whether you like it yourself or not. The newspapers have been raking up this case in connection with—mine—and I see that one theory was that the man in this broken negative committed suicide. Well, if he did, I firmly believe that Dr. Baumgartner was there and willed him to do it!"

"He must have been there if he took the photograph."

"Is there another man alive who tries these things? I've told you all he told me about it, but I haven't told you all he said about the value of human life."

"Nor need you! He makes no secret of his opinion about that!"

"Then put the two things together, and where do they lead you? To these murders committed with the mad idea of taking the spirit in its flight from the flesh; that's his own way of putting it, not mine."

"But I thought your case was an accident pure and simple?"

"On my part, certainly; but how do I know he couldn't get more power over me in my sleep than at any other time? He saw me walking in my sleep with this wretched revolver. He said himself I'd given him the chance of a lifetime. You may be sure he meant before that poor man's death, not after it."

"It isn't possible," declared Phillida, as though she had laid hold of one solid certainty in a sea of floating hypotheses. "And I know he hasn't a pistol of his own," she added, lest he should simplify his charge.

But there they were agreed.

"He hadn't one on him that morning; that I can swear," said Pocket, impartially disposing of the idea. "Mine was the only one in that cape of his, because I once jolly nearly had it out again when he came back into the room. There was nothing of the sort in his other coat, or anywhere else about him, or I couldn't have helped seeing it." Phillida accepted this statement only too thankfully. She beamed on the boy, as if in recognition of a piece of downright magnanimity towards an enemy whom she could now understand his regarding in that light. If only he would go before the enemy returned! If her uncle had such a power over him as he himself seemed to feel, then that was all the more reason for him to go quickly. But Pocket was not the man to get up and run like that. Perhaps he enjoyed displaying his bravery on the point, and keeping his companion on tenter-hooks on his account; at any rate he insisted on finishing his breakfast, and gave further free expression to the wildest surmises as he did so. And yet he was even then on the brink of a discovery which was some excuse for the wildest of them all, while it demanded a fresh solution of the whole affair.

He had been fingering the recovered weapon in his pocket, almost fondling it, though with mingled feelings, as the Prodigal Son of his small possessions; suddenly it leapt out like a live thing in his hand, and clattered on the table between the girl and boy. It was a wonder neither of them was shot dead in his excitement. His whole face was altered; but so was his whole life. She could not understand his incoherent outburst; she only knew that he was twisting the chambers round and round under her nose, and that there appeared to be live cartridges in all six.

"Don't you see?" the words came pouring. "Not one of them's been fired—it's as I loaded it myself the other night! It can't have been this revolver at all!"

"But you must have known whether you fired or not?"

"I tell you I was walking in my sleep till the row woke me. I'd only heard it once before, in a room. It sounded loud enough for the open air, though I do remember wondering I hadn't felt any kick. But I was so dazed, and there was this beastly thing in my hand; and he took it from me in such a rage that of course I believed I'd let it off. But now I can see I can't have done. It wasn't my revolver and it wasn't me!"

"Yet you say yourself my uncle didn't carry one?"

"I'll swear he didn't; but there's another man in all this! There was the man they arrested on Saturday—the man I was so keen to set free!"

The boy's laugh grated; he was beside himself with righteous joy. What was it to him that his innocence implied another's complicity? Only too characteristically, he saw simply the central fact from his own point of view; but was it such an undoubted fact as he hot-headedly supposed? There was the broken negative to confirm a certain suspicion, but that was not enough for Phillida.

She asked if he had no more cartridges, and he said he had a few loose in his waistcoat pocket; he had thrown away the box. "Then my uncle might have put in a fresh one while you were asleep."

"Why should he?"

"I don't know, but it sounds quite as possible as the other."

"I'll soon tell you if he did!" cried Pocket. "There were fourteen in the box to start with, because I counted them, and we only shot away one at the Knaggses' before we were cobbed. That left thirteen—six in the revolver and seven in my pocket. There are your six, and here's one, two, three, four—and three's seven!"

He swept them over the cloth like crumbs, for her to count them for herself, while he looked on with flaming cheeks and wagging tongue. He was beginning to see what it all meant now, but still only what it meant to him and his. He could look his people in the face again; that was the burden of his loud thanksgiving. He was as sure of his innocence as though the dead man had risen to prove it.

"Very well," said Phillida, briskly; "then it's all the more reason you should go this minute, and catch the very first train home."

And in her sudden anxiety to see him safely off, she was for helping him on with the overcoat he had brought down again with his bag; but he followed her out slowly, and he would not turn his back.

"I can't leave you now," he said; and she knew that he saw it from her side at last.

"Why not?"

"Because the whole thing's altered! I'm not going to leave you with a man like that!"

So Pocket, without a moment's thought either for her immediate feelings or the ultimate consequences to himself; and yet with an unconscious air of sacrifice more wounding than his actual words. She would have flung open the door, and ordered him out, but he got his back to it first. So her big eyes blazed at him instead.

"You're very kind!" she cried. "But suppose I don't believe a word you say against my uncle behind his back?"

"I shall wait and say it to his face. That's another reason for waiting."

"Do you think you're the person to judge him—a boy like you?"

"I don't say I am. I only say that print—"

"How do you know he took the negative?"

"I don't, but—"

"But you jump to conclusions like a baby!" cried the girl, too quick for him in following up a confusing advantage. "I never heard anybody like you for flying from one wild notion to another; first you say he must have made you fire, though you own you were walking in your sleep with a loaded revolver, and then you're sure you never fired at all, simply because you find the revolver fully loaded after days and days! Then you find a photograph that needn't necessarily be what we thought it, that my uncle needn't have taken even if it was; but you jump to another conclusion about him, and you dare to speak of him to me as though you knew every horrid thing you chose to think! As if you knew him and I didn't! As if he hasn't been kind and good to me for years and years—and kind to you—far too kind—"

The strained voice broke, tears were running down her face, and in it and them there was more sincerity. Grief, and not anger, was the well of those bitter tears. And it was in simple supplication, not imperiously any more, that she pointed to the door when speech failed her. The boy's answer was to go close up to her instead. "Will you come with me?" he asked hoarsely.

She shook her head; she was past surprise as well as indignation; she could only shake her head.

"My people would be as good to you as ever he was," urged Pocket extravagantly. "They'd understand, and you'd stay with us, Phillida! You might live with us altogether!"

She smiled very faintly at that.

"Oh, Phillida, can't you see that they'd do anything for you after all we've been through together? And I, oh! there's nothing I wouldn't do if only you'd come with me now this minute! I know there's a train about ten, and I know where we could borrow the money on the way. Come, Phillida, get on your things and come away from all this horror!"

He had gone on, even into details, encouraged by the tolerance or apathy which had allowed him to go on at all. He took it for indecision; but, whatever it was, she shook it off and declared once for all that she would never leave Dr. Baumgartner, even if everything was true about him, and he as mad as that would make him out.

"But he is!" cried Pocket, with most eager conviction. "That's the only possible explanation, and you'd believe it fast enough if you'd heard all he said to me that first night, and been with me in the dark-room when he developed his negative of the man he said I shot! You'd see how it all fits in, and how this other negative this morning simply shows he was at the bottom of that other affair as well! Of course he's mad; but that's the very reason why I can't go and leave you with him."

"He would be as he's always been to me."

"I believe he would," said honest Pocket.

"Then why don't you go away and leave us?"

"Because I can't."

"Because you won't!"

"Very well, because I won't and never will! But, mind you, it'll be your fault if anything happens to either of us after this!"

He only meant it as a last argument, though he did resent her fatal obstinacy, and all the obligations which it imposed upon himself. He stood chained in fetters of her forging, as it were to the stake, but he was prepared to stand there like a man, and he did not deserve the things she said to him in a fresh paroxysm of unreasonable wrath. He might be a baby, but he was not a complete coward, or simply trying to make her miserable, as she declared; neither, on this occasion, was he thinking only of himself. But Phillida seemed suddenly to realise that, for she broke off with a despairing little cry, and ran sobbing up the stairs.

A THIRD CASE

In days to come, when the boy had schooled himself not to speak of these days, nor to let his mind dwell on their mystery and terror, it was as a day of dark hours and vivid moments that he remembered the one which Phillida and he began alone together in her uncle's house. Those endless hours were either mercifully forgotten or else contracted to an endurable minimum; but the unforgettable moments would light themselves up in his memory without a detail missing.

There was their first encounter at the dark-room door, and Phillida standing all but barefoot in the ruby light, with her glorious hair about her shoulders, a picture that could never fade. Then there was the moment of the incriminating print, which the sun wiped out even as Phillida stood with it in her hands. That moment merged itself in the greater one of his discovery that the revolver was fully loaded, his inspiration that neither it nor he had done the fatal mischief in the Park. Then she was begging him to go (she who would keep him the time before!) and he entreating her to come with him, and neither giving way an inch, so that they quarrelled just when they should have stuck together, and she ran away in tears, and he stayed below in a glow of anger which dissolved his fears like snow in May.

That was the beginning of a black hour and more. Phillida was never to be forgiven, then; he was staying there at his peril, staying absolutely on her account, and so far from giving him the slightest credit for it, or a single word of encouragement, she said all sorts of things and was off before he could answer one of them. It was not for Pocket to see the many ironies of that moment, and not for him to recognise the tonic property of his heroic grievance. He could only see himself at the foot of those stairs, first gnashing his teeth and not sorry he had made her cry, then sitting down with his eye on the front door, revolver in hand, to await the click of the doctor's key. Another click was to answer it; and at the point of the cocked revolver Baumgartner was to have made a clean breast of his crimes, not only to the giant-killer at the foot of the stairs but to the girl he meant to call to witness with her own ears.

Pocket saw himself a desperate character just then, and one not incapable of desperate action had the climax only come at once. But he had more than an hour of it alone at his post; he had a whole hot forenoon of unmitigated suspense, of sickening alarms from tradesmen's carts, boys whistling past the house as though they were not in a wicked world at all, and then a piano-organ that redoubled his watchfulness, and spoilt some tunes for him for ever. Once he did hear shambling feet on the very steps outside. Once was quite enough, though it was but an advertisement for cast-off clothing (and false teeth) that came fluttering through the letter-box. Pocket was left in such a state that he would not have backed himself to hit the door from the stairs; and he put the chain on it, thinking to interview the doctor over that, in the manner of old Miss Harbottle.

So it happened that the first significant sound was entirely lost upon him, because he was listening for one so much nearer at hand, until Phillida ran downstairs and almost over him where he sat.

He got up to make way stiffly, but a glance assured him that the quarrel was over on her side. The great eyes were fixed appealingly upon him, but with a distressing look which he had done nothing to provoke. Not before then was he aware of another duet between newsboys coming nearer and nearer, and shouting each other down as they came.

"You hear that?" she whispered, as if not to drown a note.

"I do now."

"Do you hear what it is?"

Pocket listened, and caught a word he was not likely to miss.

"Something fresh about the murder," said he grimly.

"No; it's another one," she shuddered. "Can't you hear? 'Another awful murder!' Now they're saying something else."

"It is something about the Park." Pocket stuck to his idea.

"And something else about some 'well-known'—I can't hear what!"

"No more can I."

"I'll open the door."

She opened it on the chain as he had left it. That did not help them. The shouting had passed the end of their quiet road. It was dying away again in the distance.

"I must go out and get one," said Phillida. "Some well-known man!"

"You're not thinking of the doctor, surely?"

"I don't know! I can't think where he is."

"But you're worse than I am, if you jump to that!" said Pocket, smiling to reassure her. He did not smile when she had run out as she was; he had shut the door after her, and he was waiting to open it in a fever of impatience.

Dr. Baumgartner had left the house before six o'clock in the morning; now it was after twelve. If some tragedy had overtaken him in his turn, then there was an end to every terror, and for him a better end than he might meet with if he lived. The boy remembered Him who desireth not the death of a sinner, and was ashamed of his own thought; but that did not alter it. Unless his fears and his surmises were all equally unfounded, better for everybody, and best of all for Phillida, if this criminal maniac came to his end without public exposure of his crimes. Pocket may have misconceived his own attitude of mind, as his elders and betters do daily; he may have been thinking of his own skin more than he knew, or wanted to know. In that case he had his reward, for the murdered man was not Dr. Baumgartner. Phillida's first words on returning were to that effect; and yet she trembled as though they were not the truth.

"Who was it, then?" the schoolboy asked suspiciously.

"Sir Joseph Schelmerdine."

"So he was the well-known man!"

He was well known even to the boy by name, but that was all. He had seen it in newspapers, and he thought he had heard it execrated by Baumgartner himself in one of his little digs at England. Pocket was not sure about this, but he mentioned his impression, and Phillida nodded with swimming eyes.

"Did the doctor know him?"

"Not personally; but he thought him a European danger."

"Why?"

"I can't tell you. It was something to do with politics and gold-mines, and some financial paper. I never understood."

"May I see the paper you've brought in?"

The girl held it tight in her hand, and tighter still as he held out his.

"I'd rather you didn't," she said.

"Then there's something you haven't told me."

"There is!"

"I shall know it sooner or later."

"I know you will, and I know what you'll think! You may think what you like, and still be wrong!"

There was a pause between the sentences, and in the pause the boy found the paper at his feet. There was no need to open it at the place; it was so folded already, the news standing out in its leaded type, and more of it in the late corner. Sir Joseph Schelmerdine, Bart., M.P., the well- known proprietor of the Money-maker, had been shot dead in front of his house in Park Lane. The murder had been committed in the early hours of the morning, before anybody was about except Sir Joseph and his groom, and the person whom the groom described as the only possible murderer. The man had just seen his master mounted for the early morning ride, and had left him in conversation with a photographer representing himself as concerned with the press, and desirous of obtaining an equestrian photograph for his paper. The groom thought it was to be taken in the Park, and was himself on his way back to the mews when the riderless horse overtook him. Mounting the animal, he had galloped round to find Sir Joseph dead in the road, and no trace of the "photographer" but a false beard and spectacles which he had evidently discarded in his flight, and which unfortunately precluded a close description of his appearance. But a hue and cry had been started, and it was believed that the criminal was still in hiding in the immediate neighbourhood, which was being subjected to a thorough search under the direction of responsible officers from Scotland Yard.

Such was the news which the young girl had shrunk from showing to her companion. She had left him, indeed, to read it by himself. And the next thing he remembered was finding her quite insensible in the big chair in the back room.

The afternoon was a blank broken by no more moments such as these. It was a period of dull misery and gnawing dread; but the pair saw each other through it, they were not divided any more. Now they listened for his step no longer, but for more newsboys crying his capture to the world. And in the hours that they spent thus listening, and listening, the girl had much to say, that it did her good to say, about this Dr. Baumgartner as she had known and almost loved him in the past.

Lovable, however, he had never been, though more than good and kind to her for all that. He had never taken her into his life, or entered into hers, in the many years they had been more or less together. All she really knew of him was from her mother, whose elder sister he had married soon after the Franco-Prussian War, and lost soon after marriage. He must have been settled in England many years before Phillida's mother, herself an Englishman's widow, came to keep house for him. The girl could not remember her father, but her mother had lived to see her in her teens, and in her lifetime Dr. Baumgartner had seemed much as other men. It was only of late years that he had withdrawn from a world in which he was justly honoured, and buried himself ever deeper in his books and his photographic experiments. His niece had never known anything of these; he had told her nothing, and she had always gone in awe of him. But he had sent her to school, he was going to send her to college, he had only just given her six months in Switzerland. It was during those months that all his eccentricities had become pronounced; that he had given up servants, and taken to doing half the work of the house himself, with the casual aid of charwomen, and saving the other half by having the meals in from a restaurant. Phillida had no influence with him in these or any other matters. She only blamed herself for not having realised the change in him and done more to save him from himself. He had done so much for her, whatever madness might have overtaken him in the end; her own kinsfolk so much less, for all their opulent integrity. Nothing could make her forget what he had done. She never could or would desert him; it was no use asking her again; but she took her callow champion's hand, and wrung it with her final answer, which was unaccompanied by further prayers for his departure.

And Pocket could understand her now, though it was no consecutive tale that he heard, but a very chaos of excuses and extenuations, regrets, suppositions, and not always revelant recollections, of which he had to make what he could in his own mind. What he made was a narrative so natural that he could not believe it was the life-story of a murderer. His own convictions became preposterous in his own eyes. What had he been thinking about all day? Was that the way a murderer would behave? Was this the way a murderer would live, in these surroundings, with those books about him, with that little billiard-table in the next room? Had those waxen murderers in the garish vault lived ordinary lives as well? Pocket had only thought of them as committing their dreadful deeds, yet now he could only think of Baumgartner as living this ordinary life.

The mood passed, but it would recur as sure as Phillida thought of something else to be said for Dr. Baumgartner; it was the creature of her feeling for him, and of the schoolboy's feeling for her. If he could have convicted himself of the fatal affair in the Park, and so cleared Baumgartner of all blood-guiltiness whatsoever, in that or any other case, he would have done it for Phillida's sake that afternoon. But with every hour of the doctor's absence suspicions multiplied. Phillida herself was a prey to them. She was almost as ready to recall symptoms of incipient insanity as instances of personal kindness; if one lost one's reason, she broke a long silence to contend, there could be no question of regret and wrong. She was not so sure about crime and punishment. Pocket, of course, said there could be no question of that either; but in his heart he wondered how much method they must prove to hang a madman.

The evening meal had been taken in, but that was all. The girl and boy had no thought of sitting down to it; she had made tea not long before; and strong excitement is its own meat and drink. They were sitting silently together in the room at the back. The scented summer dusk was deepening every minute. Suddenly there was a sound of small branches breaking in the garden. Pocket peeped out, standing back from the window at her entreaty.

The laburnum by the wall was shaking violently, pouring its golden rain into both gardens, and the bush beneath it looked alive; a tall figure rose out of it, and came creeping towards the little conservatory, bent double, and brushing the soil from his clothes as he advanced with long and stealthy strides. It was Dr. Baumgartner, in a cap pulled down over his eyes, and the old alpaca jacket. He had a newspaper parcel under his arm.

The boy and girl were in the dark angle between the window and the door; but it was only comparative darkness, and Baumgartner might have seen them; they were clasping hands as they shrank away from him with one accord. But he did not seem to see them at all. He stretched himself, as though he found it a relief to stand upright, and more mould trickled from his garments in the act; he took off the alpaca jacket, and shook it as one shakes a handkerchief. There could have been nothing in the pockets, certainly no weapon, and if he had a hip-pocket there was none in that, for his gaunt figure stood out plainly enough in the middle of the room. There was still the newspaper parcel; he had put it down on one of the walnut-tables. He now removed the paper; it fell at Pocket's feet, a newspaper and nothing more; and nothing had come out of it but the stereoscopic camera, that either watcher could detect.

And he passed through the room without taking the least notice of either of them, whether he saw them or not; and they heard him go upstairs, and shut the door, and then his footsteps overhead.

"I'll go up and tackle him at once," said Pocket, through his set teeth; but Phillida would not hear of it.

"No! I must go first and see if there's nothing I can get him; he mayn't have had anything all day. There's no need for you to come at all—I believe he's forgotten all about us both!"

"Not he!" whispered Pocket, as the door opened overhead. "Here he comes!"

He could not help gripping his revolver as the stairs creaked again under Dr. Baumgartner; he had gripped it more than once already with the hand that was not holding Phillida's. The doctor was coming down in a hurry, as though he had indeed forgotten something. But he passed the open drawing-room door; they saw him pass, jingling a bunch of keys, and never so much as glancing in on the way. It was the dark-room door he opened. Now he would find out everything! They heard a match struck, and saw the faint light turn into a strong deep crimson glow. The door shut. The children stood listening in the dark.

Running water, and the chink of glass; the tapping of a stoppered bottle; the opening of the dark slide; these stages the younger photographer followed as though he were again looking on. Then there was a long period without a sound.

"He's developing now!" whispered Pocket, close to the folding-doors. He caught the sound of laboured breathing on the other side. "There it is—there it is—there it is!" cried the doctor's voice in mingled ecstasy and mad excitement. A deep sigh announced the blackening of the plate at the conclusion of the first process. A tap ran for a moment; interminable minutes ensued. "It's gone! It's gone again!" cried the wild voice, with a sob; "it's gone, gone, gone like all the rest!"

One listener waited for the passionate smashing of the negative as before; but that did not happen again; and then he wondered if it was being put straight into the rack with the others, if the damage to the locker had been discovered at last. He never knew. The door opened. The red glow showed for a moment in the passage, then went out. The door shut behind Baumgartner, and again he passed the drawing-room, a bent figure, without looking in. And the flagging step on the stairs bore no resemblance to the one which had come hurrying down not many minutes before.

"I must go to him!" said Phillida in broken undertones, and her grief communicated itself to the other young sympathetic soul, for all the base fears he had to fight alone. Personal safety, little as she might think of it, was the essence of her position as opposed to his; and he was of the type that thinks of everything. She left him listening breathless in the dark. And in the dark she found him when at length she returned to report the doctor busy writing at his desk; but a pin's head of blue gas glimmered where there had been none before, and a paper which had been trodden underfoot now rustled in Pocket's hand.

"Does he know I'm here?" he asked.

"I don't think so. We never mentioned you. I believe he's forgotten your existence altogether; he began by looking at me as though he'd forgotten mine. He says he wants nothing, except time to write. He seems so strange—so old!"

Again the break in her voice, and again the boyish sympathy in his. "I wonder if something would be any comfort to you?"

"I don't think so. What is it?"

"Something I saw in the paper he brought in with him. I lit the gas while you were upstairs."

Phillida turned it out again without comment.

"Nothing that you saw can make any difference to me," she sighed.

"Do you remember my saying there must be another man in these—mysteries?"

"I think I do. What difference does it make? Besides, the man you meant is in prison."

"He isn't!"

"You said he was?"

"He was let out early this morning! Let me light the gas while you read it for yourself."

But Phillida had no desire to read it for herself. "I doubt if there's anything in that," she said; "but what if there were? Does it make it any better if a man has an accomplice in his crimes? If he's guilty at all, it makes it all the worse."

THE FOURTH CASE

The boy and girl sat long and late in the open window at the back of the house. The room would have been in darkness but for a flood of moonlight pouring over them. The only light in the house was in the room above, and they only saw its glimmer on the garden when a casual cloud hid the moon; but once Pocket had crept out into the garden to steal a look at the lighted window itself; and what he saw was the shadow of a huge bent head smoking a huge bent pipe, and dense clouds of shadow floating up the wall and over the ceiling.

It seemed hours since they had heard footstep or other sound upstairs or anywhere. There had been a brisk interval—and then an end—of more or less distant hansom-bells and motor-horns. There was no longer even a certain minute intermittent trembling of trifles on the walnut-tables, to which Pocket had become subconsciously accustomed in that house, so that he noticed its absence more than the thing itself. It was as though the whole town was at rest, and the tunnels under the town, and every single soul above or below ground, but those two white faces in the moonlight, and perhaps one other overhead.

Pocket wondered; it was so long since a single sound had come down to their ears. He wanted to steal out and look up again. Phillida was against it; perhaps she was wondering too. Pocket, as usual, saw what he did see so very vividly, in his mind's eye, that he shivered and was asked if he felt cold. The whispered debate that followed was the longest conversation they had that night. The window was not shut as a result of it, but Pocket fetched his overcoat on tiptoe, and it just went over both their shoulders, when the chairs were drawn as near together as they would go.

The ragged little garden was brimming over with moonlight from wall to wall. The unkempt grass looked pale and ghostly, like the skin of some monstrous wolf. The moon rolled high in the sky and clouds flew above and below the moon, varying in pace as well. Yet it was a still night, and Pocket did not think that he had broken the stillness, until the door burst open behind them, and Baumgartner stood there, holding his lamp aloft. The wick was turned too high, the flame ran up the chimney in the draught, and for an instant a demoniac face flared up behind it. Then the chimney cracked, and fell in a tinkling shower, and the doctor was seen whirling a naked tongue of fire about his head. The boy drew back as the lamp flew through the open window, within an inch of his nose, and crashed upon the path outside.

The trio stood without a word in the moonbeams; but the doctor was breathing hard through his teeth, like a man wrestling with himself; and at last he laughed sardonically as though he had won.

"A lamp like that's a dangerous thing," said he, with a kind of forced solemnity and a shake of the head; "you never know what may happen when a lamp does that! I'm glad the window was open; it didn't go very near my young fellow, I hope?"

And he took Pocket playfully by the ear, but pinched it so hard that the boy could have screamed with pain.

"It would have served you right," continued the doctor, before Pocket could find his tongue, "for sitting up so late, and keeping a young lady from her bed to bear you company. Come, Phillida! I shall have another word with you, young fellow."

The two words to the girl were in a different key from all the rest. They were tolerant, conciliatory, tenderly persuasive. The rest was suavely sinister; it made her hesitate; but Pocket had the presence of mind to bid her a cheery good-night, and she went, closely followed by Baumgartner.

Posted once more at the open door, the boy heard Baumgartner on the next flight, soothing and affectionate still, allaying her fears; and his own surged into his throat. He looked wildly about him, and an idea came. He opened the front door wide, and then stole back through the conservatory into the moonlight. He heard Baumgartner coming down before he gained the garden. He tore to the end of it, and cowered in the shadow of the far wall.

The doctor came running into the moonlit room, but not for a minute; it looked as though he had run out first into the road. In the room he lit the gas, and Pocket saw him have a look in all the corners, but hardly the look of a seeker who expects to find. Some long moments he stood out horribly at the open window, gazing straight at the spot where the fugitive crouched a few inches out of the moonlight and hugged the revolver in his pocket. He seemed to see nothing to bring him out that way, for he closed that window and put out the gas. The trembling watcher heard the front door shut soon after, and saw another light in Baumgartner's room the minute after that, and the blind drawn down. But on the blind there lagged a cloud-capped shadow till the doctor's pipe was well in blast.

There were no more shadows after that. The moon moved round to the right, and set behind the next house. The sky grew pale, and the lighted blind paler still, until Baumgartner drew it up before putting out his light. Pocket was now too stiff to stir; but it was not necessary; the doctor had scarcely looked out. There was a twitter of sparrows all down the road, garden answering to garden. The sun came up behind Pocket's wall, behind the taller houses further back. And Baumgartner reappeared at his window for one instant in his cap.

The front door shut again.

Down the garden ran Pocket without the least precaution now. There was a gravel passage between the tradesmen's entrance, on the detached side of the house, and the garden wall. This passage was closed by a gate, and the gate was locked, but Pocket threw himself over it almost in his stride and darted over into the open road.

Just then it was a perfectly empty road, but for a gaunt black figure stalking away in the distance. An overwhelming curiosity urged the boy to follow, but an equal dread of detection kept him cowering in gateways, until Baumgartner took the turning past the shops without a backward glance. Pocket promptly raced to that corner, and got another glimpse of his leader before he vanished round the next. So the spasmodic chase continued over a zigzag course; but at every turn the distance between them was a little less. Neither looked round, and once the boy's feet were actually on the man's shadow; for half the streets were raked with level sunlight, but the other half were ladders of dusk with rungs of light at the gaps between the houses. All were dustier, dirtier, and emptier than is ever the case by night or day, because this was neither one nor the other, though the sun was up to make the most of dust, dirt, and emptiness. It was before even the cleansing hour of the scavenger and the water-cart. A dead cat was sprawling horribly in one deserted reach of wood-paving. And a motor-car at full speed in a thoroughfare calling itself King's Road, which Pocket was about to cross, had at all events the excuse of a visible mile of asphalt to itself.

Pocket drew back to let it pass, without looking twice at the car itself, which indeed was disguised out of knowledge in the promiscuous mire of many countries; but the red eyes behind the driver's goggles were not so slow. Down went his feet on clutch and brake without a second's interval; round spun the car in a skid that tore studs from the tyres, and fetched her up against the kerb with a shivered wheel. Pocket started forward with a cry; but at that moment a ponderous step fell close behind him; his arm was seized, and he was dragged in custody across the road.

"Your boy, I think!" cried one whom he had never seen before, and did not now, being locked already in the motorist's arms.

"When did you find him?" the father asked when he was man enough, still patting Pocket's shoulders as if he were a dog.

"Only last night when I wired."

"And where?"

"In the house where you and I couldn't make ourselves heard."

The schoolboy flared up through all his emotion.

"Why, I never saw you before this minute!"

"Well, I've had my eye on you, more or less, for a day or two."

"Then why didn't you wire before?" demanded Mr. Upton, quite ready to mask his own emotion with a little heat. "I didn't get it till after nine o'clock—too late for the evening train—but I wasn't going to waste three hours with a forty-horser eating its head off! So here I am, on my way to the address you gave."

"It was plumb opposite Baumgartner's. I mounted guard there the very night you left. He came out twenty minutes ago, and your boy after him!"

"But what does it all mean, Thrush? What on earth were you doing there, my dear boy?"

The notes of anger and affection were struck in ludicrously quick succession; but the first was repeated on the boy's hang-dog admission that he had been hiding.

"Hiding, Tony?"

Thrush himself seemed surprised at the expression. "But at all events we found you better employed," he said to Pocket, "and the sooner we all take up the chase again the more chance we shall have of laying this rascal by the heels."

"Take it up, then!" snapped Mr. Upton. "Jump into the motor, and bring the brute to me when you've got him! I want to speak to my boy."

He did not realise the damage done to his car, or listen to a word that passed between Thrush and his chauffeur; he had eyes only for those of his child who had been lost but was found, and not a thought in his head outside the story he extracted piecemeal on the spot. Poor Pocket told it very volubly and ill; he would not confine himself to simple facts. He stated his suspicion of Baumgartner's complicity in the Hyde Park affair as though he knew it for a fact; cited the murders in Holland Walk and Park Lane as obvious pieces of the same handiwork, and yet declared his conviction that the actual hand was not Dr. Baumgartner's at all.

"But why should you think he had an accomplice, Tony?"

"He was unarmed the other morning. I'm quite positive of that. And his niece, who lives with him, has never seen a firearm of any kind in the house."

"Well, he's villain enough to hang, if ever there was one! It's time we laid hold of him. Where's Mr. Thrush? I thought you'd taken him on in the car?"

This to the chauffeur, now the centre of the carrion crowd that gathers about the body of any disabled motor. The chauffeur, a countryman like his master, was enjoying himself vastly with a surreptitious cigarette and sardonic mutterings on the cause of his scattered spokes; the facts being that he had nearly fallen asleep at his wheel, which Mr. Upton had incontinently taken into his own less experienced hands.

"The car won't take anybody anywhere to-day," explained the chauffeur, with his cigarette behind his back. "I shall have to get a lorry to take the car." He held his head on one side suddenly. "There's a bit o' tyre trouble for somebody!" he cried, grimly.

Indeed, a sharp crack had come from the direction of the river, not unlike the bursting of a heavy tyre; but Pocket Upton did not think it was that. He caught his father's arm, and whispered in his father's ear, and they plunged together into a side street broader than the asphalt thoroughfare, but with scarcely a break in either phalanx of drab mediocre dwellings, and not a creature stirring except themselves and a few who followed. The hog's back of a still more deserted bridge arched itself at the foot of the street, its suspension cables showing against the sky in foreshortened curves. As they ran a peculiarly shrill whistle cut the morning air like a streak of sound.

"P'lice!" screamed one of those bringing up the rear, and they easily spurted past father and son, each already contending with his own infirmity. Mr. Upton was dangerously scarlet in the neck, and Pocket panting as he had not done for days. In sad labour they drew near the suspension bridge, to a crescendo accompaniment on the police whistle. It was evidently being blown on the Embankment to the right of the bridge, and already with considerable effect. As the pair were about to pass an intermediate turning on the right, a constable flew across it on a parallel course, and they altered theirs with one accord. Pocket panted after the constable, and his father thundered after Pocket, into a narrow street debouching upon a fenced strip of greenery, not too dense to hide broad pavement and low parapet on its further side, with a strip of brown river beyond that, and a skyline of warehouses on the Surrey shore.

The narrow garden had not been opened for the day. There was a gate opposite the end of the road, another gate leading out on the Embankment opposite that. Between the two gates a grimy statue rose upon a granite pedestal, a meditative figure clad to the heels in some nondescript garment, and gazing across the river as he sat with a number of discarded volumes under his chair. It was a peculiarly lifelike monument, which Pocket would have been just the boy to appreciate at any other time; even now it struck him for an instant, before his attention was attracted to the group of commonplace living people on the Embankment beyond the narrow garden. They were standing together on the far side of one of the fixed seats. There was the policeman who had blown the whistle, and a small but motley crew who had answered to the call. Conspicuous units were a gentleman in dressing-gown and pyjamas, a couple of chimneysweeps, and a labouring cyclist on his way to work. They had formed a circle about some hidden object on the ground; and long before the new-comers could run round and join them, the schoolboy had steeled himself to look upon another murdered man. He was in no hurry to look; apart from a natural dread of death, which he had seen for the first time, and then unwittingly, only the other morning, it was the murderer and not his victim of whom the boy was thinking as he arrived last upon the scene. It was Dr. Baumgartner whom he half expected to see swimming the river or hiding among the bushes in the enclosed garden; for he was not one of the group on the Embankment; and how else could he have made his escape? The point was being discussed as Pocket came into earshot; all he could see of the fallen man was the soles of his boots upright among living legs.

"Is he dead?" he asked of one of the chimneysweeps, who was detaching himself from the group with the air of a man who had seen the best of the fun.

"Dead as an 'erring," replied the sweep cheerfully. "Sooicide in the usual stite o' mind."

"Rats!" said the other sweep over a sooty shoulder; "unless 'e shot 'isself first an' swallered the shooter afterwards! Some'un's done 'im in."

Pocket set his teeth, and shouldered his way into the group. His father was already in the thick of it, talking to the stout man in spectacles, who had risen miraculously from the ground and was busy brushing his trouser-knees. Pocket forced himself on with much the same nutter he had taken into the Chamber of Horrors, but with an equal determination to look just once upon Dr. Baumgartner's latest victim. A loud cry escaped him when he did look; for the murdered man, and not the murderer, was Dr. Baumgartner himself.

WHAT THE THAMES GAVE UP

Phillida was prepared for anything when she beheld a motor-car at the gate, and the escaped schoolboy getting out with a grown man of shaggy and embarrassed aspect; but she was not prepared for the news they brought her. She was intensely shocked and shaken by it. Her grief and horror were not the less overwhelming for the shame and fear which they replaced in her mind. Yet she remained instinctively on her guard, and a passionate curiosity was the only emotion she permitted herself to express in words.

"But have they no idea who did it? Are they quite sure he didn't do it himself?"

Mr. Upton broke through his heavy embarrassment with no little relief, to dispose of the question of suicide once and for all.

"It's the one thing they are sure about," said he. "In the first place no weapon was to be found, and we saw no sign of a camera either, though this boy tells me your uncle had his with him when he went out. That's more or less conclusive in itself. But there was a doctor on the spot before we left, and I heard him say the shot couldn't have been fired at very close quarters, and that death must have been instantaneous. So it's no more a suicide than the case in Park Lane yesterday or the one in Hyde Park last week; there's evidently some maniac prowling about at dawn, and shooting down the first person he sees and then vanishing into thin air as maniacs seem to have a knack of doing more effectually than sane men. But the less we jump to conclusions about him—or anybody else—the better."

The girl was grateful for the covert sympathy of the last remark, and yet it startled her as an index of what must have passed already between father and son. It was a new humiliation that this big bluff man should know as much as the boy whom she had learnt to look upon as a comrade in calamity. Yet she could not expect it to be otherwise.

"What must you think!" she cried, and her great eyes filled and fell again. "Oh! what must you think?"

"It's no good thinking," he rejoined, with almost a jovial kindness. "We're all three on the edge of a mystery; we must see each other through before we think. Not that I've had time to hear everything yet, but I own I can't make head or tail of what I have heard. I'm not sure that I want to. I like a man's secrets to die with him; it's enough for me to have my boy back again, and to know that you stood by him as you did. It's our turn to stand by you, my dear! He says it wasn't your fault he didn't come away long ago; and it shan't be mine if you stay another hour alone in this haunted house. You've got to come straight back with us to our hotel."

They happened to be all three standing in the big back room, a haunted chamber if there was one in the house. With his battle-pictures on the walls, his tin of tobacco on the chimney-piece, and the scent of latakia rising from the carpet, the whole room remained redolent of the murdered man; and the window still open, the two chairs near it as they had been overnight, and the lamp lying in fragments on the path outside, brought the last scene back to the boy's mind in full and vivid detail. Yet the present one was in itself more desolate and depressing than any in which Dr. Baumgartner had figured. It might be that the constant menace of that portentous presence had thrown his simple middle-class surroundings, at the time, into a kind of reassuring relief. But it was the case that the morning had already clouded over; the sunshine of the other mornings was sadly missing; and Phillida looked only too eager to fly from the scene, until she declared she never could.

"But that's absurd!" cried Mr. Upton bluntly. "I'm not going to leave a young girl like you alone in the day of battle, murder and sudden death! You needn't necessarily come with us, as long as you don't stay here. Have you no other relatives in London?"

"None anywhere that I know much about."

"That doesn't matter. It's time they knew more about you. I'll hunt them up in the motor, if they're anywhere within a hundred miles, but you simply must let me take their place meanwhile."

He was a masterful man enough; it did not require the schoolboy's added supplications to bring about an eventual compromise. The idea had indeed been Pocket's originally, but his father had taken it up more warmly than he could have hoped. It was decided that they should return to their hotel without Phillida, but to send the car back for her later in the morning, as it would take her some time to pack her things and leave the deserted house in some semblance of order.

But her packing was a very small matter, and she left it to the end; most of the time at her disposal was spent in a hurried investigation of the dead man's effects, more especially of his store of negatives in the dark- room. The only incriminating plates, however, were the one she had already seen on its discovery by Pocket the day before and another of a man lying in a heap in the middle of a road. This one had been put to dry openly in the rack, the wood of which was still moist from the process. Phillida only held it up to the light an instant, and then not only smashed both these negatives, but poured boiling water on the films and floated them down the sink. The bits of glass she put in the dust-bin with those of the broken lamp, and had hardly done so when the first policeman arrived to report the fatality. He was succeeded by a very superior officer, who gained admittance and asked a number of questions concerning the deceased, but in a perfunctory manner that suggested few if any expectations from the replies. Neither functionary made any secret of his assumption that the latest murder was but another of the perfectly random series which had already thrilled the town, but on which no light was likely to be shed by the antecedents of the murdered men. A third official came to announce that the inquest was to be opened without delay, at two o'clock that afternoon, and to request Phillida to accompany him to the mortuary for the formal identification of the deceased.

That was a dread ordeal, and yet she expected a worse. She had steeled herself to look upon a debased image of the familiar face, and she found it startlingly ennobled and refined. Death had taken away nothing here, save the furrows of age and the fires of madness, and it had given back the look of fine courage and of sane integrity which the girl was just old enough to associate with the dead man's prime. She was thankful to have seen him like this for the last time. She wished that all the world could see him as he was, so noble and so calm, for then nobody would ever suspect that which she herself would find it easier to disbelieve from this hour.

"You do identify him, I suppose, miss?" the officer whispered, impressed by her strange stare.

"Oh, yes!" said Phillida. "But he looks as I have not seen him look for years. There are worse things than death!"

She said the same thing to Mr. Upton at luncheon in his private sitting- room at the hotel, whereupon he again assured her that he had no desire to know a dead man's secrets. He had found his boy; that was quite enough for him, and he was able to deliver himself the more freely on the subject since Pocket was not at table, but in bed making up for lost sleep. Not only had he succeeded in finding his son, but he had found him without the aid of police or press, and so not more than a dozen people in the world knew that he had ever disappeared. Mr. Upton explained why he had deemed it essential to keep the matter from his wife's ears, and added almost equally good reasons for continuing to hush it up on the boy's account if only it were possible to do so; but would it be possible to Phillida to exclude from her evidence at the inquest all mention of so recent a visitor at her uncle's house? Phillida promised to do her best, and it proved not only possible but easy. She was questioned as to the habits of the deceased so far as they explained his presence on the Embankment at such a very early hour, but that was all. Asked if she knew of a single person who could conceivably have borne such a grudge against Dr. Baumgartner as to wish to take his life, the witness answered in the negative, and the coroner bowed as much as to say that of course they all knew the character of the murder, but he had put the question for form's sake. The only one which caused her a moment's hesitation arose from a previous answer, which connected the doctor's early ramblings with his hobby of instantaneous photography. Had he his camera with him that morning? Phillida thought so. Why? Well, he always did take it out, and it certainly was not in the house. Mr. Upton wiped his forehead, for he knew that his boy's name had been on the tip of the witness's tongue. And there was a sensation in court as well; for here at last was a bone for the detectives, who obtained a minute description of the missing camera, but grumbled openly that they had not heard of it before.

"They never told me they hadn't got it," explained Phillida to the coroner, who made her his courteous bow, and permitted her to leave the court on the conclusion of her evidence.

On the stairs Mr. Upton paid her compliments that made her wince as much as the crude grip of his hand; but he was tact itself compared with his friend Mr. Thrush, who sought an interview in order to ply the poor girl there and then with far more searching questions than she had been required to answer upon oath. She could only look at Mr. Upton in a way that secured his peppery intervention in a moment. The two men had scarcely seen each other since the morning, and the ironmaster thought they had enough to say to each other without bothering Miss Platts just then; they accordingly adjourned to Glasshouse Street, and Phillida was to have gone on to the hotel; but she made them drop her at a shop near Sloane Square on the pretext of seeing about her mourning.

Phillida had promised to drive straight back to Trafalgar Square and order tea for herself if Tony had not appeared; but she did not drive straight back. She had a curious desire to see the place where the murder had been committed. It had come upon her at the inquest, while listening to the constable who had found the body, her predecessor in the witness-box. She had failed to follow his evidence. He had described that portion of his beat which had brought him almost on the scene of the murder, almost at the moment of its commission. It included only the short section of Cheyne Walk between Oakley Street and Cheyne Row. The houses at this point are divided from the Embankment by the narrow garden which contains the Carlyle statue. He had turned up Cheyne Row, at the back of the statue, but before turning he had noticed a man on the seat facing the river on the far side of the garden. The man was sitting down, but he was said to have turned round and watched the policeman as he passed along Cheyne Walk. There might have been a second man lying on that seat, or crouching on the flags between the seat and the parapet, but he would have been invisible from the beat. Not another creature was in sight anywhere. Yet the policeman swore that he had not proceeded a dozen yards up Cheyne Row before the shot was fired. He had turned round actually in time to see the puff of smoke dispersing over the parapet. It was all he saw. He had found the deceased lying in a heap, nearer the seat than the parapet, but between the two. Not another soul did he see, or had he seen. And he had not neglected to look over the parapet into the river, and along the foreshore in both directions, without discovering sign or trace of human being.

Such was the story which Phillida found so hard to credit that she proceeded to the spot in order to go over the ground for her own satisfaction. This did not make it easier to understand. It had come on to rain heavily while she was in the shop; the shining Embankment was again practically deserted, and she was able to carry out her experiment without exciting observation. She took a dozen steps up Cheyne Row, pretended she heard the shot, turned sharp round, and quite realised that from where she was the body could not have been seen, hidden as it must have been by the seat, which itself was almost hidden by the long and narrow island of enclosed garden. But a running man could have been seen through the garden, even if he stooped as he ran, and the murderer must have run like the wind to get away as he had done. The gates through the garden, back and front of the statue, had not been opened for the day when the murder took place, so Phillida in her turn made a half-circuit of the island to get to the spot where the body had been found, but without taking her eyes off the spot until she reached it. No! It was as she had thought all along; by nothing short of a miracle could the assassin have escaped observation if the policeman had eyes in his head and had acted as he swore he had done. He might have dashed into the garden, when the policeman was at his furthest point distant, if the gates had been open as they were now; but they had been locked, and he could not have scaled them unobserved. Neither would it have been possible to take a header into the river with the foreshore as described by the same witness. Yet the murderer had either done one of these things, or the flags of the Embankment had opened and swallowed him.

The girl stood on the very spot where the murdered man must have fallen, and in her utter perplexity it was no longer the tragedy but the problem which engrossed her mind. What had happened, had happened; but how could it have happened? She raised her umbrella and peered through the rain at a red pile of many-windowed flats; had that Argus of the hundred eyes been sleeping without one of them open at the time? Her own eyes fell as far as the black statue in the narrow garden, standing out hi the rain, like the greenery about its granite base, as though the blackened bronze were polished marble. How lifelike the colossal scholar in his homely garb! How scornful and how shrewd the fixed eternal gaze across his own old Father Thames! It assumed another character as the girl gazed in her turn, she seemed to intercept that stony stare, to distract it from the river to herself, and to her fevered fancy the grim lips smiled contemptuously on her and her quandary. He knew—he knew—those grim old eyes had seen it all, and still they stared and smiled as much as to say: "You are looking the wrong way! Look where I am looking; that way lies the truth you are poor fool enough to want to know!"

And Phillida turned her back towards the shiny statue, and looked over the wet parapet, almost expecting to see something, but never dreaming of what she actually saw. The tide, which must have been coming in that early morning, was now going out, and between the Embankment masonry and the river there was again a draggled ribbon of shelving foreshore, black as on some volcanic coast; and between land and water, at a point that would necessarily have been submerged for the last eight or nine hours, a small object was being laid more bare by every receding wavelet. It was black and square, perhaps the size of two large cigar-boxes side by side; and it had one long, thin, reddish tentacle, finishing in a bulb that moved about gently in the rain-pocked water.

Phillida felt the parapet strike cold and wet through her rain-coat sleeves as she leant far over to make doubly sure what she object was; but indeed she had not a moment's doubt but that it was the missing camera of the murdered man.

AFTER THE FAIR

Mr. Upton was dumfoundered when the top-floor door in Glasshouse Street was opened before Eugene Thrush could insert his key; for it was the sombre Mullins who admitted the gentleman as though nothing had happened to him except a fairly recent shave.

"I thought he was in prison?" exclaimed the ironmaster when the two were closeted.

"Do you ever read your paper?"

"I haven't looked at one since Plymouth."

"Well, I howked him out first thing yesterday morning."

"You did, Thrush?"

"Why not? I had need of the fellow, and that part of the game was up."

Mr. Upton showed symptoms of his old irritability under the Thrush mannerism.

"My good fellow, I wish to goodness you'd explain yourself!"

"If I cared to be profane," returned Thrush, mixing drinks in the corner, "I should refer you to the first chapter of the Book of Job. I provided the prisoner, and I'd a perfect right to take him away again. Blessed be the song of the Thrush!"

"You say you provided him?"

"In other words, I laid the information against my own man, but only with his own consent."

"Well, well, you must have your joke, I suppose. I can afford to put up with it now."

"It wasn't meant as a joke," returned Thrush, and drank deep while his client sipped. "If it had come off it would have been the coup of my career; as it didn't—quite—one must laugh it off at one's own expense. Your son has told you what that poor old sinner made him think he'd done?"

"Of course."

"Would it surprise you to hear that one or two others thought the same thing?"

"Not you, Thrush?"

"Not I to quite the same positive extent as my rascal Mullins. He jumped to it from scratch!"

"He connected Tony with the Park murder?"

"From the word 'go.' "

"On the strength of an asthma cigarette and my poor wife's dream?"

"No; he didn't know about the dream. But he refused to believe in two independent mysteries at one time and on one spot. The eternal unities was too many measles for Mullins, though he never heard tell of 'em in his life."

Mr. Upton was no longer irritated by the other's flippancy. He looked at Thrush with a shining face.

"And you never told me what was in your minds!"

"It was poison even in mine; it would have been deadly poison to you, in the state you were in. I say! I'll wear batting-gloves the next time we shake hands!" and Thrush blew softly on his mangled fingers.

"You believed he'd done it, and you kept it to yourself," murmured Mr. Upton, still much impressed. "Tell me, my dear fellow—did you believe it after that interview with Baumgartner in his house?"

Thrush emptied his glass at once.

"Don't remind me of that interview, Mr. Upton; there was the lad on the other side of so much lath-and-plaster, and I couldn't scent him through it! But he never made a sound, confound him!"

"Tony's told me about that; they were whispering, for reasons of their own."

"I ought to have seen that old man listening! His ears must have grown before my purblind eyes! But his story was an extraordinarily interesting and circumstantial effort. And to come back to your question, it did fit in with the theory of a fatal accident on your boy's part; he was frightened to show his face at school after sleeping in the Park, let alone what he was supposed to have done there; and that, he believed, would break his mother's heart in any case."

"By Jove, and so it might! It wouldn't take much just now," said Mr. Upton, sadly.

"So he thought of the ship you wouldn't let him go out in—and the whole thing fitted in! Of course he had told the old ruffian—saving his presence elsewhere—all about the forbidden voyage; and that gentleman of genius had it ready for immediate use. I'm bound to say he used it on me with excellent effect."

"Same here," said the ironmaster—"though I'd no idea what you suspected. I thought it a conceivable way out of any bad scrape, for that particular boy."

"It imposed upon us all," said Thrush, "but one. I was prepared to believe it if you did, and you believed it because you didn't know your boy as well as you do now. But Miss Upton, who seems to know him better than anybody else—do you remember how she wouldn't hear of it for a moment?"

"I do so, God bless her!"

"That shook me, or rather it prevented me from accepting what I never had quite accepted in my heart. That's another story, and you're only in the mood for one at present; but after seeing Baumgartner on Saturday, I thought I'd like to know a little more about him, not from outsiders but from the inside of his own skull. So I went to the British Museum to have a look at his books. It was after hours for getting books, but I made such representations that they cut their red tape for once; and I soon read enough to wonder whether my grave and reverend seignior was quite all there. Spiritualism one knows, but here was spiritualism with a difference; psychic photography one had heard about, but here was a psychical photographer gone mad or bad! When a gifted creature puts into admirable English his longing to snap-shoot the souls of murderers coming up through the drop, like the clown at Drury Lane, you begin to want him elected to a fauteuil in Broadmoor. Will you believe me when I tell you that I stumbled mentally on the very thing I shall presently prove to have been the truth, and that I dismissed it from my mind as the wildest impossibility?"

"I don't see how you're going to prove it now," remarked Mr. Upton, who hoped there would be no such proof, for the sake of the girl who had been good to his boy; but that was a private consideration which there was no necessity to express.

"I shall want another chat with your lad when he's had his sleep out," replied Thrush, significantly; "he's told me quite enough to make me eager for more. But you haven't told me anything about your own adventures?"

And he got another drink to help him listen; for as a rule the ironmaster was only succinct when thoroughly irate. But now for once he was both brief and amiable.

"What have I to tell compared with you?" he asked. "Those damned old wooden walls only cleared the Thames on Sunday morning, and they weren't near Plymouth when I left last night; but my little aluminium lot broke all her records before I broke one of her wheels. What I want to know is what you did from the time I left on Sunday night to that great moment this morning."

"I sat down to watch Baumgartner, his house," replied Thrush. "The merit of those quiet little streets is that there are always apartments of sorts, though not always the most admirable sort, to be had in half the houses. There was quite a choice bang opposite Baumgartner's, and I'd taken a front room before you were through Hammersmith. Of course I explained that I had lost a last train, and the landlady's son embarrassed me with pyjamas of inadequate dimensions. Well, I sat at the front window all night, for no better reasons than my strong feeling about the doctor's writings, and your daughter's disbelief in his yarn about her brother. Soon after five in the morning the old bird came out, and I was after him like knife. I tracked him to Knightsbridge without much difficulty, excepting the one of avoiding being spotted, but there that happened by the merest accident. He was passing under the scaffolding outside the church they're pulling down there, and he's so tall he knocked his hat off. I admit I was too close. He saw, and must have recognised me; but I shouldn't have recognised him if I hadn't seen him start out. He was wearing a false beard and spectacles!"

"That's proof positive," said ingenuous Mr. Upton, under his breath.

"Well, I confess it's something like it in this case; but it was a very awkward moment for me. I hadn't to let him see I knew him, nor yet that I was following him, and the only way was to abandon the chase as openly as possible. It was then I decided that it was no use leaving poor old Mullins in pawn to the police. I redeemed him without delay. We went back to my new rooms together, which I needn't tell you I liked so much that I brought a suit-case and took them for a week. Of course, as we had lost the run of Baumgartner, the next best thing was to watch for his return. Mullins took that on while I got some sleep; when I awoke the Park Lane murder was the latest, and I won't say I didn't suspect who'd done it. Perhaps I didn't tell you he had his camera with him as well as beard and goggles, and all three figured in the first reports."

"But all this time you had no idea my boy was in the house?"

"None whatever; we saw the girl once or twice, but that was all until I wired last night. What I never saw myself was Baumgartner's return; but in the afternoon I sent Mullins round to another road to try and get a room overlooking the place from the back. Well, the houses were too much class for that; but one was empty, and he got the key and risked going back to prison for the cause! Suffice it that he set eyes on both man and boy before I sent that wire."

"And you left my son in that murderer's clutches a minute longer than you could help?" It was a previous incarnation of Pocket's father that broke in with this.

"You must remember in the first place that I couldn't be in the least sure it was your son; in the second, if murder had been intended, murder would have been done with as little delay in his case as in the others; thirdly, that we've nothing to show that Dr. Baumgartner is an actual murderer at all, but, fourthly, that to raid his place was the way to make him one. Poor Mullins, too, as the original Sherlock of the show, was desperately against calling in the police under any circumstances. He assured me there was no sign of bad blood about the house, until the small hours, and then he saw your son make his escape. I told him he should have collared the lad, but he lost sight of him in the night and preferred to keep an eye on that poor desperate doctor."

Thrush treated this part of his narrative with the peculiar confidence which most counsel reserve for the less satisfactory aspects of their case. But Mr. Upton was not in a mood to press a point of grievance against anybody. And the name of Mullins reminded him that his curiosity on a very different point had not been gratified.

"Why on earth did you have Mullins run in?" he inquired, with characteristic absence of finesse.

"I'm not very proud of it," replied Thrush. "It didn't come off, you see."

"But whatever could the object have been?"

"I must have a damn-it if I'm to tell you that," said Thrush; and the ironmaster concluded that he meant a final drink, from the action which he suited to the oath. "It was one way that occurred to me of putting salt on the lad."

"Tony?"

"Yes."

"You puzzle me more and more."

"Well, you see, I gathered that he was a particularly honourable boy, of fine sensibilities, and yet Mullins thought he had shot this man by accident and was lying low. I only thought that, if that were so, the news of an innocent man's arrest would bring him into the open as quick as anything. Mullins proving amenable to terms, and having really been within a hundred miles of both murders at the time they were committed, the rest was elementary. But what's the good of talking about it? It didn't come off."

"It very nearly did! I can tell you that straight from Tony; he was going to give himself up yesterday morning, if he hadn't accidentally satisfied himself of his own innocence."

Mr. Upton said more than this, but it was the explicit statement of fact that alone afforded Thrush real consolation. His spectacled eyes blinked keenly behind their flashing lenses; the button of a nose underneath twitched as though it scented battle once again; and the drink with the opprobrious name was suddenly put down unfinished.

"If only I could find that camera!" he cried. "It's the touchstone of the whole thing, mark my words. If it's an accomplice who did this thing, he's got it; even if not—"

He stood silenced by a sudden thought, a gleam of light that illumined his whole flushed face.

"Mullins!" he roared. Mullins was on the spot with somewhat suspicious alacrity. "Get the almanac, Mullins, and look up Time of High Water at London Bridge to-day!"

He himself flopped down behind the telephone to ring up the cab-office in Bolton Street. But it takes time even for a Eugene Thrush to consume all but three large whiskies and sodas; and the afternoon was already far advanced.

THE SECRET OF THE CAMERA

The camera had been placed upon a folded newspaper, for the better preservation of the hotel table-cloth. Its apertures were still choked with mud; beads of slime kept breaking out along the joints. And Phillida was still explaining to Pocket how the thing had come into her possession.

"The rain was the greatest piece of luck, though another big slice was an iron gangway to the foreshore about a hundred yards up-stream. It was coming down so hard at the time that I couldn't see another creature out in it except myself. I don't believe a single soul saw me run down that gangway and up again; but I dropped my purse over first for an excuse if anybody did. I popped the camera under my waterproof, and carried it up to the King's Road before I could get a cab. But I never expected to find you awake and about again; next to the rain that's the best luck of all!"

"Why?"

"Because you know all about photography and I don't. Suppose he took a last photograph, and suppose that led directly to the murder!"

"That's an idea."

"The man threw the camera into the river, but the plate would be in it still, and you could develop it!"

The ingenious hypothesis had appealed to the eager credulity of the boy; but at the final proposition he shook a reluctant head.

"I'm afraid there's not much chance of there being anything to develop; the slide's been open all this time, you see."

"I know. I tried to shut it, but the wood must have swollen in the water. Yet the more it has swollen, the better it ought to keep out the light, oughtn't it?"

"I'm afraid there isn't a dog's chance," he murmured, as he handled the camera again. Yet it was not of the folding-bellows variety, but was one of the earlier and stronger models in box form, and it had come through its ordeal wonderfully on the whole. Nothing was absolutely broken; but the swollen slide jammed obstinately, until in trying to shut it by main force, Pocket lost his grip of the slimy apparatus, and sent it flying to the floor, all but the slide which came out bodily in his hand.

"That settles it," remarked Phillida, resignedly. The exposed plate stared them in the face, a sickly yellow in the broad daylight. It was cracked across the middle, but almost dry and otherwise uninjured.

"I am sorry!" exclaimed Pocket, as they stood over the blank sheet of glass and gelatine; it was like looking at a slate from which some infinitely precious message had been expunged unread. "I'm not sure that you weren't right after all; what's water-tight must be more or less light-tight, when you come to think of it. I say, what's all this? The other side oughtn't to bulge like that!"

He picked the broken plate out of the side that was already open, and weighed the slide in his hand; it was not heavy enough to contain another plate, he declared with expert conviction; yet the side which had not been opened was a slightly bulging but distinctly noticeable convexity. Pocket opened it at a word from Phillida, and an over-folded packet of MS. leapt out.

"It's his writing!" cried the girl, with pain and awe in her excitement. She had dropped the document at once.

"It's in English," said Pocket, picking it up.

"It must be what he was writing all last night!"

"It is."

"You see what it is!" urged Phillida, feebly. But she watched him closely as he read to himself:—

"June 20,190-."

"It is a grim coincidence that I should sit down to reveal the secret of my latter days on what is supposed to be the shortest night of the year; for they must come to an end at sunrise, viz., at 3.44 according to the almanac, and it is already after 10 p.m. Even if I sit at my task till four I shall have less than six hours in which to do justice to the great ambition and the crowning folly of my life. I used the underlined word advisedly; some would substitute 'monomania,' but I protest I am as sane as they are, fail as I may to demonstrate that fact among so many others to be dealt with in the very limited time at my disposal. Had I more time, or the pen of a readier writer, I should feel surer of vindicating my head if not my heart. But I have been ever deliberate in all things (excepting, certainly, the supreme folly already mentioned), and I would be as deliberate over the last words I shall ever write, as in my final preparations for death—".

"What is it?" asked Phillida, for his eyes had dilated as he read, and he was breathing hard.

"He practically says he was going to commit suicide at daybreak! He's said so once already, but now he says it in so many words!"

"Well, we know he didn't do it," said Phillida, as though she found a crumb of comfort in the thought.

"I'm not so sure about that."

"Go on reading it aloud. I can bear it if that's the worst."

"But it isn't, Phillida. I can see it isn't!"

"Then let us read it together. I'd rather face it with you than afterwards all by myself. We've seen each other through so much, surely we can—surely—"

Her words were swept away in a torrent of tears, and it was with dim eyes but a palpitating heart that Pocket looked upon the forlorn drab figure of the slip of a girl; for as yet, despite her pretext to Mr. Upton, she had taken no thought for her mourning, that unfailing distraction to the normally bereaved, but had put on anything she could find of a neutral tint; and yet it was just her dear disdain of appearance, the intimate tears gathering in her great eyes, unchecked, and streaming down the fresh young face, the very shabbiness of her coat and skirt, that made her what she was in his sight. Outside, the rain had stopped, and Trafalgar Square was drying in the sun, that streamed in through the open window of the hotel sitting-room, and poured its warm blessing on the two young heads bent as one over the dreadful document.

This was the part they read together, now in silence, now one and now the other whispering a few sentences aloud:—.

"What I have called my life's ambition demands but little explanation here. I have never made any secret of it, but, on the contrary, I have given full and frank expression to my theories in places where they are still accessible to the curious. I refer to my signed articles on spirit photography in Light Human Nature, The Occult Review and other periodicals, but particularly to the paper entitled 'The Flight of the Soul,' in The Nineteenth Century and After for January of last year. The latter article contains my last published word on the matter which has so long engrossed my mind. It took me some months to prepare and to write, and its reception did much to drive me to the extreme measures I have since employed. Treated to a modicum of serious criticism by the scientific press, but more generally received with ignorant and intolerant derision, which is the Englishman's attitude towards whatsoever is without his own contracted ken, my article, the work of months, was dismissed and forgotten in a few days. I had essayed the stupendous feat of awaking the British nation to a new idea, and the British nation had responded with a characteristic snore of unfathomable indifference. My name has not appeared in its vermin press from that day to this; it was not mentioned in the paragraph about the psychic photographer which went the rounds about a year ago. Yet I was that photographer. I am the serious and accredited inquirer to whom the London hospitals refused admittance to their pauper deathbeds, thronged though those notoriously are by the raw material of the British medical profession. Begin at the bottom of the British medical ladder, and you are afforded the earliest and most frequent opportunities of studying (if not accelerating) the phenomena of human dissolution; but against the foreign scientist the door is closed, without reference either to the quality of his credentials or the purity of his aims. I can conceive no purer and no loftier aim than mine. It is as high above that of your ordinary physician as heaven itself is high above this earth. Your physician wrestles with death to lengthen life, whereas I would sacrifice a million lives to prove that there is no such thing as death; that this human life of ours, by which we set such childish store, is but a fleeting phase of the permanent life of the spirit. One shrinks from setting down so trite a truism; it is the common ground of all religion, but I have reached it from the opposite pole. Religion is to me the unworthy triumph of instinct over knowledge, a lazy substitution of invention for discovery. Religion invites us to take her postulates on trust; but a material age is deserving of material proofs, and it is these proofs I have striven to supply. Surely it is a higher aim, and not a lower, to appeal to the senses that cannot deceive, rather than to the imagination which must and does? But I am trenching after all upon ground which I myself have covered before to-day; it is my function to-night to relate a personal narrative rather than to reiterate personal views. Suffice it that to me, for many years, the only path to the Invisible has been the path of so-called spiritualism; the only lamp that illumined that path, so that all who saw might follow it for themselves, the lamp of spirit photography. It is a path with a bad name, a path infested with quacks and charlatans, and by false guides who rival the religious fanatics in the impudence of their appeal to man's credulity. Even those who bear the lamp I hold aloft are too often jugglers and rogues, to whose wiles, unfortunately, the simple science of photography lends itself all too readily. Nothing is easier than the production of impossible pictures by a little manipulation of film or plate; if the spiritual apparition is not to be enticed within range of the lens, nothing easier than to fabricate an approximate effect. And what spiritualist has yet succeeded in summoning spirits at will? It is the crux of the whole problem of spiritualism, to establish any sort or form of communication with disembodied spirits at the single will of the embodied; hence the periodical exposure of the paid medium, the smug scorn of the unbeliever, and the discouragement of genuine exploration beyond the environment of the flesh. There is one moment, and only one, at which a man may be sure that he stands, for however brief a particle of time, in the presence of a disembodied soul. It is the moment at which soul and body part company in what men call death. The human watcher sees merely the collapse of the human envelope; but many a phenomenon invisible to the human eye has been detected and depicted by that of the camera, as everybody knows who has the slightest acquaintance with the branch of physics known as 'fluorescence.' The invisible spirit of man surely falls within this category. To the crystal eye of science it is not so much invisible as elusive and intractable. Once it has fled this earth, the sovereign opportunity is gone; but photography may often intercept the actual flight of the soul."

"I say no more than 'often' because there are special difficulties into which I need not enter here; but they would disappear, or at least be minimised, if the practice received the encouragement it deserves, instead of the forbidding ban of a sentimental generation. It would hurt nobody; it would comfort and convince the millions who at present have only their Churches' word for the existence of an eternal soul in their perishable bodies. It would prove more, in the course of a few experiments, than all the

Churches have proved between them in nineteen centuries. Yet how are my earnest applications received, in hospitals where men die daily, in prisons where they are still occasionally put to death? I am refused, rebuffed, gratuitously reprimanded; in fact, I am driven ultimately to the extreme course of taking human life, on my own account, in order to prove the life eternal. Call it murder, call it what you will; in a civilisation which will not hear of a lethal chamber for congenital imbeciles it would be waste of time to urge the inutility of a life as an excuse for taking it, or the misery of an individual as a reason for sending him to a world which cannot use him worse than this world. I can only say that I have not deprived the State of one conceivably profitable servant, or cut short a single life of promise or repute. I have picked my few victims with infinite care from amid the moral or material wreckage of life; either they had nothing to live for, or they had no right to live. Charlton, the licensed messenger, had less to live for than any man I ever knew; in the course of our brief acquaintance he frequently told me how he wished he was dead. I came across him in Kensington, outside a house to which an unseemly fracas had attracted my attention as I passed. Charlton had just been ejected for being drunk and insolent, and refusing to leave without an extra sixpence. I befriended him. He was indeed saturated with alcohol and honeycombed with disease; repulsive in appearance, and cantankerous in character, his earnings were so slender that he was pitifully clad, and without a night's lodging oftener than not. He had not a friend in the world, and was suffering from an incurable malady of which the end was certain agony. I resolved to put him out of his misery, and at the same time to try to photograph the escape of his soul. A favourable opportunity did not present itself for some time, during which Charlton subsisted largely on my bounty; at last one morning I found him asleep on a bench in Holland Walk, and not another being in sight, and I shot him with a cheap pistol which I had purchased second-hand for the purpose, and which I left beside him on the seat. Yet the weapon it was that cast a doubt upon the authenticity of the suicide, despite my final precaution of stuffing a number of cartridges into the dead man's pocket; pot-house associates came forward to declare that he could never have possessed either the revolver or its price without their knowledge. Hence the coroner's repudiation of the verdict at the inquest. Yet it is to be feared that the fate of such as poor Charlton excites but little public interest in its explanation, and that the police themselves never took more than an academic interest in the case."

"To me it was a bitter disappointment on other grounds. I had lost very few seconds between pulling the revolver trigger and pressing the bulb of my pneumatic shutter; but one had to get back into position for this, and the fact remains that I was too late. The result may be found among my negatives. It is dreadfully good of the dead man, if not a unique photograph of actual death; but it lacks the least trace of the super- normal. The flight of the soul had been too quick for me; it would be too quick again unless I hit upon some new method. I had not only failed to leave convincing evidence of suicide, but the fatal pause between pistol- shot and snap-shot was due entirely to my elaborate attempt in that direction. It was not worth making again. The next case should be a more honest breach of the Sixth Commandment; the shot to be fired, and the photograph taken, at the same range and all but at the same instant. There would be no further point in leaving the weapon behind, so I was free to choose the one best suited to my purpose, and to adapt it at my leisure to my peculiar needs. Eventually I evolved the ingenious engine which, no doubt, has already explained itself better than I could possibly explain it; if not, the discoverer of the camera need not hesitate to experiment with the pistol, as it will not be loaded when found."

There was a brief discussion here. The children could not understand about the pistol; but only one of them cared what had become of it. For Phillida it was enough to know that the writer of this shameless rigmarole, with its pompous periods and its callous gusto, must long ago have lost his reason. She had no doubt whatever about that, and already it had brought a new light into her eyes. She would pause to discuss nothing else. It was her finger that pointed the way through the next passages.

"The perfection or completion of my device was the secret work of many weeks; it brings me down almost to the other day, and to what I have described as the supreme folly of my life. I had everything in readiness for another attempt to liberate and photograph a human soul in consecutive fractions of a second. But the right man was never in the right place at the right time; one saw him by the dozen in a crowd, but the people one met all by themselves, in the early summer mornings, stayed one's hand repeatedly by the eager brightness of their eyes or a happy elasticity of step. Once an out-patient at the Brompton Hospital, whom I had dogged all the way down to Richmond Park, was cheated of a merciful end by dusk falling just as I had him to myself. No; the dawn and the drunkard were still my best chance. So it was that the wretch whose name I forget met with his death in Hyde Park last Tuesday morning. I knew him by sight as a pot-house loafer of the Charlton circle, but it was quite by chance that I followed his uncertain footsteps through the Park, and saw him go deliberately to bed in the drenching dew. His face filled in his tale; it was another farrago of privation and excess. This was the type that caused me no compunction: having aimed and focussed at the same time, as my invention provides, I despatched the poor devil as he lay on his side, with his hat over his eyes, and exposed my plate as he rolled over on his face. It may be reckoned an offensive detail, but the click of my instantaneous shutter coincided with the last clutter in his throat."

"I need hardly say that I had looked about me pretty thoroughly before firing, and my first act after taking the photograph was to make another wary survey of the scene. It had the advantage that one could see a considerable distance in three directions, and in none of these, neither right nor left along the path, nor yet straight ahead across the grass on the edge of which my victim lay, was a living creature to be seen. This was very reassuring, as I felt that I could see a good deal farther than the report of my small automatic pistol was likely to be heard; for it is a remarkable feature of most shooting cases, especially where a pistol has been used, and in the open air, how seldom it is that a witness can be found who has actually heard the fatal shot. In the fourth quarter, where there was a bank of shrubbery behind some iron palings, I looked last, for I was standing with my back that way. How shall I describe my sensations on turning round? There was a young lad within a few feet of me, on the other side of the palings; and this young lad was flourishing a revolver in his right hand!"

"At first I made certain he had seen everything; but his blank and frank bewilderment was more reassuring at a second glance, and at a third I guessed what had happened to him. His crumpled clothes were dank with dew. His eyes were puddles of utter stupefaction. He had been sleeping in the Park, and walking in his sleep, and in all probability it was my shot which had brought him to himself; of this, however, I was less sure, and in my doubt I was disastrously inspired to accuse him of having fired the shot himself. It never struck me that he could mistake the body behind me for a living man; it was with a wild idea of being the first to accuse the other, that I asked him if he knew what he had done, and seized his revolver at the same moment. I had the wit to grasp it in my hot hand until the barrel was just warm enough to help me convince the child that he really had fired the shot; but, since he could not see it for myself, I was not going out of my way just then to tell him it was a fatal shot. Already I regretted that I had gone so far, and yet already I saw myself committed to a course of action as rash as it was now inevitable. The boy became convulsed with asthma; I could not leave him there, to tell his story when the body was discovered, to have it disproved perhaps on the spot, at the latest on a comparison of bullets, and the truth brought home to me through his description. Again, when I had taken him to my house, with all sorts of foolish precautions, and still more foolish risks, I had to keep him there. How could I let him loose to blurt out his story and implicate me more readily than ever after what he had seen of me at home? I had to keep him there—I repeat it—alive or dead. And I was not the kind of murderer (if I am one at all) to take a young and innocent life, if I could help it, to preserve my own; on the contrary, I had, and I hope I always should have had, humanity enough at least to do what I could for a fellow-creature battling with an attack which almost threatened to remove him from my path without my aid."

There followed a few remarks on Pocket's character as the writer read it. They were not uncomplimentary to Pocket personally, but they betrayed a profound disdain for the typically British institution of which Pocket was too readily accepted as a representative product. His general ignorance and credulity received a grim tribute; they were the very qualities the doctor would have demanded in a chosen dupe. Yet he appeared to have enjoyed the youth's society, his transparent honesty, his capacity for enthusiastic interest, whether in the delights of photography or in the horrors of war. Baumgartner seemed aware that he had been somewhat confidential on both subjects, and that either his contempt of human life, or his ambitions in the matter of psychic photography, would have been better kept to himself; but, on the other hand, he "greatly doubted whether they taught boys to put two and two together, at these so-called public schools"; and, after all, it was not detection by the boy, but through the boy, that he had to fear.

"The madness of keeping him prisoner, as he had been from the beginning, in spite of all pretences and persuasions to the contrary, was another thing to which Baumgartner had been thoroughly alive all along. He had regarded it from the first as 'the certain beginning of the end'; from the first, he had been prepared with specious explanations for any such inquisitor as the one who had actually arrived no later than the Saturday afternoon. He wrote without elation of his interview with Thrush, whose name he knew; the doctor had not been deceived as to the transitory character of his own deception. It was the same with the letter which he had pretended to post, which could only have kept the boy quiet for a day or two, if he had posted it, but which the boy himself had discovered never to have been posted at all. There was a sufficiently cool description of the desperate mood into which Baumgartner's intuition of the boy's discovery had thrown him on the Sunday night."

"It was then," he wrote, "that I formed a project which I should have been sorry indeed to carry out, though I should certainly have done so if he had given me the chance I sought. It must be understood that my second attempt to photograph the flight of the soul had proved as great a fiasco as the first. Suddenly I hit upon a perfectly conceivable (even though it seem a wilfully grotesque) explanation of my failure. What if the human derelicts I had so far chosen for my experiments had no souls to photograph? Sodden with drink, debauched, degraded, and spiritually blurred or blunted to the last degree, these after all were the least likely subjects to yield results to the spirit photographer. I should have chosen saints instead of sinners such as these, entities in which the soul was a major and not a minor factor. I thought of the saintliest men I knew in London, of some Jesuit Fathers of my acquaintance, of a 'light' specialist I know of who is destroying himself by inches in the cause of science, of certain missioners in the slums; but I did not think twice of any one of them; their lives are much too valuable for me to cut them short on the mere chance of a compensating benefit to mankind at large. Last, and longest, I thought of the boy upstairs. I had not meant to sacrifice him; a young life, of some promise, is only less sacred to me than a mature life rich in beneficent activities. But this young fellow was going to be my ruin. I could see it in his eyes. He had found me out about the letter; he would be the means of my being found out and stopped for ever in the work of my life. It was his life or mine; it should be his; but I was not going to take it there in the house, for reasons I need not enter into here, and I intended to take more than his life while I was about it. But he never gave me the chance. I did my best to get him to go out with me this morning. But he refused, as a horse refuses a jump, or a dog the water. He said he was ill; he looked ill. But I have no doubt he was well enough to make his escape soon after my back was turned. I see he has broken into my dark-room for the clothes I took away from him before I went out; he would scarcely remain after that; but, to tell the truth, I have hardly given him a thought since my return."

The readers shuddered over this long paragraph. More than once the boy broke in with his own impulsive version of the awful moments on the Sunday night and the Monday morning, in his bedroom at the top of the doctor's house. He declared that nothing short of main force would have dragged him out-of-doors that morning, that he felt it in his bones that he would never come back alive. Then he would be sorry he had said so much.

It only increased his companion's anguish. She was reading every word religiously, with a most painful fascination; it was as though every word drew blood. There was a brief but terrible account of the murder of Sir Joseph Schelmerdine outside his own house in Park Lane. It was the rashest of all the crimes; but, apparently, the one occasion on which the doctor had disguised himself before hand; and that only because Sir Joseph and he knew and disliked each other so intensely that a "straight" interview was out of the question. As it was he had escaped by a miracle, after lying all day in a straw-loft, creeping into a carriage at nightfall, and getting out on the wrong side when it drove round to its house. Baumgartner described the incident with a callous relish, as perhaps the most exciting in his long career; he was going on to explain his subsequent return, in propria persona, and yet by stealth, when he paused in the middle of a sentence which was never finished. And his statement concluded as follows, in less careful language and a more flowing hand:—

"I thought the fool had cleared out long ago. The day's excitement must have driven him clean out of my head. I never thought of him when I got back, never till I saw the damage to the darkroom window and missed his clothes. I didn't waste two thoughts upon him then. I had my negative to develop. A magnificent negative it was, too, yet another absolute failure from the practical point of view, perhaps from the same reason as its predecessors. South African mines may produce gold and diamonds (licit and illicit!) but their yield in souls is probably the poorest to the square mile anywhere on earth. Schelmerdine never had one in his gross carcass. So there was an end of him, and a good riddance to rotten clay. I have not thought of him again all night. I have thought of nothing but this perhaps passionately dispassionate statement that I have made up my mind to leave behind me. It has given me strange pleasure to write, a satisfaction which I have no longer the time to attempt to analyse; all night long my pen has scarcely paused, and I not conscious of a moment's weariness of mind, body, or hand. Only sometimes have I paused to light my pipe. I had made such a pause, perhaps half an hour ago, when in the terrible stillness of the night I heard a footstep in the hall. My nerves were somewhat on edge with all this writing; it might be my imagination. I stole to my door, and as I opened it the one below shut softly. I waited some time, heard nothing more, went down with my lamp, and threw open the drawing-room door. There was my young fellow, not gone at all, but sitting in the dark with one whose name there is no need to mention. I do not wish to be misunderstood. It was all innocent enough, even I never doubted that. But somehow the sight of that boy and girl, sitting there in the dark without a word, afraid to go to bed—afraid of me—made the blood boil over in my veins. I could have trampled on that lad, my Jonah whom I had pictured overboard at last, and I did hurl the lamp at his head. I am glad it missed him. I am glad he made good his escape while I was seeing his companion safe upstairs. If I had found him where I left him, God knows what violence I might not have done him after all. The boy has good in him, and more courage than he knows himself; again I say that I am glad he has escaped unscathed. His life was not safe, but now I shall only take my own."

"Yes! I have made up my mind; it is better than leaving it to the common hangman of this besotted country. I know what to expect in enlightened England: either a death unfit for a dog, or existence worse than death in a criminal lunatic asylum. I prefer my own peculiar quietus; it has stood on my table all night long, ready and pointed at my heart; a hand upon the door, a step behind me, and I should have rolled over dead at their feet. So it will be if even now they are waiting for me outside; but, if not, I know where to go, where already it is broad daylight, where the wide open space will quicken and enhance every ray, and the broad river multiply the sun by a million facets of living fire. It is not the light that will fail me, there; and as I have served others, so also will I serve myself, and it may be with better fortune than they have brought me. Who knows? It would be in keeping with the poetic ironies of this existence. At all events, unless waylaid at once, I am giving it a chance. I shall place the camera on the parapet of the Embankment. I have fitted the shutter with a specially long pneumatic tube, and the bulb will do its double work as usual when my fingers relax. I have long had it all in my mind. I have written full instructions on the envelope which I shall stick by the flap to the open slide; if we are found by a reasonably intelligent person, the slide will be shut, and the camera handed over bodily to the police. They, I think, may be trusted to honour one's last instructions, if only out of curiosity; their eyes will be the first to read what I fear they will describe as my 'full confession.' Well, it is 'full,' and the substantive must be left to them. So long as the document does not fall into one little pair of gentle hands, I shall lie easy in whatever ignominious grave they lay me. That is why I hide it where I do: since, if it fell first into those hands, it would never see the light at all."

There was a little more, but Phillida suddenly snatched the MS. away, and wept over the end, bitterly, and yet not altogether in bitterness, while Pocket picked up the camera and set it back in its place on the muddy newspaper. Phillida folded up the packet, and after a moment's hesitation went away with it, jingling keys in her other hand. On her return she stood petrified on the threshold.

Pocket was seated at the table, the red bulb of the pneumatic shutter between his finger and thumb; he pressed the bulb, and there was a loud metallic snap inside the camera; he released the pressure, and the shutter snapped like a shutter and nothing else. Phillida came forward with a cry. Pocket had taken the top off the camera; it was like a box without the lid, and on the one side there was nothing between the lens and the grooved carrier for the slide, but on the other there was an automatic pistol, fixed down with wires, as a wild beast might be lashed, and its muzzle pointing through the orifice intended for the second lens of the stereoscopic camera.

Pocket pressed again, and again the mild clash of the shutter was preceded by the vicious one that would have been an explosion if there had been another cartridge in the pistol.

"And we never guessed it!" said he. "That's why he went in for this sort of double camera, and rigged it up to take both kinds of shot in quick succession. It's the cleverest thing I ever heard of in my life."

He spoke as if it were only clever! Phillida stared at it and him without a word.

"The cleverest part is the way you aim. I do believe he relied altogether on that spot about the middle of the focussing screen. I've been trying it against the window, and where that spot comes the pistol's pointing every time. It's a fixed focus, about ten to fifteen feet, I fancy, and the spot isn't quite in the middle of the screen, but just enough to the left to allow. I don't quite see how the one bulb works everything, but these springs and things are a bit confusing. We shan't understand everything till we take it to pieces."

"You mean the police won't!" said Phillida, bitterly.

"The police! I never thought of them."

"What do you mean to do with this—this infernal machine?" the girl asked, her voice breaking over the perfectly applicable term.

"What do you mean to do with—the writing?" demanded Pocket in his turn.

"Burn it! I've asked for a fire in my room; it's locked away meanwhile."

"Well, this is yours, too," said Pocket, deliberately, "to do what you like with as well."

"They wouldn't think so!"

"They'll never know."

Phillida shook her head, and not without some scorn. "You couldn't keep it to yourself," she said. "You would have to tell."

"Well, but not everybody," said poor Pocket. "Only my father, if you like!" he added, valiantly.

"Mr. Upton would feel bound to tell."

"I don't see that. Didn't you hear what he said about a man's secrets dying with him?"

"He's so kind! He says that; he said it again to me; but this is the mystery of the day. It'll be the talk for months, if not years. And as yet only you and I, in all the world, have found it out!"

She looked at him so wistfully, so sweetly and sadly and confidentially, that he would have been either more or less than human boy if he had failed to see her heart's desire, and how it was still in his power to save her the supreme humiliation and distress of sharing their secret with the world. He made up his mind on the spot; and yet it was a mind that looked both ways at every turn of affairs, and even then he saw what he was going to lose. Fred and Horace would not sit nearly so spellbound as they might have done, would probably back their penetration of the mystery against his! There would be no boasting about it in front of the hall fire at school, no breathing it even to Smith minor out for a walk; no adventure to recount all his days; and Pocket was one to whom the salt of an adventure would always be its subsequent recital. But he could "play the game" as well as Horace himself, when he happened to have no doubt as to the game to play. And now he had none whatever.

"Phillida, if you wish it, I'll never breathe a syllable of all this to a single soul on earth, I don't care who they are, or what they do to me!"

He wanted them to put him on the rack that moment.

"Oh, Tony, do you mean it?"

Her eyes had filled.

"Of course I mean it! I'll swear it more solemnly than I've ever sworn anything in my life so far."

"No, no! Your word's enough. Don't I know what that's worth, after this terrible week?"

And she cried again at its hideous memories, so that Pocket turned away and put the camera together again, and wrapped it up in her waterproof, so that he might not see her tears.

"I'll never breathe a single word to a single soul," he vowed, "except yourself."

She caught at that through her tears. He could talk to her about it, always, as much as ever he liked; it would be a bond between them all their lives. And not until she said it, to be just to Pocket, did he think of a reward or look beyond those days.

But what were they to do with a stereoscopic camera containing an automatic pistol? It was not to be burnt in a grate like a sheaf of MS. They thought about it for some time with anxious faces; for it was getting on towards evening now, though the sun was out again, and it was lighter than the early afternoon; but Mr. Upton might be back any minute. It was Phillida who at last said she knew. She would not tell him what she meant to do; but she put on her waterproof again, little as it was wanted now, and the camera under it as before; and together they sallied forth into the noisy and crowded Strand.

Pocket did not know where he was, and Phillida would not tell him where she was going, neither could he question her in that alarming throng. He felt a frightful sense of guilt and danger, not so much to himself as to her, with that lethal weapon concealed about her; every man who looked at them was a detective in his eyes, and past the policemen at the corners he wanted to run. But they gained the middle of Waterloo Bridge undetected and ensconced themselves in a recess without creating a sensation.

"Now, then," said Phillida, "will you focus Westminster Bridge and the Houses of Parliament, or shall I?"

There they were before them against the sunset, the long lithe bridge, the stately towers. But Pocket could not see Phillida's drift until she aimed herself, and, aiming, let the square black box slip clean through her fingers into the depths of the river from which she had only retrieved it a couple of hours before, as a body is committed to the deep.

She bewailed her stupidity; he had the wit to echo her then, and in a loud voice, that any eye-witness or passer-by might be struck with the genuine severity of their loss. But there had been no eye-witness who thought it worth while to rally them on the occurrence, and the busy townsfolk hastening past were all too much engrossed in their own affairs to take any interest in those of the boy and girl who seemed themselves in something of a hurry to get back to the Strand.

And in the Strand the first thing they saw was a yellow poster bearing but four words in enormous black letters:—

CHELSEA INQUEST
CAMERA CLUE!

Phillida slipped her hand within Pocket's arm. Pocket was man enough to press it to his side.

Ernest William Hornung was born on 7th June 1866 at Cleveland Villas, Marton, Middlesbrough. He was the third son, and youngest of eight children, to John Peter Hornung and his wife Harriet née Armstrong.

By the age of 13 Hornung had joined St Ninian's Preparatory School in Moffat, Dumfriesshire before enrolling at the exclusive Uppingham School, in Rutland, in 1880.

Hornung suffered from a general state of bad health, including asthma and poor eyesight but managed to be well-liked at school and to develop a life-long passion of cricket. He loved to play despite the obvious fact that his talents were rather limited.

At 17 his health worsened, and he left Uppingham to travel to Australia, where a sunnier climate was deemed to be better for his various ailments.

Upon arriving he worked as a tutor to the Parsons family in Mossgiel, in New South Wales. As well as teaching he spent time working in remote sheep stations in the outback and began to contribute materials to the weekly magazine; The Bulletin. It was also at this time that he began work on his first novel.

After two years of very valuable life experiences Hornung returned to England in February 1886, a few months before the death of his father, in November, whose deteriorating business interests had become a constant worry.

Hornung found work in London as a journalist and story writer. In 1887 he published his first story under his own name, 'Stroke of Five', which appeared in Belgravia magazine. His work as a journalist coincided with the reign of terror brought about by Jack the Ripper's grisly murders. From this Hornung developed an interest in criminal behaviour.

He had completed the manuscript of the novel he brought back from Australia and, between July and November 1890, the story, 'A Bride from the Bush', was published in five parts in the respected Cornhill Magazine. It was released later that year in book form. This, his first novel, was well received by critics.

Hoping to further his talents in cricket Hornung, in 1891, became a member of two cricket clubs: the Idlers, whose members included Arthur Conan Doyle and Jerome K. Jerome, and the Strand club.

Hornung knew Doyle's sister, Constance ('Connie') from when he had visited Portugal. Connie was described as attractive, "with pre-Raphaelite looks ... the most sought-after of the Doyle daughters".

They were married on 27th September 1893, although Doyle was not at the wedding and relations between the two writers were occasionally difficult. The Hornung's had their only child, a son, Arthur Oscar (but always called just Oscar), in 1895.

In 1894 Doyle and Hornung began work on a play for Henry Irving, on the subject of boxing; Doyle was, at first, eager to begin and paid Hornung a £50 advance but then withdrew before the first act had been completed: the play was never finished.

Like Hornung's first novel, 'Tiny Luttrell' had Australia as a backdrop and the device of an Australian woman in a culturally alien environment. This theme ran through his next four novels: 'The Boss of Taroomba' (1894), 'The Unbidden Guest' (1894), 'Irralie's Bushranger' (1896), in this Hornung introduced the character of Stingaree, an Oxford-educated, Australian gentleman thief. In 'The Rogue's March' (1896) Hornung began to show a growing fascination with the motivation behind criminal behaviour and was sympathetic to the criminal hero as a victim of events. It was different thinking but caused some consternation for others.

In 1898 Hornung's mother died and he dedicated his next book, a series of short stories; Some Persons Unknown, to her memory.

Later that year Hornung and Connie spent six months in Posillipo, Italy. An account of this trip was published in the May 1899 issue of the Cornhill Magazine.

The fictional character Stingaree was re-written to become his most famous creation; A. J. Raffles; the gentleman thief, first used in six short stories published in 1898 in Cassell's Magazine. Modelled on George Cecil Ives, a Cambridge-educated criminologist and talented cricketer who, like Raffles, lived in the Albany, a gentlemen's only residence in Mayfair. The first tale of the series 'In the Chains of Crime' was published in June that year, titled 'The Ides of March'.

Another account adds to the richness by asserting that Raffles and his sidekick, Bunny Manders, were based not only on Doyle's Holmes and Watson but also on his friends Oscar Wilde and his lover, Lord Alfred Douglas. Whatever the exact amalgam the characters were warmly embraced by the reading public who turned it into both a popular and financial success, although some critics echoed Doyle's own fears of the dubious nature of a criminal being used as a hero.

In early 1899, the Hornung's returned to London, and resided in Pitt Street, West Kensington, for the next six years.

After publishing two novels, 'Dead Men Tell No Tales' (1899) and 'Peccavi' (1900), Hornung published a second collection of Raffles stories, 'The Black Mask', in 1901. The critics again complained about the criminal aspect. The public who bought them had no such qualms.

In 1903 Hornung collaborated with Eugène Presbrey to write a four-act play, 'Raffles, The Amateur Cracksman', which was based on two previously published short stories, 'Gentlemen and Players' and 'The Return Match'. The play was first performed at the Princess Theatre, New York, on 27th October 1903 and ran for 168 performances.

In 1905, after publishing four other books in the interim, Hornung brought back the character Stingaree. Later that year, in response to public demand he published a third collection of Raffles stories in 'A Thief in the Night', in which Manders relates some of the earlier adventures he had had with Raffles.

In 1909 the final Raffles story was published, the full-length novel 'Mr. Justice Raffles'. It was poorly received. The Observer reviewer asking if "Hornung is perhaps a little tired of Raffles".

It seems not. That same year he partnered with Charles Sansom for the play 'A Visit From Raffles', which was performed in November that year at the Brixton Empress Theatre, London.

Hornung turned away from Raffles thereafter, and in February 1911 published 'The Camera Fiend', a thriller whose narrator is an asthmatic cricket enthusiast and his attempts to photograph the soul as it leaves the body. This was followed by 'Fathers of Men' (1912) and 'The Thousandth Woman' (1913) before 'Witching Hill' (1913), a collection of eight short stories in which he introduced the characters Uvo Delavoye and the narrator Gillon. In 1914 his fictional works ceased with 'The Crime Doctor'.

His son, Oscar, left Eton College in 1914, and was due to proceed to King's College, Cambridge later that year. However, the terrors of WWI were about to unleash themselves all over Europe. Oscar volunteered, and was commissioned into the Essex Regiment. He was killed, aged a mere 20, at the Second Battle of Ypres on 6th July 1915.

Although heartbroken Hornung edited and issued privately a collection of Oscar's letters home under the title 'Trusty and Well Beloved', in 1916.

Around this time Hornung himself joined an anti-aircraft unit. He also joined the YMCA and did volunteer work in England for soldiers on leave. In March 1917 he visited France, writing a poem about his experience afterwards—something he had been doing more frequently since Oscar's death—and a collection of his war poetry, 'Ballad of Ensign Joy', was published later that year.

In July 1917 Hornung's poem, 'Wooden Crosses', was published in The Times, and in September, 'Bond and Free' appeared. A few months later he was accepted as a volunteer in a YMCA canteen and library just a few miles behind the Front Line.

Hornung was concerned about support for pacifism among troops and wrote to Connie about it. She spoke to Doyle and, rather than discussing it with Hornung, he informed the military authorities. Hornung was naturally angered by Doyle's action and relations between the two men were further strained as a result. He continued to work at the library until a German offensive overran the British positions and he was forced to retreat, firstly to Amiens and then, in April, back to England. He stayed in England until November 1918, when he again took up his YMCA duties, establishing a rest hut and library in Cologne.

In 1919 Hornung's account of his time spent in France, 'Notes of a Camp-Follower on the Western Front', was published. Doyle later wrote of the book that "there are parts of it which are brilliant in their vivid portrayal". That year Hornung also published his third and final volume of poetry, 'The Young Guard'.

Hornung finished his YMCA work and returned to England in early 1919. He worked on a new novel but was hampered by poor health. But Connie's was of greater concern. In February 1921 they took a holiday in the south of France to recuperate. Whilst travelling there on the train Hornung fell ill with a chill that progressed to influenza and finally pneumonia.

Ernest William Hornung died on 22nd March 1921, aged 54.

He was buried in Saint-Jean-de-Luz, in the south of France, in a grave adjacent to that of George Gissing.

E. W. Hornung – A Concise Bibliography

Periodicals
Stroke of Five (1887, Belgravia)
Spoilt Negative (1887, Belgravia)
Nettleship's Score (January 1890, Cornhill Magazine)
A Bride From the Bush (5 Parts. July-Nov, Cornhill Magazine, 1890)
Thunderbolt's Mate (4 Parts. March 1892, Chambers's Journal)
Kenyon's Innings (April 1892, Longman's Magazine)
The Burrawurra Brand (November 1893, The Idler)
The Unbidden Guest (6 Parts. May-Oct 1894, Longman's Magazine)
The Governess at Greenbush (4 parts. February 1895, Chambers's Journal)
After the Fact (3 Parts. January 1896, Chambers's Journal)
The Ides of March (June 1898, Cassell's Magazine)
A Villa in a Vineyard (May 1899, Cornhill Magazine)
No Sinicure: More Adventures of the Amateur Cracksman (January 1901, Scribner's Magazine)
A Jubilee Present: More Adventures of the Amateur Cracksman (February 1901, Scribner's Magazine)
The Fate of Faustina: More Adventures of the Amateur Cracksman (March 1901, Scribner's Magazine)
The Last Laugh: More Adventures of the Amateur Cracksman (April 1901, Scribner's Magazine)
To Catch a Thief: More Adventures of the Amateur Cracksman (May 1901, Scribner's Magazine)
An Old Flame: More Adventures of the Amateur Cracksman (June 1901, Scribner's Magazine)
The Wrong House: More Adventures of the Amateur Cracksman (Sept 1901, Scribner's Magazine)
Chrystal's Century (June 1903, Atlantic Monthly)
Charles Reade (June 1921, London Mercury)

Novels and Short Story Collection
A Bride from the Bush (1890) Novel
Under Two Skies (1892) Short story collection
Tiny Luttrell (1893) Novel; two volumes
The Boss of Taroomba (1894) Novel
The Unbidden Guest (1894) Novel
Irralie's Bushranger (1896) Novel
The Rogue's March: A Romance (1896) Novel
My Lord Duke (1897) Novel
Some Persons Unknown (1898) Short story collection
Young Blood (1898) Novel
The Amateur Cracksman (1899) Short story collection
Dead Men Tell No Tales (1899) Novel
The Belle of Toorak (1900) Novel; published in the US as The Shadow of a Man
Peccavi (1900) Novel
The Black Mask (1901) Short story collection; republished as Raffles: Further Adventures of the Amateur Cracksman
At Large (1902) Novel
The Shadow of the Rope (1902) Novel
Denis Dent: A Novel (1903) Novel
No Hero (1903) Novel
Stingaree (1905) Novel

A Thief in the Night (1905) Short story collection; republished as A Thief in the Night: Further Adventures of A. J. Raffles, Cricketer and Cracksman
Raffles: The Amateur Cracksman (1906) Short story collection; stories taken from The Amateur Cracksman and The Black Mask
Mr. Justice Raffles (1909) Novel
The Camera Fiend (1911) Novel
Fathers of Men (1912) Novel
The Thousandth Woman (1913) Novel
Witching Hill (1913) Short story collection
The Crime Doctor (1914) Short story collection
Old Offenders and a Few Old Scores (Published posthumously) Short story collection

Plays
Raffles, The Amateur Cracksman (27th October 1903) By Hornung and Eugéne Presbrey; first performed at the Princess Theatre, New York
Stingaree, the Bushranger (1st February 1908) First performed at the Queen's Theatre, London
A Visit From Raffles (1st November 1909) By Hornung and Charles Sansom; first performed at the Brixton Empress Theatre, London

Non-Fiction
'Trusty and Well Beloved', The Little Record of Arthur Oscar Hornung (1915) Privately published
Notes of a Camp-Follower on the Western Front (1919)

Poetry
Ballad of Ensign Joy (1917)
Wooden Cross (1918)
The Young Guard (1919)